Bill Stenlake 2018

It's
W

Copyright © 2018 William (Bill) Stenlake
Createspace edition

It's Dark in Wenlock by Bill Stenlake

All rights reserved. No part of this book may be reproduced, distributed or transmitted in any form, by any means without the prior consent of the author.

All characters in this publication are fictitious and any resemblance to persons, living or dead is purely coincidental. Some places named in the book exist and are real and some do not exist and are not real. The placement of all things geographical is relevant to this story only and as such should be deemed fictional.

Book Cover Photo:
© Bobrooky/Dreamstime.com

Other books by Bill Stenlake:

HOLLOW MILL
THE KEEPER
KENAN'S LEGACY
CORNERSTONE
THE GRAND MASTER
DETECTIVE BRAMLEY BOOK 1
RANDOLPH
VOICES IN MY HEAD
LOWARTH TOLL
THE CORIDAE KEY
BRAMLEY BOOK 2
THE MANNACHS
DIMENSIONS
THE ROOTS
A PAIR OF SHORTS
THE WATCHER
THE KEEPER TRILOGY
COMING SOON: JOHNSTONE

It's Dark in Wenlock by Bill Stenlake
Chapter 1

It was last night I saw her for the first time. Just a fleeting glimpse, but that was enough. Then she disappeared. She kept me awake for the rest of the night, wondering who she was and what she was doing in the church graveyard. That's what I get for walking home in the dark, at 3 o'clock in the morning.

It's dark at night in Wenlock. Well of course it is! I am not meaning to be obvious like that; it is just the way it struck me last night. I have been out at night in Wenlock before, of course I have. It is just that I haven't been out that late, walking home in complete darkness. It is the fact that they turn off the street lights overnight that made the difference, as I walked home last night.

It is not as if I haven't been out during the night. I have, but I have been out in the car. The car has lights on it, so even though it is dark outside, it doesn't feel so dark in the car, with the lights on.

I got a call about ten o'clock. I had forgotten that I was the contact for Mary when she presses her emergency alert button. That goes to the call centre and then they try the local nominated responder. That is me. She got stuck on the floor. I won't bore you with the story of why she was on the floor. It is just too silly. Anyway, I couldn't get in, so I called the police and they broke in for me. Mary was on the floor. She was alright, but couldn't get up. Three people managed to rectify that. That was the emergency over, except that the paperwork had to be done by the police, and the ambulance people. They had come along too. Oh and then there was the little matter of waiting for someone, to come and board up the door. He didn't turn up until 2 o'clock, which was long after Mary had turned in for bed. It is not a problem; it is just the reason why I was walking home in the dark, at 3 o'clock in the morning.

I turned out of the lane onto Sheinton Street, or is it Shineton Street? It all depends on which sign you read. At one end of the street it is one spelling and at the other end, the other spelling. I realized then just how dark it was without any streetlights on and with no lights on in any of the houses. I felt it was quite creepy, so I was already a little bit on edge.

I crossed over by the Bull Ring and started walking up past the church. I heard a noise to my left. I can't explain what sort of noise exactly, but it was like a swooshing noise. I stopped and turned. I felt my heartrate go up a few notches. I could just make out the outline of the nearest gravestones. I could also make out the shape of the big tree beyond that. That was about the extent of my view.

Then she appeared from the doorway of the church and walked along the path and away from me. She must have been hiding in the doorway as I approached. The whoosh, I took to be her movement. She had a long cloak on, as far as I could make out. Beyond the gravestones, she just blended into the rest of the darkness. I did call out to her, but she didn't slow down and she didn't respond. I am saying she, but to honest I am only saying that, because of her size and the cloak.

I stood there for a few more seconds and my heartrate continued at its accelerated pace. The darkness reminded me that I needed to get moving again. I started walking, but keeping one eye to my left and the church green and the other, ahead of me, towards the square. I reached the Guildhall and the darkened area where they hold the markets. Somehow I was spooked and I kept to the edge of the pavement as I walked past it. As I passed the end of the Guildhall, where the passage comes out, I either heard the whooshing noise again, or I imagined it. I crossed over the road towards the square and the momentary relief of the light. The Smoothie leaves one on in their café overnight. I was grateful for that relief. It may sound silly, but I needed the safety of that light, just at that moment. If she chose to come towards me, I would be able to see her.

Of course I wasn't going to be able to stand out in the square all night. So I stayed for maybe a minute or so, before I resumed my journey along Barrow Street. I live almost at the far end of Barrow Street. I had maybe about four hundred paces to overcome, before I reached my front door. Now I found myself looking back over my shoulder every few steps. There was nothing to see, but I was beyond telling that by then. The only light relief ahead of me was in the distance, just about opposite where I live. That is the sign that advises drivers of the impending sharp corner. It remains lit all night. In between there and where I was, was all in darkness. There are plenty of places where someone could stand and you wouldn't be able to see them.

I didn't hear the whooshing sound and I didn't see the dark figure again. But I did think I could hear a faint footstep, somewhere behind me. But I couldn't see anyone, when I turned to investigate. I kept my pace to a brisk one. The sooner I got home, the sooner this torment would be over. How I wished I had taken a torch along, but I hadn't given it a thought when I left home at 10 o'clock. Next time, if there is a next time, I will take a torch with me.

As you can imagine, I had forgotten to leave the outside light on, outside my front door. It is dark in our little cul-de-sac. The light from the road sign does little to penetrate across the road to where we are. I fumbled with the key for far too long, before I found the key hole and managed to get the door open. It was with an immense relief that I stepped through the doorway, to be greeted by the dogs. I put the kettle on and made a cup of coffee. I let the dogs out while the water boiled and then sat in my armchair, thinking about what I had seen and heard, on my walk home through the village. They call it a town, but the size of it is really only that of a village. I finished up and retired to bed, but I didn't sleep well at all. The whooshing noise and the vision of her walking through the graveyard, over-ruled my need for sleep.

Chapter 2

As can be expected I got the best sleep, just before it was time to get up. A cold nose against my cheek and the feeling of doggie breath on my face, ensure my eyes open to the dawning of the new day. As usual, they are impatient for their morning walk. I have to get up first and have a bit of breakfast before we go. This is expected of me by the dogs, but they only accept it, because they also share some toast for their breakfast.

It is a reminder of the night before, when I step out of my front door into the warm early morning sunshine. It is a reminder, because in the daylight, I can see everything around me; last night I could not. Seeing it this morning, makes me realize how little I had been able to see, in the pitch black I had walked home in. I know the road I live in well, but in the dark I may as well have been walking somewhere new to me.

We walk along Barrow Street as usual and it is only as we get to where the road narrows in Wilmore Street, that I see the flashing blue lights ahead of me. There are two patrol cars and an unmarked car, all with their lights still flashing. Along with them, there is a white van and an ambulance. My first thought is that there has been a traffic accident, but as I draw nearer, I can see that there are no vehicles in an odd position, that may be the cause of this. There is a policeman, standing in the road by one of the cars. The way they are all parked, no one will be able to get past them.

Naturally, as we are walking past him, I acknowledge his presence. He looks at me, but doesn't say anything. I carry on along Sheinton Street (I am coming from home, so it is that spelling this way) and on the bend I pass another policeman, walking back towards the cars. He too doesn't give any greeting and I keep walking with the dogs. When I get to the end of the road, I see that he has placed a road closed sign, at the junction with the main road.

We have our walk round the old railway line and up onto Windmill Hill, before making our way back towards the town centre again. When I reach the junction to the main road, where he has placed the road closed sign, we are stopped from walking down there, by the policeman posted there. He just says to me, that I will have to find another way round. That is after he has established that I don't actually live on Shineton Street (We are at the other end now). We make our way up the main road and turn into Queen Street and down past the bus station (it is only a bus stop and shelter). Then we turn up Back Lane and through onto the High Street. I decide I'll pop into the newsagent, Mrs P's, and ask Paul if he knows what all the police activity is about.

He tells me that one of the early morning regulars had been on his way up, to fetch his paper. He noticed a front door was wide open, which he says is most unusual for the house in question, as no one lives there. It has been empty for years. He popped his head in and had only taken a few steps, when he found someone dead on the floor. He says he doesn't know who it is. He had got a shock and backed quickly out, before running up to Paul, to call the police.

I don't mention it to Paul as he tells me this, but I walked right past that house, on my way home in the dark last night. That, and the figure I saw, gives me a funny feeling in my stomach. It gives me a completely different feeling in my head, as I think about it too. I buy my paper and walk the dogs home. I look left at the bottom of High

Street. The road is closed now there too. There are more vehicles there blocking the road, than before.

Over a mug of coffee, my wife suggests that maybe I had better walk back down and talk to the police. After all, it is only a few hours since I walked right past that door, in the dark at 3 o'clock this morning. It is not so much that part of my walk home I need to tell them about, rather it is about the figure I saw by the church. He, or she, may be significant in their investigation, not that I will be able to tell them much.

I finish my coffee and amble, rather reluctantly, back along Barrow Street. There is a policeman on duty, at the point the road is closed by the church. I walk up to him and say that I was walking home at 3 o'clock this morning and that I saw someone in the church grounds. He tells me to wait where I am, while he tries at first to use his radio and when he gets no response to that, he walks down the road to the cars. I see him standing at the door to the house. He is there for maybe a minute, before he comes back towards me.

'One of the detectives will be along in a minute or two, to talk to you.'

It is more like ten minutes later, when he walks towards me. In the meantime, several of the locals have walked up to the road closed sign and asked what is going on. I don't answer them, as the policeman does.

'They've found a body in one of the houses.'

We have to move out of the way, as another vehicle wants to get through to the scene. By the time that has happened, the detective has made it up to where I am standing. He waves me through and we walk back past the Guildhall, to the wall by the church grounds.

'Tell me what you saw.'

He listens to me for a few seconds, before deciding I am worthy of him taking some notes. He takes my name, address and telephone number for starters, before he allows me to continue with my report.

I explain what I was doing out at that time of the morning. It is easily confirmable, assuming it will have to be done. He is more interested when I get to the bit, about the figure appearing from by the church door. It is hard to get him to understand that it was so dark then; compared to the brilliant daylight now, as we are sitting on the wall. He asks me for a description. I only have that it was a person in a cloak. I can only say that I think it was a woman, because I don't really know. It could have been a slight man. The whooshing sound I heard is treated with a little scepticism, which really isn't surprising. He asks me if I had been drinking. I'd had a glass of wine earlier, before I got called out, but I was far from being intoxicated. He makes me run through what I have told him, a couple of times more, before he decides that he has heard enough from me. He says that he might be in touch with me again. He hands me a card and says that if I think of anything else I might have seen and heard, then I am to give him a ring.

I think he believes I was drunk, from the way he is sort of dismissing what I have said, about the character I saw by the church. I know what I saw and I was definitely not drunk in the slightest. He watches me as I make my way back towards the High Street junction. I know that, because I turn, just before I reach the road closed sign. He is still watching me. The policeman there watches me as I walk by too. I decide I need a cup of coffee, so I walk up High Street and into the Deli, which is opposite Mrs P's, the newsagent. There are a few locals in there, for an early morning coffee. I sit down with them, as they are talking about the police presence in the town. I decide that I won't tell them that I was walking home in the middle of the night. It is not that they would talk about me or anything, but it is easier not to add any fuel to any fire that might get lit.

Twenty five minutes later, I am walking home once more. I need to get started on the day's tasks.

Chapter 3

I take a wander back down the town, just before lunch time. As I get to the square, I see that there is still a lot of activity going on, beyond the police cordon. It is still being manned by a single copper. There are a few locals standing talking to him, but it doesn't appear to me that he is giving out any answers. I pop into one of the shops, to see if my wife needs a coffee to keep her going, and something to eat of course too. She tells me that the incident is the talk of the town. She also tells me that something else appears to be going on. At about eleven o'clock, the number of people investigating appears to have swollen in number. Several more vehicles had arrived about then, with their sirens blaring. She says that the word is that something else has happened, but she can't tell me what it is. No one really knows, so the rumour mill is in full production. The best one she has heard so far; is that the body has disappeared. Others tell of multiple bodies being found upstairs and blood all over the place. It all has to be taken with a pinch of salt, until the facts are made known.

Town is busy and I have to wait a while for my takeaway sandwiches. I am not sure what has brought people to the town today, but maybe it is something to do with the incident.

I think they have been rather slow on the take up, considering that it is now lunch time, but a couple of camera crews turn up and drive down the High Street. I watch as they stop at the bottom of the street and set themselves up for a broadcast. I'm guessing that quite possibly something has changed and turned this into something much more newsworthy.

I leave my wife, to get on with things. I wander back down to the junction, at the bottom of High Street. The camera crew has wasted no time in setting things up. They are busy talking to the locals and trying to get some good pictures beyond the cordon. I am not going to learn anything here, so I start to walk home along Barrow Street. I have only got as far as the Raven, when a car coming towards me, suddenly swings in to the edge and screeches to a stop. Two men get out quickly. I recognize the passenger as being the detective I spoke to earlier.

'We need to have another talk to you.' Is all that is said initially. Their stance is anything but relaxed. I have a feeling I am not going to like the talk they want to have. It is not because I have done anything wrong, but more the manner in which they have stopped and got out of their car.

'Here?' I ask.

'Somewhere a little quieter would be better.'

The road and pavement isn't exactly bustling with people, but there are a few people walking along the pavement and a few cars driving by.

'Do you want to come back to my house then?' I offer.

'That will do for now.'

I don't like the sound of that, but I am not going to be in control, is the feeling I get. I start walking away. They get into their car and do a three point turn in the road, much to the annoyance of a car coming along the road.

They drive at a speed that matches my walking pace, annoying another driver who is following them. As I turn into my drive, they swing in and stop near to my front door. The dogs bark as I unlock the door. Neither of them is too enamoured with my visitors. That is a surprise, because they are generally friendly dogs. I walk through to the kitchen and put the kettle on to boil. They follow me through. I get the distinct feeling, as they ask me to go through things again, that something has indeed changed. I am not sure where I and my story fit into this change, but it is obvious that they think it is relevant. I can only say what I have seen. I don't think my story has changed from the first time I told it. I don't think he thinks it has either. We drink our coffee and then he says that we need to go. Not that they need to go, but that we need to go. That includes me. I let the dogs out, to do their business in the garden and while I am out there, I send my wife a text, telling her what is happening, just so she knows. We are apparently going down to Sheinton Street, so I can walk them through that part of my journey home last night. I don't get a reply before we leave. When I am down there, it is unlikely I will receive any reply, as the signal is so poor in that part of town. At least it is with my phone provider.

We go round the town and come in from the far end. It is better that way. I am sure loads of gossip would start up, if they saw me in the back of a police car, albeit an unmarked one, going through the cordon. That is all I need, to be at the centre of the rumour mill's production. .

We pull to a stop in the Bull Ring and we all get out of the car. We walk along Sheinton Street, past the old Priory Tea Rooms and the Hairdresser's shop, right up to the lane that goes up to the Pottery. It is this lane I came out of at 3 o'clock this morning, in the dark. It is a private lane, but there is a gate that leads through to Chapel Close, where I had to go regarding the panic button call out.

They tell me to do exactly as I had done last night. That is quite strange and also very hard to do. They want me to look in the direction I would have been looking at then. It is hard to do, because it is daylight now and I can take in everything I can see. It was pitch black when I walked here last night. It was all I could do to look ahead of me in the dark, and avoid the steps to houses, that are dotted along the first section.

When I get to the old Priory Tea Room, they ask me to stop. They say it is important I now do exactly as I did last night. Did I notice if the door was open? No I didn't. I have never known it to be open and the only way I would have been able to see that last night, is if there had been a light on inside. Did I hear any noise, as I passed the house? No I didn't. The only noise I heard was the whooshing sound, but that was up by the church.

I walk the section past the house where the body was found, and then cross over at what I judge to be almost the same point I crossed the road last night. Why did I cross the road there? To be honest I don't really know. I just wanted to cross the road at this point. It might be because there are a couple of alleys that come out onto the pavement, if I had stayed on the other side of the road. But it wasn't really a conscious decision I made; I just crossed the road when I did.

We move on to the point where I noticed the figure. There is so little to tell them about what I saw. I saw the figure and heard the whooshing sound. That is pretty much the extent of it. They run through that a couple of times, but my story isn't going to be any different. We wander back down towards the car. Someone comes out of the house and walks towards us. He stops as he gets to us. His look asks if they have found out any more. Their look tells him that I haven't managed to throw any more light on anything. Then he just utters these words. They are directed at me I think, but are meant for them.

'Something really odd happened. I wouldn't have believed it if I hadn't been here. It has just disappeared into thin air. We left the room and stood outside for a minute, to let the SOCO team in. We stepped out of the front door and it slammed shut behind us. We had to break the door down to get back in. The place is locked from the inside. There are piles of letters on the floor inside the door. They weren't there earlier. The body has gone. There is no way anyone could have taken it. We just can't see how it went. Another thing is that the floor is clean where he lay. It wasn't when we got there. It couldn't have been cleaned up like that so quickly. Well I say clean, but from the body I mean. It is dusty as hell now, as if no one has been in there for years. We only stepped outside to let the others in!'

Chapter 4

I think they suddenly realize that I am still standing with them.

'You mustn't say anything of this to anyone.'

He is looking at me, realizing I shouldn't have been told all this.

'I won't say a word, until it is public knowledge of course' I reply.

I am thinking about what he has just said. It doesn't make any sense, but then they don't think what I told them about the figure I saw is true either. But, I am thinking, if you take the two together, then maybe they are easier to believe.

'Thanks for your help' he says after a minute or two of silence, or was it only a few seconds? 'And remember, please don't tell anyone about what I have just said.'

'I won't.'

As I leave them, I see that someone else is being led through the cordon, on foot. I recognize Bob. I see him in Mrs P's sometimes, if I am covering for Paul. He must be the regular who found the door open and the body. Is it all part of an elaborate hoax, is the first thought that goes through my mind. It is doubtful. Firstly, Bob doesn't strike me as that sort of a bloke. Secondly, what is the point? Thirdly, it is a bit much and how did they do it? Fourthly, is the fact I saw the figure by the church, on the way home. I don't know for sure that the two incidents are connected, but in my mind they definitely are. Even more so, now I know what has happened this morning, with the front door and the body.

Bob nods to me as he walks past. I can see he is not happy with being brought down here again. I very much doubt he has anything he can tell them, about what has happened since he called the police, just like my information hasn't changed anything for them either.

I pop back into the shop and chat to Kate for a bit, before I walk slowly back towards home. She is covering the shop while the owner is away.

By the time I come back up at shop closing time, I am surprised to see that the police presence has disappeared. The cordon has gone, as has the squad of police cars and other vehicles that had clogged up the area round the Bull Ring, earlier in the day. I wander down to the house where all the fuss was. The door has been mended. It is easy to see where it has been patched up. I needed to see this, as I was getting the idea that maybe I have been experiencing a long daydream. I know I haven't, but sometimes you start to doubt yourself. On my way back up towards the High Street; I bump into Bob. We stop for a chat. I ask if he knows anything. He knows even less than I do, as it turns out. We part and life goes on in Wenlock.

I don't give it any more thought, as the days and then the weeks roll by. Nothing came of the incident and nothing was mentioned about them getting locked out and the body disappearing. There were some rumours. They said that the body was actually a dummy that had been dressed and made to look like a murdered corpse. But it soon all died down.

It is maybe two months later I am in Mrs P's, talking to Paul. I bring the subject up, as to whether he has heard anything since. He hasn't. I ask if Bob has said anything about what he found that morning. He tells me that Bob came in every morning for about a week after the incident, but he hasn't seen him since. He says it is most unlike him, now that I have brought his name up. We talk about it for another couple of minutes, until Paul gets loads of customers in, so I leave him to it.

Something is nagging at me, about Bob. I don't know why and I can't pin it down either. I grab a couple of coffees from the Deli and go to sit with Kate, to drink them. She is helping out again in the town. I tell her about what Paul has said about Bob. She asks me why I am so bothered about it. She knows how I sometimes get feelings about things. She knows that I sometimes see things, that maybe others don't, or can't. She can see that I am mithered about it. She knows it won't just go away. I will stick with it, until I know what the reason for it is.

'You'd better go up and see if Paul knows where he lives. You won't rest until you settle what is in your head. And that means I won't get any peace either. It will keep eating at you, until you have the answer.'

'Ok' I don't put up any resistance. That is because she is right of course and I do need to know where Bob is.

I wander back up the road and wait for a few minutes, while Paul deals with his queue of customers. When he has finished, I ask him if he knows where Bob lives. He doesn't know exactly where he lives, but he thinks it is up on the Stretton Road. I thank him and walk out of the shop. Once outside, I suddenly think that the road he has said he lives on, doesn't make sense to me. If it is on the Stretton Road, then Bob would not have been walking along Sheinton Street that morning, to get his paper. He would have been coming along Victoria Road and into High Street, that way. I have the thought, that it was suggested that Bob always walked along Sheinton Street to get to Mrs P's. I debate whether to go back and ask Paul about this, but decide that I should keep this to myself, for the moment. There is probably nothing wrong, so I don't need to spread my concerns with the world. It will probably all come to nothing and that I have been mithering for no reason. I don't need any more people thinking I am 'different'.

I wander up slowly towards the Stretton Road, wondering how I am going to approach this. I don't know Bob, other than a fleeting meeting when he picks up his paper. I haven't seen him that often either, as I only occasionally do an early for Paul. I start along Stretton Road. I knock at a couple of doors, but don't get an answer. The first one I do get an answer at; does not know where Bob might live. I get the feeling they don't know him at all. I don't give up, but try the next door and the next one after that. Mary answers that door and she knows who I mean. I don't tell her why I want to see Bob. I thank her and walk along to Bob's house. I don't get a reply. I try round the back, but can see no life in there. I don't think Bob works. He strikes me as being retired, but again I am only guessing at this.

I try his neighbour on the one side. There is no reply there, but there is on the other side. I recognize the woman who answers the door, but I don't know her name. She appears to know my name though. I ask her when Bob is normally in. She replies, telling me that he is always in. Other than getting his paper every day and then doing a bit of shopping in town; he doesn't go anywhere much since his wife died, five years ago. I thank her and say I will come back later and see if Bob is back from wherever he has gone. Just before I leave, she says something to me. It does nothing to settle that strange feeling I have in my head and now in my stomach too.

'Now that you mention it, I haven't heard him for days. He hasn't been out in the garden either. He is always in the garden, well, several times a week.'

'I wonder if he is alright' I say, with a degree of concern in my voice.

'We can go and have a look if you like. I have a key. You know, just in case he locks himself out, then I keep the spare for him. He has struggled a bit at times since his wife, Alice, died.'

She goes in and returns a minute or so later, dangling a key on her finger.

'I do hope nothing has happened to him. I will feel ever so guilty if it has and I haven't noticed it.'

She puts her front door on the latch and we walk around, to have a look at Bob's house.

Chapter 5

As we reach Bob's front door, she hands me the key. I had a feeling that this was going to happen. I am surprised actually that she has come this far with me. I expect that when we open the front door, she will stay on the doorstep, while I investigate. I am wrong about that.

I push the door open and shout out Bob's name. I wait and there is no reply, so I do it one more time. I get the same response as the first time; nothing.

I look at Jean who is standing beside me now. We both know the next move is the one we have been dreading. I step into the hallway. The house is not a bright one. That isn't helped by the fact the doors are all closed. I shout out his name again, as I step along the hall. Still I get no response. I open the living room door and step in. I am surprised to find that Jean has braved it in with me. As she puts it:

'It will be better with two of us together, if we do find anything.'

The anything being; finding Bob of course! He is not in the living room. I briefly think about the irony of him not being found in here. In fact Bob isn't to be found anywhere downstairs. The back door is firmly shut and locked too, from the inside.

I make my way back to the hall, where the stairs are. To be honest this is the part I have really been dreading. My head says that if I am going to find him dead, it is either going to be in the bedroom, or the bathroom. Jean is still with me as I climb the stairs. Once again I am shouting Bob's name, in case he hasn't heard me so far. We reach the landing and I see the bathroom door is open. I step in, but the coast is clear. Two bedroom doors are closed and one is open. I check the closed door rooms first. They are spare rooms and empty. I feel my heart rate increase, as I get to the main bedroom. I don't delay, but walk right in. Jean, to be fair, is right on my heels. The first thing I can see is that there is no one in the bed. I check round the other side, but there is no Bob. The bed is unmade and there are some clothes lying around. It is a lived in room and Bob probably isn't the tidiest, but then he doesn't need to be, if he lives on his own. I am relieved I haven't found his body here, but I still have the feeling that not everything is right.

'We may as well check out the garden properly, while we are here' I suggest.

'But the back door was locked' Jean says.

'I know, but it seems silly not to check anyway, seeing we have checked everywhere else.'

'There are no letters on the mat' Jean says.'

'No there aren't, but I saw a mailbox on the wall by the front door.'

'Oh yes, that's right. They used to have a dog that chewed everything that came through the letter box.'

We make our way downstairs and through the dining room to the kitchen, where we unlock the door and make a tour of his well-kept garden. The grass is a little long, but other than that, it is very tidy and Bobless. I then go back through the house, to check on the mail box. As expected it is locked and there is some stuff in there. I have a quick look for the key, but can't see it hanging anywhere. I don't think it right that I rummage through the drawers, to see if I can find the key, so I try to pull the letters out from the top with my fingers. I get enough, to be able to see that there is more than one week's mail in there. I relay that information to Jean, before putting the ones I have retrieved back into the box.

'I don't know where he could have gone' Jean says. She has a slightly worried tone to her voice. 'I mean, I think he would have said if he was going away for a few days. It is most unlike him.'

For sure, it doesn't look like he has gone away. We have gone back through to the kitchen, to lock up the back door. I have looked in the fridge. The milk is off and the bread in the bread bin is mouldy. There are some dishes in the sink, waiting to be washed. The food is dried on the plates and the drink dregs have evaporated in the mugs. All these things point out that he hasn't been around here for a couple of weeks, in my opinion.

'What do we do now?' Jean asks me.

'I guess we should maybe ring the police and at least enlighten them, as to our concern for his whereabouts and safety.'

We use Bob's phone. I check it first, but the last call is weeks ago, according to 1471. He hasn't got an answer phone, but I am guessing it would be empty, even if he had. I am not sure if he had any children, but we haven't seen any evidence of that as we've searched his house. I haven't seen any photos or the like.

Our call is taken and I give both Jean's contact information and my own. They are not too impressed, when we tell them that we don't know if he might have gone away, just that we don't think he has. I suspect they might check the hospitals and then wait until we contact them again, before they take it more seriously. I give Jean my address and telephone number and lock up Bob's house. Jean returns to her house, along with Bob's key.

I take a last look at Bob's house, before I wander back down into the town again. I stop off to talk to Kate. She can see straight away, that I haven't resolved my problem. I tell her what has transpired.

'What do you think has happened?' she asks.

I note she isn't asking where I think that Bob is. It is too early for that. From experience, she knows that will most likely come, but just not yet.

'I really don't know. The house looks like it should. Nothing has happened there. It is just that he probably hasn't been there for a couple of weeks, at least.' I explain why I have come to that conclusion.

'So what is next?'

'I'm going to check in the Spar and Nisa, I suppose, too. I gather he shopped mostly in the Spar though.'

'Try not to get too caught up in it' are her parting words, as I leave her to continue with my enquiries.

The girls in the Spar know who I am talking about. After a quick discussion between themselves and a phone call or two, to other staff who aren't in work right now; they come up with that they haven't seen him for a couple of weeks or so. I move on up to the Nisa at the petrol station. It is harder there, as they don't appear to know who I am talking about. I leave with an inconclusive response. My gut feeling tells me that he hasn't switched his paper and shopping buying to there. I think they would know if he has.

There is nothing else I can do about it. I walk home, down St Mary's Lane and turning right at the Raven. I need some fresh air, so I decide to take the dogs for an extra walk. They aren't going to complain about it. They love going for a walk. I walk through the town and cut down past the Priory and along the lane. Rather than go onto the old railway line, I follow the road round and along the lane, past the mill and through the fields beyond. I then turn left and come back along the old railway line, from Farley Halt back to Station Road. I haven't really thought about much as I have walked. The dogs have enjoyed themselves, investigating all the different smells they have found on our journey. I let them have a final run around the Gaskell field, before calling it a day on their freedom. We walk back through the town, calling in at the shop, to say hello to Kate again. She doesn't bring up the subject of Bob again. She can see it etched on my face, that I haven't made any progress with it.

I haven't achieved much on the day. Well I suppose I have in one sense. I have found out that Bob isn't at home and has been missing for over 2 weeks.

Chapter 6

Nothing happens for a few days and I drift back into routine. I still have a feeling that something isn't quite right, but I don't know what it is and I don't know how to find the answer. I have found, in the past, that if it wants to, then the answer will come to you, in its own time and in its own way.

I go up to the Stretton Road, to see if Bob has come back. He isn't there at his house and Jean tells me she hasn't seen or heard him at all. We ring the police again and this time they send someone out. Well someone is in the area and comes along to see us, pretty much straight away. Our argument isn't that convincing, particularly when we show him around Bob's house. It is not as if it has been broken into or something, or been ransacked. It is all pretty much in order; it is just that Bob has disappeared. The policeman does go through some of the drawers. He finds an address book. There doesn't appear to be any children, or family, listed in there. Nothing is marked like that. The writing is in a woman's hand. We expect it was his wife's address book. We ring some of the numbers, but no one has seen Bob. No, he doesn't visit. They haven't seen him since his wife's funeral. The story is the same with everyone we reach. He doesn't appear to be that close to anyone. There is nowhere that he might have gone off to, visiting.

The policeman is satisfied that he is missing and says it will be logged in the appropriate places. If he turns up on his own volition, could we let them know? If not, they will be in touch, when they have something to report.

That night I get another alarm call. I have had the lock changed on the door since the last time. No longer can the key be left in the lock on the inside, by Mary. It is a key lock on the outside and a knob that turns to lock it, on the inside. This time I am able to get in, without having to call out the police to break in for me. Mary isn't feeling well; she has been a bit off colour since the last call out, not that the two are connected. I call the paramedics, when it becomes clear to me that she isn't easily sorted, just by me answering the alarm call. By the time they come and assess her, a couple of hours have gone by. By the time they have decided that she isn't bad enough to take in and have settled her down again, another hour has gone by. By the time I leave her, after putting her to bed and giving her another cup of tea, it is well past the hour of three o'clock. I lock her front door and walk down her path. I have remembered to bring my torch with me this time. It is a good job I have, because if anything, this night is even darker than the one, the last time I did this middle of the night walk home.

I go through the gate, shutting it as quietly as I can behind me. I walk down the rough lane to the bottom, where it joins Sheinton Street. For some reason, I cross over to the other side. The pavement isn't quite so narrow this side and with my torch on as well, I can see a bit further round the shallow bend of the road. There is nothing to see in my torchlight. I am feeling much more comfortable within myself as I walk along. I get to the point where I am walking past the old police station, which is opposite the house where the incident was before.

My torch suddenly gives up the ghost. That may be truer than the words are meant to be. My torch goes out though and I am thrust back into the darkness of the night in Wenlock. I hear a whoosh and then I think I see a cloaked figure, rushing across the road ahead of me, crossing over at the Bull Ring. It is so dark and I don't see the figure clearly. It is soon gone from my limited vision.

My torch then flickers and comes on. I don't know why I do it, but I shine my torch over the road, towards that front door. I stop straight away. I had stopped when my torch went out and restarted when it came back on. The door to the house over the road is wide open. I feel my heart start to race. I admit to be feeling a little bit afraid. I don't know what of, but I can feel my nervousness of the situation rising. Despite that, I cross the road and walk up to the front door. The floor is littered with old mailings. I shine my torch in, but I can't see very far. The door to the first room is open, but not enough for me to see into it. I call out a softish 'hello'. There isn't any response. I doubt anyone would have heard me anyway. I try a little louder, but again nothing happens. It is at this point, the smell starts to hit me. It is not a nice smell. I don't know what it is, but it isn't nice. I probably shouldn't be doing this, but I step through the doorway. I take a couple of steps forward, towards the next door. The smell is getting stronger and there is a buzzing sound that comes to my ears now too. This is not good, what I am going to find in here. I am pretty sure about that. I have just about made it to the door, to see what awaits me, when there is a crash from behind me. The front door crashes shut. I jump out of my skin and my heart rate must easily double. I go back quickly to the front door, to open it again. I can't do it. It is either jammed by the crashing shut it has just done, or it is locked. I shine my torch at the gap where the lock goes across and I can see the metal of the lock. Somehow the door has locked, as it slammed shut.

I turn my attention back to the other little matter. That is what is making the smell and causing the buzzing noise. Both seem to be stronger, now the front door has closed. I step towards the inner door again. The smell gets stronger with every step and the noise is louder too. I push open the door and shine my torch in. I see the answer to most of this, lying in the middle of the room, on the floor. There is a body and from the looks of it, it has been there for some time. It is covered in flies, thousands of them. The smell is pretty obnoxious too. It seems to penetrate my nostrils harshly, now I am in the room. I back off into the hall. I really want to pull the door closed behind me to distance myself from the noise and the smell. I don't really want to touch the door though. I have already used my hand to push it open, but I don't want to touch it again, if I can help it.

I take my phone out of my pocket and switch it on. Whether I have signal here is going to be a marginal call. It is not good in town generally and from experience, on this side of the road, in this part of town, I am unlikely to have any. So it turns out to be. I try the front door again, but it isn't going to open to let me out. What a nightmare! I wonder if I can get out the back way, but to do that I will have to go through the living room. I really don't want to have to do that, if I can avoid it. The alternative is to go upstairs and go to the front of the house and hope I can get a bit of signal from there. Again it is not ideal, as I don't want to be trampling all over any evidence there might be in the house, but I appear to have little choice in the matter.

Reluctantly, I climb the stairs and go into the front bedroom. There is no furniture in the room and it looks like no one has been in here for years. I stand by the window and hold my phone high above my head, hoping that I will manage somehow to get even one bar of phone signal. As I stand there, the smell from downstairs seems to have followed me up here.

Chapter 7

I keep bringing my phone down, to see if I have managed to get a bit of signal. Just as I am about to give up on it, the gods smile on me and I get 2 bars. I keep the phone high and put it on speaker while I dial 999. My call is answered straight away. I ask for the police. I tell her the address straight away, well the approximate address, as I don't know the number. I am afraid I am going to lose my signal any second. Thankfully it stays with me for now. I tell her why I am calling and then tell her what I have found and that I appear to be locked in. To be fair, she doesn't dwell too long on that one. She tells me to stay on the line. I explain that I am struggling for signal and might lose it any second. I might also have to go downstairs, when the police arrive. From the sound I can hear coming towards my position, it looks like she has called out the fire brigade too. I ask her and she says she has, when I told her I was locked in.

The windows are really dirty and I don't want to touch whatever the cloth is, hanging over them. I doubt the fire brigade will be able to see me through them, even if I shine my torch at them. The decision is made for me anyway, as my call gets cut, when I lose the signal. I take the opportunity to leave the window and bring my aching arm down to my side. It is possible that I let my arm come down far enough, to lose the signal in the first place.

I hear a banging on the door, as I make my way down the stairs. The stench is even more overpowering, when I near the bottom. They bang again on the door and I step up to the door my side, to answer them. I explain quickly that the door had been open and that I'd come in to investigate. Then the door had slammed shut on me and appears to have self-locked. No I don't have a key. I don't live here. The conversation stops, as the police have just turned up now. I have to repeat the conversation to the police. I say there is a body in here and that I am locked in. I can just imagine how that sounds, to the people out there. I haven't been able to clearly tell them the whole story.

Anyway the result is that I am told to stand well back. I do so by climbing half way up the stairs. There is no way I am going into the living room again. I am barely in position and have shouted that to them, when the door crashes off its hinges. They shout in, for me to come out with my hands up. I do so willingly, even if only to get away from the smell and the buzzing. I am told to lie down on the ground. They frisk me and then allow me to stand. I am kept a hold of, by one of the policemen. One of the others, along with the firemen has entered the house. The policeman comes out first and throws up in the gutter. The firemen take a little longer before they come back out. They have checked out the whole house. There is nothing else in there, other than the body in the living room and thousands of flies.

I am put in the back of the police car, while they wait for others to arrive. It doesn't take long for several other vehicles to arrive. There are also several people on the street, who have been roused by the noise and the flashing lights. I see several people taking a note of me, sitting in the back of the police car.

Luckily, or maybe not so, it is the same detective I saw the last time the door of this house was found open, who arrives to take over the investigation. He is a little surprised to see me. I think I am already at a disadvantage, because of the previous interview. I haven't done anything wrong though, so I tell him the exact order of events. It is easy enough for him to check out that I got another alarm call, and he does. He also checks out that the paramedics turned up at the scene too. That just leaves the bit about my journey home. I'm guessing that because something strange went on here last time, he is more open to what my story tells, particularly the bit about the door slamming shut and locking.

After maybe fifteen minutes of interviewing me, we get out of the car again. I am presuming he has decided I am in the clear, for tonight at least. I can see the people looking at me. Some of them I know and some I don't. I can guess that I will be the subject of many a conversation in the morning. He asks me to walk to the house. I approach the front door with him, but when he asks me to go in; I say I would rather not. I will willingly tell him what I touched and what I haven't and where I've been, but I really don't want to smell that smell again, unless I really have to. I really have to apparently. It is almost worse now than the first time I went in. It is as if the fresh air from the door being open has ripened the smell up considerably.

There is little doubt that the person lying on the floor, has been there for a long time. We know he wasn't there when the first incident happened. Well actually, he might have been and then been taken away, but he wasn't there when they left. The flies have moved away from the body, with the attention it is now receiving. The back door has been opened, so that they have somewhere to go. Look out Wenlock; there is a swarm of flies been let on the loose, in the middle of the night.

I look down at the body. It is not in a good state, but I think I recognize the clothes. I then look at what there is to see of the face and I can't be sure. One of them is rummaging through his pockets, to see if he is carrying any id. Just as they pull his wallet out, I say to the detective that I think it is Bob.

'Bob who' he asks?

'Bob who found the door open the last time.' I also add 'It is the Bob who has been missing for a couple of weeks or so, we think. It is Bob who we reported as missing twice.'

'Bob who' he asks again.

'I don't know his last name. I just know him as Bob, when he collects his paper early in the morning.'

'When did he last collect one?'

'I don't know. I only help out there when they go away, or have a day off. You need to speak to Paul about that.'

'Where is Paul?'

'He owns Mrs P's with his wife Ness.'

'We'll check on it.'

'He is Robert Manning' a voice comes from beside the body. He has retrieved the wallet and opened it. He is holding a driving license.

'Can we get out of here now? I'd hate to muck up a crime scene any more than it is, by being sick over it.'

We move outside and stand just away from the front door. The police have moved the public further away now. I can still see them and they can see me. There are still going to be stories including me, in the morning.

Someone comes from inside the house and speaks to the detective. I don't get to hear what is being said, but I can see that it is serious. When they have finished talking, the man goes back into the house and the detective returns to my side.

'I think we should go to the station and take a statement from you.'

'Alright' I say, with some hesitation in my voice. Whatever has been said between the other man and the detective has obviously changed things somewhat. I don't know how, but I am not getting a good feeling about this.

'I need to ring my wife and tell her what has happened.'

He hesitates for a few seconds, before he says that is ok. The only problem I have is that I don't have any signal again down here. I tell him I need to go over in front of the church. There is normally signal there to be had. He escorts me over there, while I make my call.

Chapter 8

Kate is surprised by my call. She is also surprised by the content of it. Not only that I think it is Bob who I have found dead in there, but the fact I have to go to the police station, to make a statement. When you think about it though, it is not a surprise. I found the door open, in the middle of the night. I went in to see what was going on in there and I got shut in, by the front door slamming shut. It is all a bit strange. Add to that, I have been trying to check on Bob and they want to know some more. Hopefully all I will have to do is, to make a statement.

I promise to keep her posted, if I am allowed to. The small crowd that is still hovering on the peripheral of the scene watch me, as I get into the back of the police car and am driven off.

I spend many hours at the station. I do make a statement, but that is only after I have answered countless questions. They have been to Bob's house and spoken to Jean. She has backed up everything I have said, about being concerned about Bob's safety. Unfortunately it looks like I was way too late. I still don't know what was said, that made them take me to the station. I have been treated fairly, although they are still sceptical about parts of my story. Those parts being, I suspect, about the whooshing sound I have heard on both occasions and the figure I saw on both occasions too.

To be fair, there is no suggestion that I am a suspect in the death of Bob. It is just that I have been the one person who has been on the scene for both incidents. I am the one who came forward on the first incident and was involved in the second one. I am also the only person who has seen something else at the scene.

I am being taken back through to the front. They have offered to take me back home, but I have decided to wait for my wife to pick me up instead. She has something to do first, but will be here in a while.

I have been sitting waiting for only a few minutes, when the detective comes walking quickly out to where I am sitting.

'You can cancel your lift. I'm taking you back.'

'I need to call my wife first then.'

'Do it' he says and makes for the door.

I get up and follow him, making the call as I go. It is only when we are on the way back to Wenlock, that he tells me what is the cause of this journey.

'I have just had another call. It has happened again!'

I wait to be told exactly what has happened again, but it appears I am expected to know. I don't comment back for a few seconds and it is then he realizes that I am not with him in what he has said.

He glances at me. I am looking back at him.

'You are probably wondering what I am talking about?'

'I am a bit' I reply.

'Well when the guy came out of the house to talk to me earlier, just before we came here for you to make your statement. He came out to tell me that he believed the body had been moved. He hadn't moved it from where it lay, but he was looking closely and he could see that the body had been moved there, probably after death.'

There is another little pause. I don't know what to say about that anyway. And also, I suspect, there is more to come. He still hasn't told me what has happened again. I decide to let him tell me in his own time. It doesn't take him long before he continues.

'So, because that is what he thought, he sent for some other equipment. The vehicle bringing that over broke down on the way. The team in the house decided to leave it until it arrived. The smell was quite strong in there, as you know. They left a constable on guard at the door. The door, if you remember, was pretty much off its hinges, when the firemen smashed it open. The others went off to get some breakfast. Now the constable says he was on the door all the time. He maybe moved a foot or two, but he says he was never more than a yard away from it. He hears a noise behind him and by the time he has turned, the door is back on and shut firmly again. Initially he thought someone had got past him, but he asked the people watching and they said no one had been near him. The back door had been closed again, once the flies were out, so it wasn't that. The door was now back on its hinges and shut. He sent for the team having breakfast and with the help of the firemen, again forced entry into the property. The body has gone. There is no sign of where it lay on the floor.'

He waits for my reaction. The only thing that is going through my head at this precise second; is that I am pleased I wasn't there. I was being interviewed and having a statement taken at the police station. He senses what I must be thinking.

'I bet you're glad you were with me at the station.'

'Something like that' I reply.

'Any ideas what has happened?'

I stay quiet for a few seconds. It is all beyond me and a bit bizarre.

'Not really. I was starting to think it was something connected to me, if you know what I mean. I mean with me seeing the figure and hearing the whooshing sound, but then now something has happened and I was nowhere near.'

'But you were looking for Bob!'

'I was, but that only started when I asked Mr P, a couple of months after the first incident, if Bob was alright. It was then he told me he hadn't been in since the week after it.'

'Yeah, I get that, but why go look for him?'

'I just got a feeling that it wasn't right. I can't explain it fully, but I sometimes get feelings about stuff. My wife can see when it happens. She knows that the best thing is to let me try to get to the bottom of whatever it is. I went to see if Bob was alright. You know the rest.'

We chat a little bit more about what has happened, until we reach Wenlock. It doesn't take long to get there. We park up in the Bull Ring. There isn't a space for us, as there are quite a few vehicles attending the scene. We park up and get out. Andy, the detective, obviously is expecting me to go with him. I get out of the car and walk with him, over the road to the house. There are two constables on the door now. There is also a small crowd, standing in the road in Wilmore Street, watching the proceedings. The constables let us pass and we go into the house. The first thing that strikes me is the smell. The smell now is of dust and of being empty for years. The smell from earlier, of the body, has disappeared. The only tell-tale I can see from the hall, is that there are a few flies still around. We walk into the living room. There are three other people in there. They are standing at the edge of the room talking. That stops when we come in.

'It has just disappeared' the one man says.

He was the one who came up to Andy earlier and told him about the body had been moved here after death. It has moved again apparently and no one has a clue who did it either time.

'There is no sign of it ever having been here either. Look at the floor. There is no way it could look like that, if we had removed the body. There is nothing, except for some flies of course. If it wasn't for them, I would have believed that I was dreaming about it being here. There is no way anyone could have got in from the back. And then there is the little matter of the front door. How on earth did that get back on its hinges, with a constable standing only a few feet away and a crowd of people watching, just up the road?'

'What about the rest of the house?'

'It is just as it was. It is only the body that has gone and the door that was fixed again. The firemen have had to break in again. I really don't know what to make of it.'

Chapter 9 Anne

The ground trembles in the darkness. There isn't a storm outside or anything like that. It could be a minor earth tremor, but then it is only happening here. It is extremely localized. The trembling carries on for several minutes. It is occurring away from any town or village. It is occurring deep down in the ground, way beneath the escarpment. The trembling stops and there has been some movement of the ground too, but not at the surface. It has happened deep underground, in a cave. Where the cave had been sealed in before, there is now an access out of it. The access is only small, but it is there. There hasn't been an access to this cave for a very long time. There hasn't been one, since it was blocked off completely. Now it isn't totally blocked off any more.

Anne opens her eyes. The first thing she realizes is that it is dark; it is very dark. She waits for a minute or so, to give her eyes some time to accustom to the darkness. There is very little that she can see. It isn't totally dark where she is. There is a little bit of less dark, about ten feet from her. She moves towards this area of less intense darkness. It is above her now. She turns and looks back to where she has walked from. She can just about make out a shape on the floor, but that is the extent of it. She can't remember where she was and what she was doing before she woke up, well before she went to sleep she means.

The wall is cold to the touch. She moves along the wall, feeling her way carefully, wherever this is. She tries to think where she was last, but nothing is coming to her to help with that. Where she is, isn't square like a room. The walls are made of rock. She keeps going round the walls, until she finds herself back where she started, just under the less dark area. She looks around the area again. Her eyes can see a fraction more now, but she still can't make out what the shape on the floor is. She moves towards it. It is not by the wall; it is in the middle. When she gets there, she can feel nothing at all. It must just be a shadow, or something. There is nothing at all that she can feel, of the shape. She reaches the wall beyond and turns round. She can still make out the shape on the floor, but she can't determine what it might be. She walks back across, but again when she gets to it, there is nothing that she can feel.

It is cold in here, she realizes. She shivers a little, as she stands there wondering what she should do. She looks up at the less dark area. There is no other way out that she can feel. She tries to judge the size of it, but she can't. There is only one way to find out. It isn't too far above her head, so she should be able to reach it, if she can get a couple of footholds on the wall. The wall isn't smooth, but it isn't that rough here either. There are though, a couple of places where she manages to climb onto. Once there, her feet find another couple of places. She only needs another set of footholds and she should be able to feel the hole. She can just about see that it is a hole now. It is lighter, the closer she gets to it.

One foot finds another place to get a toe onto. She pushes up when she has her toe in. The other foot can't find a foothold. And then it does, a little bit higher. Her hand reaches out towards the less dark spot. It finds something to hold onto and pull herself up higher. Her other hand reaches into the hole. It is not as big as she thought. It is not as big as she would like and she doesn't think it is big enough for her to squeeze thru. That hand finds something to hold onto. She pulls and then has to put her other hand into the hole, before she can try to squeeze through. Her feet come off their footholds as she pulls. She is in an awkward position. She doesn't want to get stuck, but she needs to try to get through. Her feet aren't supporting her any more, as she has pulled herself off the footholds. She moves one of her hands beyond and finds that there is nothing on the other side of the wall. Well there is nothing she can feel, in front of the hole. She feels down onto the other side of the wall and finds a rock her hand can get hold of. She pulls some more. She is surprised how easy it is, for her to pull herself along. The hole must be bigger than she thinks it is. It must be a trick of the darkness. Her head is in the hole now and her shoulders are starting to go through too. She is hoping that if they can fit through, then she should get the rest of her through too.

She starts to feel good about this and reaches further down. She hasn't thought about what happens when her body gets through the hole. How is she going to stop herself from falling onto the floor, on the other side? She finds another point to grab and pulls hard on it. She is going to be able to fit through. She knows that now. Her head is through, as is her torso, before she starts to think about how she is not going to get hurt, by falling onto the floor this side. Her hand reaches ahead for another place to get hold of. She finds something better than that. She has found a ledge. It isn't that wide, maybe six inches or so, but it is a ledge. It is as wide as she can feel. There is also, she can feel, something she can hold onto. It is going to be a little precarious, there is no avoiding that. She is in the dark, even though it is a little less so this side of the wall. She can't see the floor. She can guess how far down it is, which won't be that far, but she is the wrong way round.

She doesn't know if she can do it, but she is going to have a try. It is the only way she can think of, to try to land without hurting herself, well without hurting herself too much hopefully. She can feel her thighs coming through the hole now, and she can also start to feel that she is going to fall. There is more of her body through the hole now and gravity is starting to take hold of the situation. She is going to fall anyway. All she can do is to try to turn and land as best as she can. She gets herself ready and positions her arms on the ledge. She takes as much weight as she can on her hands, as her legs start to slip through the hole. Then they are through and she starts to turn her body. Her legs swing out from the wall and then start to fall. She is losing her balance as her body moves round. As her legs start to fall, she gives a big push with her hands against the ledge. This lifts her top half up briefly and allows her legs to move down, so at least she is going to land somehow on her feet and not on her head, or her hands. Her hands part from the ledge and she falls for a fraction of a second, until she hits the floor. It isn't that far down from the ledge, just a few feet. She isn't ready for the impact though and her legs quickly crumple beneath her. They have taken some of the force of the impact, so when her body hits the ground too, it is not that severe. She rolls a little, as she hits the floor and then comes to a stop. She is quite pleased with herself, for managing to complete the turn and get her legs round.

The floor is cold, so she only takes a few seconds before she tries to stand up. She is pleased to find that she is not injured at all. There isn't even a little niggle of pain anywhere. She brushes herself down, more out of habit than being able to see if she needs to do so. It is a little lighter in here, but not much.

Chapter 10 Anne

Now that she is through the hole in the wall, she feels a bit better. The thought of being trapped in there was not appealing. She is still thinking a bit about the shape on the floor. She has checked it out and there was nothing there, but it is still in her thoughts for some reason. The coolness of where she is brings her back to the here and now. She may well have come through the hole, but she is still in a dark and cool place. She feels round the walls, as she did in the last place. They are made of the same material she thinks, stone. The texture is more or less the same too. She gets round the edge and then the wall starts to lead off somewhere. It is like a passage, she thinks. She stops there. She needs to check out the other way. It is hard to keep perspective, when you are in a place with little or no light. She tries though and when she has worked her way round the wall; she comes back to the point she thinks she found where the passageway begins. It makes sense that this is the only way out of here, other than back through the hole, to the enclosed chamber.

She feels across the passageway and her hand meets the other wall. That somehow makes her feel better. She starts to walk forward, keeping one hand on one wall and the other on the other wall. The passageway isn't very wide, so she can do this quite comfortably. There isn't much light. In fact it is still nearly as dark as the first chamber, but there is the hint of something better ahead. She finds out after maybe thirty yards or so, along the passage. The hint of lightness, when she gets there, she finds is coming through a thin crack in the ceiling of the passage. She can't see much through it, but she can see that somewhere way above her, there is a tiny chink of daylight.

The floor is damp where she is. The passage has a dip just under the crack, where water must have dripped down from the surface, through the crack. It must drain through the floor and disappear. Over the years, the dripping has created the dip in the passage floor. She wonders if there is, at any time, more than just a drip of water comes down. Or in other words, does the passage flood? She doesn't have an answer for that. She can't get up to the chink of daylight, so she has to keep moving forward.

The passage maintains its little bit of less darkness. She can't see why that is, but she is not complaining. It wouldn't be so good if there was complete darkness around her. A little way further along, the passage starts to climb a little. She can feel the slope. At this point the passage becomes narrower too; to the point that she thinks she might have to turn sideways, to be able to keep going. It doesn't get that narrow just yet. The ceiling does come down as well though and soon she has to bend down some, to get through the next section. It keeps rising and then it turns to the left. It only goes about fifteen feet and then she comes to a wall. The ceiling goes up at this point and she can stand upright and then there is still some height. Her way is blocked by the wall, though. She feels round behind her and finds the place where the ceiling rises. There is the place she has just come from and then above that is another passage, going back the same way, but over the top of it. She feels up and can just touch the top of this passage. It can only be about 12 inches high. It isn't much wider than that either. It is going to be a tight fit, but she has to do it. There is no other way for her to go, well other than back.

The first problem she has to overcome; is how to get into this upper passage. It is too high to just reach, to get into. There isn't anything for her hands to get hold of and pull her up there. There aren't any footholds for her to use, to step up to it. The only thing she has is the walls themselves to try to scale. Luckily the passage isn't wide. She faces the new passage, which is above her. She then jumps and spreads her legs. She presses her feet against the side walls and her hands too. She has managed to get about a foot off the floor. If she can do the same again, she should be high enough to get into the passage easily. She tries, but slips to the floor again. Not to be defeated, she tries again. It is only on her fifth or sixth attempt that she manages to make the second jump work. Even then, she doesn't think she can hold it for long. She doesn't take long to go into the passage, arms first. She presses her hands to the side, which isn't hard, as this passage is so narrow. She soon pulls the rest of her body in.

She stops to gather herself. It is a good job she can handle enclosed spaces. This space is very tight. She can feel the walls both side of her. She can feel the ceiling with her head and her back. She puts her hands ahead of her and tries to use her feet too, to propel her forwards. She doesn't make much progress with each attempt, but she does move forward. She also gets better at it, the more she does. After just a few yards, this passage starts to climb too. The climb is a steeper one, but still a relatively gentle slope. It doesn't last long like this. She gets maybe twenty yards and the roof opens up, but the passage stops. She has to climb several feet, but it is quite easy, as there are numerous footholds for her to use. She then has to make her way along another passageway. It is more a wide crack in the rock really, as the floor is just a series of cracks in the rock.

She climbs and she twists as she moves on. The way she is going changes many times, from cracks to a low passage. It opens up into small chambers a couple of times too. All the time it is dark, but she feels that the further she goes, the lighter it is becoming. She has no idea how long she has been travelling for. She has no idea how much distance she has covered. It appears to be endless and she is starting to tire, if not physically, definitely mentally. If she just knew how much further she had to go, then it might perk her up some.

She doesn't know, so decides to stop for a rest, when she reaches a place where she can comfortably lie down on a flat floor. She lies down and closes her eyes.

She has no idea how much time has elapsed between when she closes her eyes and when she wakes up again. She doesn't know what has woken her, but she does know that something has. Then she feels it. There is a tiny breeze coming from ahead of her. She can feel it now and it is quite refreshing. Excited by the change, she starts her journey onwards again. The passage becomes narrow and shallow again after a few yards. Then the passage stops. The only way is up. She doesn't mind the prospect of that, because she can see some daylight again. It is coming through a hole in the shaft above her, about twenty feet up, she thinks. Getting up to it might not be too hard, if she can find footholds. She doesn't think she would be able to go up the wall, like she did to get into this passage. The shaft would be just too wide to do that anyway.

She is keen to get on, so starts to feel for footholds. Once she has got started, she manages to find some. They may be shallow and only hold her toes, but she is light and determined. She is soon up to the place where the light is shining in. It is nothing more than a wide crack where she joins this passage. She can see the daylight not too far away along the passage. Unless it is an optical illusion, she doesn't think it is going to be wide enough to get through. The only way to find out is to make her way there and try to squeeze through.

Chapter 11 Anne

She realizes she must have got into here some way or another, so there must be a way out. As far as she is aware, the way she has come since she woke up, is the only way she could have come. This must be the place for her to break out into the open again.

She starts along the widened crack. It is further to the daylight than it had at first appeared. It is awkward clambering over it, as the floor isn't level. She does so and approaches the daylight, albeit more slowly than she would have liked. The shape she sees now she is closer; looks a tight fit. It isn't just a case of squeezing through a foot or two to get outside. She stops just short of where this last challenging part starts and tries to work out the best way to proceed. Awkwardly, it appears to be slightly wider at the base than at the middle or the top. So, rather than go out standing up and working her way through sideways, she is now considering trying to get through the space at ground level, but turned onto her side.

She takes a minute or two to assess both options and decides that going through at ground level looks the only feasible one. She is about to start her way through, when she hears a noise from the outside. It stops her in her tracks. It stops her for two reasons. Firstly, this is the first sound from the outside world she has heard, since she started her journey out. It is unexpected and makes her worry. She doesn't know why it does that, but she feels her heart rate move up a gear. Secondly, is the type of noise it is. The noise she hears is the sound of a man's voice. It is loud and deep. It doesn't sound very friendly. Again she has no specific memory of a voice like this, but she knows it is contributing to her worry and nervousness. She steps back a little further along the passage and gathers her thoughts. As much as she is desperate to make it outside, she does not want to come into contact with anyone straight away. She wants to be able to emerge from here in privacy. She wants to emerge and be able to have the time to see where she is and to acclimatize to the surroundings out there. She doesn't know where she is; she just hasn't got any memory of where she last was and why she has found herself deep in this cave and passage system.

Her thoughts are interrupted, by the sound of the same voice coming to her ears again. This time it appears to be even louder and to her ears that means closer too. Her first instinct is to retreat further into the passage again, but she is afraid that she might make a noise, which might be heard by the owner of this voice.

She feels he might be really close by. She assumes he will not be alone and that assumption worries her some too. Then she hears the voice again and this is definitely closer.

'I'm sure we are in the right area. I can't see anything though. They did say that there is an opening on this section. I keep finding little cracks in the rock, but they are nothing more than that.'

Another voice comes back from a bit further away.

'It could be anywhere along here. It wasn't that specific. Anyway, we will have to call it a day soon. It is getting late and we need to make our way back, down to the town soon.'

'I'll give it another five minutes.'

The voices go quiet again. Anne listens and then takes a few steps back, deeper into the cave system. Ideally she needs to find a place well out of sight, but that would mean going back down into the shaft. If she can avoid doing that she will. Suddenly the voice comes again.

'I've found something. It is a bigger crack. It doesn't look big enough, certainly not big enough for me to squeeze through.'

'It can't be the one then, as the one we are looking for is big enough to get through, so they say.'

Anne sees a shadow come across the light ahead of her. That is all she can see. She was expecting to see part at least, of the outline of a man. She sees a beam of light being shone through the crack. It doesn't come as far to the place where she is cowering down, as low as she can. She does not know what this beam of light is. She hasn't seen anything like this before.

'There is no way that this is it.' The other voice she has been hearing says. It is much closer now too.

'It is too narrow for either of us. For a second or two, I thought I was onto something.'

'Come on then, let's call it a day and get back. The light will start to go soon enough.'

The beam of light disappears. She can't hear if the men are still there, as they have stopped talking. They might just be standing out there, waiting for her to come out. She knows she has heard them say that they need to get back and the light is starting to fail, but she is worried they have just said this, to lure her out of the cave.

She stays where she is for the next hour. It is not exactly comfortable, the position she has ended up in. She doesn't feel too vulnerable of being spotted, should they choose to shine their beam of light in through the crack again. The light has disappeared from outside. It hasn't gone completely dark, but the daylight, as such, has gone. She can still see where the crack is. Really, she needs to go now, while there is still some light to make out things, but she is deterred from doing so for a while longer, by her fear of who might be out there.

It is another hour later that she decides that it must be safe to leave, if she can. She has almost forgotten that the crack did not look big enough to get through. The men said it wasn't big enough either, although she is hoping that they are bigger than she is. She moves forward and then crouches down, to get into the right position for making it through at the bottom. Her face rubs the wall as she crawls in. It isn't exactly a crawl. It is more like one of the moves she did earlier. She has her hands outstretched ahead of her and she is turned sideways to the floor. It is most uncomfortable, as the floor is a bit jagged. But, even though she hasn't gone that far, she is still making forward progress. She can feel the back of her head touching the wall behind her and her nose touching this wall. She knows she has to keep going. She pulls herself a bit further. She can feel the walls pressing, not only on her head now, but also the parts of her body that are now in this section. But, she is alright so far. She can feel the walls, but she is also able to keep going. She knows she has made the right choice coming through this way. There is no way she could have got through standing up.

The section is longer than it looks and there is also a slight bend in it, which she had not noticed from her position. She is not worried about getting stuck, even though going back now would be very awkward to achieve, should it become necessary.

Suddenly the things she is feeling with her hands, changes. She feels a breath of the wind on her hands, as they move forward and out into the open. She manages to get a grip on something and pull herself forward the last few feet, to get her entire body out. For a second she thinks that she might get stuck, as her hips brush hard against the sides, but it is only a brief feeling. She is out.

She rolls over on the ground and looks up at the sky. It is a clear evening. The stars aren't in the sky as yet, but she knows they will be soon. She lies on her back and looks up and listens. There are no voices to be heard close by. There are no voices to be heard at all. That is a relief. There are, however, other noises that come to her ears. They are noises she has not heard before and she doesn't know what they are, or what they represent. But for now they are not a threat. She just lies there looking up at the sky.

Chapter 12 Anne

Anne spends longer than she was aware of, lying on the ground, looking up at the sky. She doesn't know why she is doing it, but she does know that for some reason it is important for her to take this time.

Eventually she sits up and has a look around. She can make out the trees close to her and the dark they spread across her vision. She looks the other way, only to see more trees that way too. She is on a small plateau, or so it seems. Only this area is not covered in trees. It is rock instead, that covers this ground.

She turns to look at the place she has just emerged from. It is dark, and she can't see it clearly. But when she stands up and moves over to it, she can't believe that she has managed to get through this space. Even at the bottom, it looks far too narrow for her to have made it through. But she knows she has made it through, so it must be an optical illusion of the light that is hiding something from her. It is of no matter. Now that she is out, it is not as if she is intending to go back in. On that thought, she briefly dwells on the question of why she was in there and how she got to be in there. She doesn't dwell on it long though.

She turns and walks to the edge of the plateau. The land falls away in front of her. It is too dark to see down. She has no idea how far it goes down. She turns the other way and sees that the land must rise above her too. She only works this out, because of the highlights of the tree tops against the evening sky.

The question she has in her head is; which way should she go now, down or up? She has not been able to even start to work out where she is. She does not recognize the place that she has emerged from, or into. She knows places where there are trees on the side of hills, but she doesn't know if this place is one of those.

There are other things that are puzzling her, particularly as she looks out towards the distance, on the side of the plateau where the land drops away. She can see lights moving. She can also hear sounds of something, but she doesn't know what they are. There are also some lights that she can see, that are static. She has seen lights before, but never ones so bright as these.

Her body gives a little shudder, as the cooler evening air gets to her. She needs to move from here. It may be the obvious thing to go downwards to start with, but that will take her towards these lights that move and then disappear, only to be replaced some time later by others. They are not in the same place every time, but they do appear to be following the same path. These lights are concerning her and so she chooses to take the other option open to her, to go up the slope.

There is no path to follow as such, but she does find what must be an animal track, to follow initially. That doesn't take her far, because as she enters at the tree line, she loses the ability to see which way it is running.

She makes her way up through the trees. The branches catch her many times, between her starting place and the top. They brush her hands and her face. They brush her clothes and sometimes she walks into some, which stop her in her tracks. They don't exactly hurt her, but they do come unexpectedly.

The slope is quite steep and she loses her footing on several occasions. At times she finds that she has to scrabble her way up the hillside. She only has it in her mind, to make it to the top. If she is somewhere that she knows, then she will find herself at the top of an escarpment and will be able to make her way into a settlement. If she is somewhere else, then she will find that out too, but obviously she will not know what she will find.

She breaks out of the trees at the top of the slope. She only knows that, because the ground becomes less steep and then very quickly, more or less flat. That is what she was expecting to find. The ground is rocky at this place, but in general she is faced with more trees, in every direction. The big question she needs the answer to now, is which way she should go. That will depend on which side of the escarpment she has been climbing. At this point, she does not know the answer to that one.

She stands there and looks up at the sky once more. To be fair, it is the only direction that she can see a long way in. She feels she should know which way to go, by the night sky, but she doesn't. The answer isn't coming to her, even if she stands there all night. Only if she waits until morning and there is a sunrise, will she know for sure which direction she should be going in; if she is in the place she thinks she is and should be.

She shivers again, with the cool of the night air. She can still hear some of the noises that were coming to her ears earlier, down the slope, but she can't see the lights any more. The trees are shielding her from everything in that direction. She shivers again. She is not dressed to be out at this time of night, in the clothes she is in. She has to make a decision. Should she go left, or should she go right. She doesn't know which the right one is and indecision is still controlling her thoughts.

Something swoops over her head and gives her a start. She doesn't see it clearly, as it is too dark. What she does hear is the whoosh, as it flies over her head. She can just make out a shadow, sweeping away from her. That makes up her mind. She starts walking in the direction the bird has come from.

She is soon back into the trees again. Again there is no clear path to follow, even if there had been sufficient light to do so. She walks along, aware that if she is the place she hopes she is, the land will go down, either side of where she is. It wouldn't be an abrupt change in the land, but a general slope to either side would tell her she is too near the edge.

She finds that she is tired after her climb up the slope, so her progress forwards is now at a slow pace. The terrain does not lend itself for swift movement in the dark, anyway. She had started out that way, but soon found that she tripped on roots and other things, let alone the bumping into trees that she manages to do too. Now that she has slowed down, she is more comfortable. Her careful steps ensure she does not come to any harm.

After maybe a quarter of an hour and a couple of short rests, she can feel the land beneath her starting to slope down. It is more gradual than it would be, if she was too near the edge that way, so she is not concerned. It is what she expected. That is a comfort to her. That is as far as the comfort goes though. She can feel under her feet; that she is now on a path of some sorts. She comes out of the trees and stops almost immediately. There are lights ahead. She does not remember what they might be. They do not move, so she resumes walking. The lights illuminate the ground around them. They do more than that for Anne. They illuminate buildings. She can't remember there being any buildings like these at this place. She still thinks she is in a place that she should know, but these lights on long poles and the buildings near to them, are totally unfamiliar to her.

The path beneath her feet becomes hard and as such, easy to walk on. The slope is very gentle and it leads her to a much bigger path and more of these lights on long poles. There are also more of these buildings. They are much more substantial to any she has seen before, in, or near this place. She notices too that there are things on this big path. They are not moving, but they look strange to her. She walks up to one of them and has a look. Anne hasn't seen a car before.

Chapter 13 Me

They turn and look at me. I don't know why they are doing that. If they are expecting me to come up with the answers to all this, then they are sadly looking in the wrong place. I have no more idea why all this has happened than they have. I do, however, have one of those feelings inside me; that I am going to know at one stage. But I am going to keep that to myself for as long as I can.

I am getting this feeling, because something has just sprung into my thoughts. It is about Bob. I push it away for now and mentally put it in a cupboard and shut the door. My guess is that Bob is dead and whatever I do or say at this moment, is not going to bring him back alive again. If I do say something at this moment, I can only see myself getting dragged deeper into this than I am comfortable with. Also, more to the point, it will put me right back at the top of their lists of suspects, if I am not already still there at the top. The only saving grace for me being, that I have been with the police all the time when the body disappeared.

I must have been away with my thoughts for a few seconds, maybe longer. I refocus again, to find them staring at me. They haven't been talking to me; at least I don't think I have. Andy is the one who breaks the silence.

'I know you couldn't have had anything to do this, because you were with us, but can you think of anything that could explain this?'

'The short answer is no. I don't think I'm aware of a long answer either. I just happen to have been around on both occasions something has happened here.'

'It is only two out of three actually! The body disappearing this morning was when you weren't around.'

'True' I reply. The thought comes into my head again about Bob. I need to let it process, before I say anything.

What I really want to happen, is for someone else to suggest what I am going to have to say, if no one else does.

I see them all looking at me again. I can tell by their looks that they know I am thinking about something. I suspect that they also know I have had a thought, about what has happened here in this house. On that point they are wrong, but I do have a thought about Bob. I really don't want to be the one who suggests the next course of action.

'It can't have disappeared into thin air' the other man says, giving me a break from his scrutiny.

'There is no way they could have got it out of the back door and away.' The third man says. 'I have checked out there and there is no evidence of anyone coming in that way. Anyway there is no way out of the back yard.'

'So how did it go?'

'I really don't know. This is all a little too much. Doors getting mended and closed, but no one there who has done it? Bodies here one minute and then gone the next. We aren't even certain that this last one was the Bob you say it was. We didn't get the opportunity to establish that. On top of that, we have no idea who the first body belonged to; the one that Bob found.'

Again they all turn to look at me, as if I have the answers to these puzzles.

'Something is going on here' I find myself entering the conversation. I have not done it intentionally, but I hear my voice talking. They stare at me even harder. They have been waiting for me to talk. 'I am fairly sure it was Bob I saw on the floor here. I don't know him that well, but I guess it is more likely to have been him than not. I have no idea who the first person was, because I didn't see them.'

I stop talking, which is not what they want me to do.

'So where do you think this body Bob might have gone?'

'I don't know.'

I still have enough control on what my mouth is doing, to not get drawn into saying what I really think. I can't believe they are not suggesting it themselves. At last, after a few minute's silence after I have continued not to speak, does someone suggest something to do, rather than just stand here, deliberating something that we know nothing about.

'I think we should go up to the Stretton Road and have another look at Bob's house.'

I feel a little jolt of energy course through me at this suggestion. It is what I have been trying so hard not to suggest. Imagine what the consequence of that would be, if they find what I suspect they are going to find up there. My joy is short lived though, as he adds something else to those words.

'But I already think that is what you have been thinking about.'

The cat is almost out of the bag, so to speak.

'I have to admit the thought has been coming to me for the past few minutes. I don't know why, but it seems to be the obvious place to go and look.'

I am still not going to say what I think we will find there. I need to leave that. If I am right, it won't look good and if I am wrong, it won't look good either.

We make our way to the front door. It is a short walk to the car. Andy and I go in one vehicle, while the other two follow us up in another one. It only takes us three minutes to get to our destination. I call next door for the key. I hand it to Andy and he is the one who unlocks the door. He is set to walk in, but is stopped by the smell. He steps back out and pulls the door to. He is too late to stop some of the stench coming our way. I recognize it from earlier, when I went into the house in the town. It is the same smell. I can also imagine that if we go further in, then we will hear the buzz of the flies.

'We need to get some masks, before we can go in.'

I am hoping that I am not going to be included in the 'we', but I have this dread of a thought, that I am included.

That is confirmed when we are approached, by a man holding four sets of protective clothing and masks.

'If you don't mind, I think you need to be with us.'

'I really don't see why' I answer back, but know I have a good probability of losing this argument.

'I'd like you to be with us. Firstly you know what Bob looks like and secondly, I think you have already seen this bit. It will be less shocking with these clothes on and a mask; particularly the mask. I'm asking you nicely. I know you don't have to, but this whole situation is a bit weird. Please!'

It is hard to put an argument as to why I can refuse. It is hard to argue his case of why I should too though, on the other hand.

I stop to have a think about it. If I don't go in with them, then I am certain they are going to think I know far more than I really do. I don't know anything. Well I am not aware that I know anything, is probably more precise. I am already under suspicion. I think, on balance, I will help my cause if I do as he asks, rather than try to not go in with them. To that end I don the clothes and mask I have been given.

Andy goes in first and we follow. I am third in line to go through the front door. The mask may well have a purpose, but it does little to reduce the stench that I can still smell. Sure enough the smell is soon accompanied by something else that I expected; the sound of buzzing flies. We climb the stairs, with both the noise and the stench getting louder and more obnoxious, the nearer we get to his bedroom. The bedroom door is open. We all want to get this first bit out of the way as soon as possible. To that end, there is no stopping as we get to the top of the stairs. We walk into his bedroom. There are thousands of flies and the most horrendous stench. Both are from the area of the body. Bob is lying on the top of the covers, very much dead.

Chapter 14 Me

'I need to leave' I say almost immediately. I can't confirm 100% that it is Bob lying on the bed, but I am guessing that it is indeed Bob. I intend to leave it up to them, to establish his identity officially.

Andy and I leave the other two to it. They are coming downstairs with us, but only so they can make the necessary calls for their wagon. Andy and I are not going to stay. I can't get too far away quickly enough. Well, we make it as far as his car, before he asks me something again.

'You had guessed that he would be here, hadn't you?'

'Well more or less that thought was given to me, so to speak. I found myself thinking about it and then I knew, I just knew.'

'It still doesn't explain the how.'

'I really can't help you with that one. I am not really involved. I was with you when he was moved from the other house. And as you know, he wasn't here when we looked here before that.'

'I'm trying to understand how it could have been done and I'm not getting anywhere. He was definitely not here, but he was definitely at the other house. He has somehow been moved, by someone unknown. This has been done right under our noses and I don't know how.'

As he is saying this to me, another thought decides to pop into my head. As a consequence of this, I must obviously have gone quiet. Andy nudges me, after what turns out of having been about a minute, of deliberating by me.

'Sorry, was just thinking something.'

'Is it something I need to hear?'

This is only going to involve me further, but I think I am already knee deep in being involved anyway. I decide to let him into my thought.

'That's two bodies you have lost from that house.'

'It is two bodies that have disappeared, that is true. What are you getting at?'

'I'll say it in the order it is just going to come out in. I found Bob in that house. He was still there when you came. Then he disappeared from there and reappeared back here.'

I see he wants to speak, but I hold up my finger, to make him wait. I see him relax and listen to the rest of what I want to say.

'I recognized the figure I found as being Bob. Knowing that, we are able to come to Bob's house and hey presto, we are finding Bob here. He has obviously been dead for some time. Forget for a minute or two about the logistics of how he moved, I believe from here to there and then back again. It is the other body that I have just thought about. Bob found that body. I'm guessing that Bob didn't know who that person was. As far as I am aware, you have not been able to establish who that person was. You hadn't got as far as identifying him.'

Andy is nodding his head at this. I don't know if he has made the jump, to where I am going to go with this. I get ready to continue.

'So we don't know who the first guy is. We do know that Bob saw him lying on the floor and he was dead. We know that you guys also saw him on the floor and he was dead. But we don't know who he is.'

'That's true. There is even a bit more you won't know about, but I might as well tell you. Before our guys left the house, to let the others in, they had taken some photographs of the body. When the door slammed and we had to break in, only to find the body had gone, we still thought that we should be able to track down who he was, from the photos. But when they went to look at the pictures, they were no longer on the memory of the camera. Somehow they had got wiped. Other things were on there, but not the pictures of that body. Obviously we have not been able to trace who it was. To be honest, it has all been kept very quiet.'

'Anyway, leaving that aside for a minute; that body too was there and then not. I'm asking the question, if the same thing happened to that body. Did that get moved to the house and then back somewhere again? If that is so, then there must be another body somewhere that is waiting to be found. And to make things worse, it may well have been waiting to be found for a lot longer than Bob.'

'Oh my god, you could be right about that. We certainly haven't come across someone who has been found dead at home. We have been keeping a look out for that sort of circumstance, naturally.'

'I may not be right.'

'I think unfortunately you could be right. The only thing we have to try and do; is to find someone who has not been seen for so many weeks. You'd think that someone would miss them, if they hadn't been seen for this long.'

'You'd like to think so, but things don't always work out that way, for many reasons.'

He looks at me strangely at that comment.

'Sometime people don't think. It's a small town, so you'd think that they would. If the body was a local, then I think we would have heard about it. But if it was someone who has recently moved to the town, or somewhere round here, then maybe there wouldn't be anyone to notice they hadn't been out. That is always assuming they have no family either.'

'Ok, I get that. So you think the same thing happened as with Bob. There is a body to be found. All we have to do is find it.'

'I dread to think what state it might be in.'

'Me too! I think we need to get on this. I'll have a word with my boss and get a door to door going. I can't see it can be done any other way. If we get enough manpower, then it won't take that long. We will have to check every house.'

I nod at this. I know, well I think I know, the search is going to prove fruitful.

'You know where I am if you need me.'

'Thanks' he says and turns to his car. As I walk away, I can see him already talking to someone on his phone.

Later that day we get a knock at our door. It is part of the door to door. Everyone is accounted for in our little cul-de-sac, but we already knew that. It is quite a bit later than that, when the doorbell goes again. I open it, to find Andy on my doorstep.

'Come in' I offer.

'Thanks. I'd like to run something past you, if I can. You seem to be able to see what we might need to know.'

I don't quite understand that comment, but I am guessing what is going to be asked of me in a minute.

I make us a cup of coffee, while he gets some papers out of his briefcase. We sit down, ready to discuss what they have found out, from their door to door.

'We have been round every house in town and just on the outskirts too. We haven't been able to get an answer from every door, which is not a surprise. Basically, what we have are six possibilities. I don't want to just break down people's doors. There sort of isn't that kind of urgency to this case, if you understand what I mean.'

I do understand. We are both in the belief camp that someone is dead and waiting to be found. I think this, but just nod back at him.

'Two of them are women. I don't need you to know who they are. They have not been seen for weeks, but they are both thought to be away. One has gone to Australia I believe, and the other has gone to see family.'

'Nora Salens is in Australia, if she is one on your list.'

'She is.'

'Well you can cross her off. I thought the body was that of a man.'

'That is true, but we have just been thorough. We'll put the other woman to one side, for a minute too. That leaves 4. None of them are local. Alan Birch has been away for well over a month, according to his neighbours. He hasn't left a key with anyone, but he did tell them he would be away, so we'll cross him off. That leaves us with three; Frank Bush, Simon Carson and Peter Leballe.'

He stops, to see if the names mean anything to me.

'Apparently Peter goes away a lot. He was widowed last year and he finds it hard to stay at home. He hasn't been in the habit of letting people know when he goes away. He has shut himself away since his wife died. He doesn't like attention. Frank Bush is new to the town. He hasn't been seen for weeks. No one knows much about him. He moved here about two years ago. He doesn't get involved, his neighbours say. Then there is Simon Carson. He lives alone. He has lived here the longest, but again keeps himself to himself. He fell out with his neighbours several times, so no one talks to him. We think he is the most likely.'

I don't say anything, but get up and go for a piece of paper and a pen. I don't know why I am getting it though.

Chapter 15 Me

I come back and sit down, with my pen at the ready. I ask him for the names again and he obliges. I don't know why I am doing this. I haven't got any special powers, but then something made me go to fetch the pen and paper.

I don't totally discard the women. I just keep them to one side and concentrate on the men's names. I know even before I have finished writing the four names down, which one is dead. I don't know how I know it, but I give a slight shiver and shudder as I write his name. I finish writing the four names and then look at them. Andy hasn't notice the change in me. I start with Alan and look at his name. I move onto Frank and then Simon. Only when I move onto Peter, do I get this feeling of dread come over me.

'Are we right?' Andy asks as he sees this.

'No, I fear that you are not. Where does Peter live?'

'He looks down at a piece of paper in front of him.'

'Hunter's Gate.'

Again I get the shiver, but stronger this time.

'He's your man. I think we should go there.'

'I'll get the team round. They are ready and waiting.'

I tell my wife that we are off out. She has already heard and seen all this. I give her a kiss on my way out. I don't believe we will be that long.

Two minutes sees us at his house. We are there first, but it is only just round the corner from me. Two more minutes and we are joined by the others. The door gives little resistance and entry is gained. Thankfully, I am not asked to go in with them. I am with Andy at the front door. There is no smell coming to our noses. Downstairs is clear, but I would expect that to be the case. We can hear the shouts of clear, as they check the rooms on the first floor. Then they go up to the top floor. That is where they find the body of Peter Leballe. He is locked in a small room up there. He has been there for weeks from the look of it. Certainly what they find points to that.

Through all this, I have been asking myself a question. What have I got to do with this? Bob discovered a body and is now dead. Did Peter discover a body before Bob and now he is dead. Therefore, and this is the question I have really been asking myself. Because I found Bob's dead body, am I next? I really hope not, but then I don't have a clue what is going on here.

I am allowed to walk home. Andy will talk to me, if he needs to. I am not to say anything yet, preferably not at all about the weirdness of what has happened. I admit to not being keen to either. I can guess what people might think and say about me.

I get a couple of visits over the next few weeks. I am pleased to say that first of all, I am very much alive. After that, I am also pleased to say, that the other five have all returned home safe and well and definitely all still alive. Andy has asked me how I knew it was Peter. I have no idea how I was able to pick him out of the six names offered to me.

It is about six weeks later, when I wake up suddenly in the middle of the night. I get the impression that something has woken me, rather than just a random awakening. I lie in my bed and try to listen for noises that shouldn't be there. The dogs are quiet and fast asleep, which should tell me that there isn't anything untoward going on outside the house. If there had been something, then they would have been barking, or at least growling. I listen for about five minutes, without success. Everything is normal. I snuggle down under the covers and try my best to get back to sleep. It isn't happening though. I toss and turn for the next half hour, before I have to give up on it. If this happens normally, I would keep trying, but tonight I am not in the mood for that. If I toss and turn much more, I am going to disturb my wife.

I slip out of bed and put my dressing gown on. The dogs hear me moving and so as I come out the bedroom, they are there, waiting for me to let them out into the garden. I go downstairs and do just that. If there is someone or something out there, then they will sound their warning. That doesn't happen either. I stand at the back door, with the light on, and watch them sniff their way round the back garden. After a few minutes they have had enough and return to me. I let them past me and lock the door.

I sit in the living room and have a cup of coffee. It is decaf and at the end of it, I feel no more ready to go back to bed, than I did when I got up. In fact I am wide awake. I also have a feeling inside of me. I hadn't noticed it coming on. It has just surfaced there. I need to get dressed.

My wife is still sleeping soundly and the dogs have gone back to their beds and settled down again. I write a note and leave it on the side in the kitchen, that I have felt the need to go out for a walk, even though it is the middle of the night. I put the time on my note.

It is dry, which I knew from standing at the back door, watching the dogs. I walk out of our little cul-de-sac and look to my right. There is nothing to see that way. It is dark. The only light near me; is coming from the street sign, telling traffic there is a bend. This sign is on the other side of the road. I start to walk slowly towards town. It is dark in front of me. I thought I remembered that they leave a street light on by The Raven, but there is no light to be seen ahead at all. It is quite eerie as I walk, hearing the sounds of my shoes on the pavement. It is very quiet. Sometimes I would imagine that there might be lights left on in some of the houses I am passing, but not tonight. They are all in darkness. I can make out outlines of buildings, but that is about the extent of it. It is certainly dark in Wenlock.

I am not normally a nervous person if I have to walk in the dark, but something is getting to me tonight. I am feeling more than just a little uncomfortable about this walk. I could of course, turn round and walk home. That is actually what I should probably do, but I don't. Something is drawing me forward, further into the dark and gloom ahead of me. I keep imagining I can hear another set of footsteps. I keep turning around, but there is nothing to see. I can't see far, so that doesn't do a lot to make me feel better.

I get to the corner at The Raven. I look up St Mary's Lane. It is dark up there too. There is not a single light in any window. I walk across the road and continue past The

Raven and on towards the square. I am just going past one of the houses, when I hear a whoosh behind me. As I turn, I catch sight of something running, or at least moving quickly towards me. My heart jumps into my mouth and I back up to the wall. I recognize the cape that I have seen before. The figure does not even slow at my presence. I start to walk quickly after it, but I don't think I am doing anything like the pace this figure is doing. I am in the square in less than thirty seconds, but I have already lost sight of where this figure has gone. I seek refuge in the light of the Smoothie's window. I need a few seconds of safety in the illumination. I need that before I move forward. There is a reason why I have had to come out for this walk.

Chapter 16   Me

I sit on one of the benches and take a few seconds, to bring things back to normal. Actually I'm not sure what normal is, in relation to all this. I have been out at this time of night three times and on each occasion I have seen this figure, but not in the same place. I'm guessing that I'm not the only person who has walked through town in the middle of the night. Have they all seen the figure in the long cloak too? Something inside me tells me that they haven't. Surely it would have been told.

I am looking around me as I am thinking. I can't say that I'm settled while I'm sitting here. I'm not on edge either. It is a weird feeling, because I know I am now waiting for something to happen. I'll give it another five minutes and then if it hasn't, then I'll get up and walk along past the Guildhall and the church, down towards the Bull Ring.

Suddenly a movement catches my eyes. It is over by the passage, by the Guildhall. It is darker over there and I can't be absolutely sure I have seen anything. Maybe it was a trick of the light. I concentrate on trying to see what is there, in that dark corner. Then I see something flapping, just a little. If I am not mistaken, it is the cape. I stand up slowly and wait to see what happens next. I am not rewarded straight away.

I give it a few seconds, before I take my first steps, roughly in that direction. I step forward towards the clock. That is on the edge of the square, between me and the Guildhall. I reach the clock and stop. I can see the cloth flapping, but I can't see any more than that. I am just about to close the gap even more, when the figure moves out. I can't see much more, as it is so dark. It is darker where the figure is. I can tell that they are looking at me, as they take several steps away from the Guildhall. The figure is not walking directly towards me, but it is looking at me. I know I am being watched. Despite the darkness, I am going to land on the side that this is a girl or a woman. The figure is slight too. She crosses the road and walks on. She is now level with me, but she is in front of the museum. She does not stop looking at me, until she reaches the front of the Spar. At that point, she turns her head to face the direction she is walking in. She isn't rushing, but she isn't dawdling either. She has reached the front doors of Foden's, before I find my legs have started to move and I am following her. I am probably a good twenty paces behind and on the other side of the road.

I can see ahead of me, on my side of the street; that the clothes shop has its window lights on. If she carries on that far, opposite the Copper Kettle, then I will get a better view of her. She doesn't give me that opportunity though. When she reaches the Corn Exchange, she ducks out of sight. You can go along the passage and out into the car park behind. It is not an ideal scenario, as it will be dark down there and I am not totally comfortable, following her down there.

There is normally a light in the passage, but I can see it is not lit. I can't see if she is hiding in the shadows. I stop, look and listen. I am still on the other side of the road. It is even darker under the Corn Exchange. I am just on the point of thinking that she must have gone through the passage, when I hear a whooshing sound. She must have been standing in the far corner, beyond the library door. She whooshes out onto the pavement at that end, and then down the front and back in. I watch, as I vaguely see her disappear down the passage.

I don't hesitate and start to cross the road. I am afraid, but then I am not. I don't think she is out to harm me. I can't hear her moving as I enter the passage. I have to feel my way along and then turn at the corner. I am soon out the back of the building, at the top end of the car park. I can just make her out, standing at the bottom of the car park, by the road. She waits until I am about half the way down the car park, before she moves off again. She goes to the right, not hurrying, down Back Lane. I don't try to catch her up. I get the feeling that would be pointless. She has been waiting for me, but not to let me catch her.

It is dark down Back Lane and I am not sure that I am seeing her or not. I'm guessing she will go down to the corner, where it joins Queen Street. When I get there, it is a fraction lighter, but not by much. She is standing outside the gateway of Wenlock Mews. That was an old stable. It has been redeveloped in a lovely house. As I start walking in Queen Street, she also starts to move again. I have a funny feeling that I know where she might be going. I am not sure I am going to like this. Sure enough, at the corner she takes a left. By the time I get to the corner, she is nowhere to be seen. I cross over the road. I don't want to stay on this side. I stop in front of the Old Police Station and face across the road.

She is standing in the doorway of the house. She is looking directly across at me. I know it can't really be, but it feels lighter here than anywhere else we have been walking. I can make her out quite clearly. She lifts her hands up and then takes hold of the hood and pulls it back, to reveal her face. I get a bit of a shock. I don't know what I am expecting. What I see is someone who looks very much like Tara. Tara works at the Deli in High Street. The only difference, my mind is telling me, is that Tara is taller than this girl. There is no doubt it is a girl. If it wasn't for the height difference, this is Tara standing in front of me.

She pulls the hood back over her head and her face is hidden from me again. She turns quickly. I notice that the door she has been standing beside is open. It wasn't open when I arrived. I haven't seen her open it, but it is definitely very much open now. She moves through the doorway and disappears somewhere inside. There is no way I am going to follow her in. I have been in there before and I don't like it in there.

I can't hear her inside there. There isn't another sound to be heard, as there hasn't since the whooshing up at the Corn Exchange. I wonder if she expects me to go in after her. She is going to be disappointed. I feel I have done quite well, following her this far. I'm not going to follow her in!

I stand there for a good ten minutes. If anyone were to drive by, it would look quite suspicious I'm sure. I am just standing by the wall of the Old Police Station, watching the open door on the other side of the road. I don't know what to do next. I don't feel I can just walk away from this. Clearly something is meant to happen. I have been meant to follow her and she has brought me here, albeit by a slightly circuitous route.

Then she appears at the door. Once again she removes the hood and stares at me. Once again I see Tara's face. Suddenly the hood is back on and her face is hidden again. I hear the whoosh, as she starts to move. She moves so quickly, across the road towards me. I don't even have the time to get worried, or move out of the way. She is making straight for me. She runs into me, but I don't feel any impact. I feel a micro second of coolness, as her figure collides with mine and then she is gone. I quickly turn my head to the left and then to the right, but there is nothing there to be seen. She isn't there. I almost feel she must have gone through me and through the wall of the Old Police Station.

Chapter 17 Me

I stand there, almost mesmerized, for a few seconds. I know she was coming straight at me. I am sure she didn't deviate from her path. She must have collided with me, but I did not feel an impact in the slightest. I guess I knew she wasn't real all along, but only now, at this second, have I actually seen that with my own eyes.

I return my attention to the house, on the other side of the road. She was standing in the open doorway, the last time I saw her, before she came at me. The open doorway is still there, but obviously she is not. A feeling of dread comes over me. The last two times that door has been open; there has been a body in the house. I am not expecting anything different today. On that basis I have absolutely no intention of going in, at least not on my own I don't.

I take my phone out of my pocket and look at the screen. Not surprisingly, it is showing that I don't have any signal. That in itself is not unusual for this particular spot in town. It has not been helped by the fact my phone has been in my pocket. From experience, that takes the possibility of having signal here from low, to pretty much guaranteed zero. I wish it was not the case, but it is. I am fairly certain that if I give it a minute or so, then the signal will show up on my phone. I could move to a place where I have an almost guaranteed better chance of having signal. But I don't want to do that, because I would then lose sight of the doorway, not by distance, but by the fact that at this moment, it is Dark in Wenlock.

I'm impatient and keep glancing at my phone, whilst keeping a really good eye on the door opposite. I am half expecting to look up at any time and see that it has closed on its own again. It hasn't and it doesn't. That in itself is not good news, because I feel that there is another story to unfold here.

I've got two bars appearing on the screen. That is enough for me to dial 999 and wait less than five seconds for the pick-up. I ask for police and say that I have found this door is wide open. That in itself is insufficient information to move my call into a priority one. I have to tell them that this is the same place that two bodies have been found in the past few weeks, when the front door has been found open. Can I confirm that there is a body in there this time? No, I cannot. I haven't been in and I have no intention of going in, at least until there is someone else with me, preferably the police.

I have said enough. A police vehicle will be dispatched, I am told. I resume my position, standing with my back to the wall. I am sort of tempted to move to a slightly different position, in case she comes back through the wall and through me once again. I opt not to, because she doesn't appear to have done me any harm on the way through. I am starting to wonder why it is me that is the witness to these actions though.

I don't have to wait long, before I am joined by a policeman. I haven't seen him before. After a brief discussion, I discover that, although he has heard something of the goings on here, he does not know anything about the previous occasions. He is undaunted by the prospect of going into the house on his own. I do actually offer to go in with him, but that offer is refused. I am fine with that. I know he is going to find something. Otherwise why would the door be open?

He switches on his torch and makes his way into the house. I can see the light move away from the hallway and go into the living room. Two seconds and he is making his way out from the doorway, rather hurriedly. He stops to retch in the gutter and then turns on his radio, to message for assistance. Even in the lack of light we have here; I can see that he has gone very pale.

He walks over to stand with me. It hasn't crossed his mind that I might be responsible for whatever has gone on in there. He clearly wants to be standing with me, rather than be standing alone.

Less than ten minutes later, there is a small convoy of vehicles turning up. Not for the first time in this street recently, the air is lit up by the flashing blue lights from police cars and an ambulance. From what the policeman has told me, there will be no need for the ambulance to be used. This body is well beyond the help of that service. It will be a different vehicle that takes this one away, if it remains there this time.

To that end, two people are put in the living room, with nothing else to do, but to ensure that no one takes the body away. The house is all lit up now, from top to bottom. There is someone standing inside by the back door; another person standing at the bottom of the stairs and another one standing in the front doorway itself.

A small crowd has turned up, no doubt woken by all the activity. I am sure I have been noticed and it will not be lost on some people, that here I am again, standing outside the scene of an unexplained death in Wenlock.

As I have been expecting, another two people arrive, a while after the main crews. Andy is looking quite sleepy as he gets out of his vehicle. The other man from the SOCO team is looking more alert. They come to talk to me first, before taking me with them across the road and into the house.

We walk through the front door and then turn into the living room. There against the far wall is the body. The main difference that even I can see straight away; is that this is the body of a woman. Even to my untrained eye, I can see that she has been dead for some considerable time. Her clothes are ragged and ripped. Her hair is tangled and covered in dust and dirt. There is nothing left of a face that is recognizable. She is very slight. I can see rings on one hand. I would say on her fingers, but there isn't any flesh on her hand. The rings are there still.

We have stopped, once we are all in the room. The smell is pretty obnoxious and there is another odour in the air that I cannot place. It is making me start to gag a bit. I can understand why the police patrol man was sick outside.

I am just about to say I am going back outside again, when something happens. It catches us all by surprise. It shouldn't have done really, considering the history we have with bodies in this house. At almost the same instant the lights go out, not only in the house, but also the lights on the vehicles outside. As that is happening, I hear the familiar whoosh from somewhere. Even though we have lost the lights in the room and my eyes have not had the chance to acclimatize to this light, I see her. It is as if she has emerged from within me! I can only see her vaguely, but what I do see, is her move from me towards the body. She bends down quickly and touches the body. She hasn't picked it up, but it goes just like that, in an instant it is not there. She whooshes past me; she does not go through me this time. She goes through the door into the hall and out of the front door. A split second later, the front door slams shut. I don't hear it shutting, but I know she has slammed it shut. The lights flicker and come back on, both inside and outside the house. We are in an empty room once more. The body of the woman has gone and there is no evidence our eyes can pick up, to show she has ever been found dead in here.

A look in the hall by Andy, confirms what I know has happened. The door has slammed shut on its own, slamming the person guarding it to the ground, on the pavement outside.

The smell has all but gone too. There were no flies this time. I still need to get out of here.

Chapter 18 Me

Not for the first time, the fire crew has to break the door open, so we can get out. I am almost tempted to ask the carpenter who is going to have to fix it again, if he will let me have one of the new keys, so I have it handy. That thought, of course, presumes that I think there is going to be another occasion. I would not be so bold as to rule that out.

There is much less fuss this time. The crews disperse relatively quickly. I find that I have to go to Telford again, to give my explanation to Andy and others. They want to know just how I came to be out in the middle of the night. And in particular, how I came to find that this door was left open once more; for us to find another body. They receive my story relatively well. As expected, they are a little sceptical when it comes to the figure I was following and what happened in the house. There I am, assuming that everything will be alright, as he has witnessed the scene, because he was there right beside me. The problem is that he didn't hear the whoosh and he didn't see her appear from within, as I put it. All he experienced was the lights going out and then coming back on.

I am not sure if he believes me. He is prepared to run with it for now. He wants to concentrate on who it might be that we need to find. Like before, I have no idea who it could be, but I get the feeling I am going to be the one who is best equipped to shorten the search process.

Do I have any ideas whose body it is I have discovered? To be precise about it, all I did was to find the door open. It was the police patrol man who technically found the body. That doesn't answer their question. Also, I am not getting away with that for an answer. What does my intuition have, to input her real name and whereabouts?

I give it a bit of thought for five minutes. I don't know for sure, but I know where I would check first.

'There were six people we unearthed in the hunt for Peter, the last body,'

'Ok, go on' he encourages me.

'We had six names on that list.'

'Yes, but we discarded two and then found Peter.'

'That's right. But we discarded two, because they weren't men and the body we were looking for was that of a man. This time we are looking for a woman. I can remember that one of them had gone to Australia. I don't know, but I am not expecting it to be her. It is the other woman I believe we should be looking for.'

He takes his phone out of his pocket and looks it up.

'Nora Salens was the woman who had gone to Australia. We can check to see if she is back. But you are saying we should look for the other woman first. She is Joan Potts.'

'I am, even though I believe she came back, as did Nora.'

I accompany them to where we have Joan listed as living. It is in one of the houses in Swan Meadow. We don't all descend on her, but there are still maybe six of us at, or very close to, her front door.

The short of it being, that we wait for the firemen to do the work on this front door. They get it open in no time and the rest of the crew goes in. I am left standing on the front drive for a considerable amount of time, on my own. If I had been the type to do something, I had the opportunity. I could have wandered off and there was no one to stop me leaving. All that would have done is to bring them down on me even more. At the moment they don't understand the things I am saying are happening. I think it is only because I wasn't present at one time; that keeps me from being given a more severe interview with them.

Needless to say they find Joan in the house. She has been dead for weeks. They find her wrapped in a sheet, on the far side of the bed. There is a good chance she has been there just as long as Peter and Bob have been deceased.

I know I have not had anything to do with their deaths, but there is little to disguise the fact that I am involved somehow, in the discovery of their dead bodies. To that extent, I am subjected to another interview. This time it is held in the front room of Joan's house. I am not held. I am certainly not charged. I also get the distinct impression that I am not a suspect in their unexplained deaths. I am therefore allowed to leave, about an hour and a half after the body has been discovered. I emerge from Joan's house, to see that a small crowd has gathered outside, to see what is going on. I can already see the tongues wagging about my presence.

I pay them no heed and walk through their midst and out the other side. I cut through Park Road and into the park. I go down the footpath and out onto Barrow Street. From there it is a short walk to my house. I have to tell my story all over again, naturally, before I go up to have a long soak and a shave.

Refreshed, I take the dogs for a walk. There is nothing outside the house in Sheinton Street, to show for the action that occurred there in the night. We walk past the house and turn up Station Road, to walk the dogs round the Gaskell Field.

The one thing about the night's excitement that keeps coming back to me, other than the fact we found another body, is about the figure I saw. The figure that moves with a whoosh. The figure that looks so much like Tara from the Deli. Maybe I am just fitting her face with someone I know. To that end, I decide that when we have taken the dogs back home again, we will walk down town and go into the Deli for a coffee. I am not sure if Tara will be working today. I can only hope so.

When we walk in there, it is Claire who is behind the counter. She owns the Deli, along with her husband Paul. I am slightly disappointed, as I had been hoping that it would have been Tara working today.

'On your own' I ask, as we sit down at one of the tables.

'No. It is just that Tara's Mum has rung in, to say she will be late. Apparently she had a bad night and overslept. She's on her way in now.'

As I hear the words, I feel something inside me. I don't know what it is, but it is the reference of it being a bad night that has done it for me. Claire continues talking to us.

'A few months ago, this would never have happened. She has been very good. Then she started having 'bad nights'. It isn't happening often, but it changes things here for us.'

Claire stops to think about something for a few seconds. She obviously decides to let us into her thoughts.

'You know, when she comes in on these days when she is late, after 'the bad night'. She has this look in her eyes. It is a dark look. There is something unsettling about the look. She is a nice girl, but that look shows that there is another side to her we don't really see in here, except when she has a late day.'

Claire decides that she has probably said enough. She takes our coffee order and goes through to the back, to make the coffees. Another couple of regulars come in and sit down at the same table as us. Claire brings our coffees and takes their orders too. She then serves some people at the counter.

We are just about finished our coffees, when Tara comes through from the back. She says good morning to us all. She stops for a little chat, as she normally does. I am not really listening to her. I am watching her instead. The first thing that I have confirmed is that I was right. The face of the girl I saw whooshing around last night; is incredibly like Tara's. The other thing I am noticing; is about what Claire said about Tara, on these late mornings. There is most definitely a dark look, not only in her eyes, but in the whole expression on her face. I feel a pit in my stomach as I look at her. It isn't just the dark look that does it to me. It is the realization that the girl and Tara must be connected.

Chapter 19 Anne

Anne feels quite odd. There are these things she has found, just standing there. There are lights high up on long poles, but there doesn't appear to be a burning flame. There are houses built all together, but these ones she does not recognize. This is not the place she remembers. In fact she remembers very little. She can't remember anything, before the time she woke up in the dark place; the place she has just managed to find her way out of. Now she has come across these things, which are alien to her. And yet the way she walked to this place, has some familiarity for her. It is just here, that she is floundering to understand exactly where she is.

She is uncomfortable standing in the light, so she moves to a place where there is more shadow. That is better for her. She doesn't feel quite so exposed there. She stays where she is for a few minutes, before deciding it is time to move on from here. She isn't picking up any more information that would be helpful to her, in establishing where she is. There is this weird thought that is coming to her, that she may be in the same place as she last was, but not in the same time. The more she thinks about that, the more convinced she is that this may be true. She does not dwell on it, because a sound comes to her ears. It is the sound of someone walking and they are coming towards her.

She moves deeper into the shadows and reaches for the hood on her cloak. Was she wearing a cloak when she was in the caves? She can't remember, but she is wearing a black cloak now and there is a hood for her to pull up over her head and down over part of her face.

The sound of the footsteps draws nearer, but she still cannot see who it is walking. Then they come into her view. What strange clothes they are wearing. She hasn't seen folks wearing clothes like these before. It is a man. He isn't walking particularly fast and he isn't walking in a straight line either. In fact if she was to describe the way he is walking, it would be to say that he is worse the wear for drinking. No doubt he has been in one of the many drinking houses that the old town has to offer.

The man stops suddenly. For a second or two, Anne thinks that maybe he has spotted her. He has certainly stopped for a reason. He is looking around, as if he has heard a sound and it has unsettled him. He moves forward, until he is standing under one of the lights on long poles. He is more leaning on it, than standing by it, she realizes. She does not move a muscle. She keeps her head down, so that he won't see any reflection of her face, not that she thinks he can see her at all, where she is in the shadows.

He isn't facing her at first, but after a few minutes, he starts shuffling round the light pole. He does a little shuffle and then looks out in that direction. It doesn't take long for him to be leaning against the part of the pole that is facing where she is standing. For the first time she sees his face lit up properly, by the light shining down on it.

She realizes that she may have made a noise. What makes her do that, is because it is a face she recognizes! It is the face of a man who lives in the town. It is the face of a man who has done things to her in the past. It is funny that she can remember this thought. She desperately wants to move deeper into the shadows, but she can't, as he has stayed in the same position, facing her, for well over a minute now. Even in his drunken state, she thinks that maybe he can see her. She certainly thinks he knows that there is someone standing watching him. She thinks she can feel his eyes, boring into her. Something has got to give. She prepares herself to start to run away, should he even take one step towards her. There is no way that she wants him to come anywhere near her again. What he has done to her, no man should do to a woman, against her will. And then it is even worse against a child, which is what she was, she now remembers.

She feels something welling up inside her. It is not fear, as she expected it to be. It is something else that she feels now. For some strange reason, she doesn't think he can hurt her now. She doesn't know why she is thinking this, but she isn't afraid of him. Certainly when she first saw his face, it gave her a start. When she saw his face, she can even say that she was momentarily scared for her safety. But now a couple of minutes have gone by, she is more assured that it won't happen again.

The man by the light stands upright, and stops using the light pole for support. He peers into the darkness towards her, but he can't see anything in the gloom. It would be more helpful if he wasn't so full of drink, but he is and so that is that. He has little to console him, now that he lives on his own. Drinking is about the only thing that gives him pleasure. Sometimes he can remember other times, when he had pleasure in other ways, but he is not feeling like that at this moment. For some odd reason he is feeling a little apprehensive. He has walked this way home before, many times in the dark, but tonight there is something different about it. He doesn't know what is different, but there is something in the gloom that he can't see. He thinks there is something there, but he isn't sure. He is thinking that he doesn't recognize where he is. Has he come the wrong way?

With one last look, he leaves the safety of the light and then stops. He turns round and starts to walk the other way again. He walks to the end of the road and then along the big road and round a corner. He takes several more turns, before he arrives in front of a house. When he gets there, he turns onto his front path and shoves his hand into his pocket, hunting for the keys. He has a little trouble getting the key into the lock, but he gets there in the end. All the while he is resisting the urge to look behind him. He has done so a couple of times, since he discovered he was in the wrong street. He hasn't seen anyone, but he feels uneasy and thinks there is something in the shadows. He doesn't want to know what might be there. He doesn't want to see who it might have been in the shadows.

He shuts the front door quickly behind him and turns on the light. He breathes a sigh of relief, now he is in the safety of his own home.

He isn't going to stay up. He needs to get to his bed and sleep the drink from him. He makes his way up the stairs and into the bedroom. He doesn't bother getting undressed. He just flops down on the bed and closes his eyes.

Anne follows the man from the shadows. At first she thinks she is just watching him, but she soon realizes that her feet are actually taking her after him. If he turned round suddenly, it is doubtful he would see her. She follows him all the way to his house. Sometimes it is hard to find a place where, if he turned round suddenly, he wouldn't have spotted her. Luckily the two or three times he did turn, she was in a place where he couldn't see her.

She watches, as he opens the door and goes in. She watches, as he turns a light on and then she can see nothing different from that. She moves out of the shadow and across the road. She walks up the path to his front door. She tries the handle, expecting it to be locked, but it is not. She opens it quietly and steps inside. She can feel that he is not still downstairs, so she starts climbing the stairs. When she reaches the top of the stairs, she stops. She can hear the sound of his breathing coming from one of the rooms. She steps forward and pushes the door open. The light isn't in the room, but there is some light coming through the window, from outside. She can make out his outline, lying on top of the bed. She moves closer to him. She isn't afraid of him anymore, if she ever was. She is sure she hasn't made a sound, but he must have sensed her presence. He opens his eyes and sees her standing there beside his bed. The words he utters to her are strange. It is not what she expects the man to say.

'Tara, what are you doing here?' is what he says.

Anne lifts her hand and pulls her cloak off her head, so that he can see who she is.

'Tara?' he says again.

Anne doesn't reply. She lifts her hand to the top of her head and removes her long hat pin. She lifts it high and then brings it down swiftly, right through his heart.

Chapter 20 Anne

Anne stands over him, as he takes his last breaths on this earth. He has a puzzled look in his eye. His last thought is; that he didn't think Tara could ever have possibly had such a dark side in her. Wenlock is a funny place. As he drifts away, he realizes that it is indeed 'Dark in Wenlock'.

She pulls the long hat pin out of him. She stares at the blood for a few seconds, before she leans forward and pulls the cover back a little. The sheet is white before she starts to clean the pin, but afterwards there is a long red streak in it. She inspects the pin, before she carefully slots it back into her hair.

Anne stands over the bed, looking at the man she has just killed. She doesn't feel anything inside, regarding the action of killing him. She feels she had the right to do so. This man paid her no respect, when he did what he did to her; and no doubt to others like her. No, she isn't feeling any remorse for her actions.

She is taking one last look at him, lying dead on the bed. She is troubled by something. She looks closely at him. This man is older than the man she thought he was. He looks like the man, but then again he doesn't, because he is an older man. He is a much older man than the one she had the trouble with. She doesn't give it any more thought and turns round, to leave the room and go back downstairs. She opens the front door and slips out, shutting the door behind her. When she turns to check it is shut, she finds the door has locked. She isn't concerned about that.

She walks down the front path and turns towards the town. She moves over the road, so that she is in the shadows. The only sound she can hear at this precise moment is; the low-level swoosh of her cloak as she moves.

Anne sort of remembers the way back to where she first saw him. She doesn't remember this hard black surface that she is walking beside. It is a little unsettling for her. She moves up onto the path, on the left hand side of the road. She hears a noise and ducks behind a tree, in one of the gardens by the footpath. From there she peeks out, to see what has made the noise. It is one of those things she had touched earlier. It is moving by itself. It does not have a horse in front to pull it; that is very strange. It passes her by and disappears into the distance. She resumes her walk.

At the sharp corner, she takes a right. The Gaskell is on her left before she turns. She knows this street. It is Spittle Street, as some call it. She feels right for the first time. The houses are not as she has remembered them, but that is of no matter. There are more of these things that move on the road, but they are by the edge right now.

The lights on the long poles were not working when she came out of the man's house. Their fires must have gone out. It makes the walk much darker, but she is more comfortable with that. It is dark here too, as she walks along and down to the bottom of the street, where she turns left into Wilmore Street. The Guildhall is now on her right. She knows where she is and she knows where she is going. She passes the church and then goes over the Bull Ring. She is nearly there now. It is not the house on the corner, but it is the next one she stops at. She does not recognize the door. It throws her a little, but she soon gathers herself. She is tired and she is confused. She needs to get inside and be safe.

Anne tries the door and finds that it opens. She looks around her, before she steps inside. The house is quite small. She can see that no one lives there. Well they do really, because she lives there. There is nothing in this house. That confuses her, but she doesn't need anything, well not at the moment. The floors are dusty and it looks like no one has been here for years. How could that be? Where has everyone gone? Where are the others?

She climbs the stairs and has a look at the rooms there too. There is nothing in these rooms either. She lies down on the floor and closes her eyes. She doesn't notice that she isn't lying on the floor at all. She is lying on some blankets, which are laid out over some straw.

As she closes her eyes, things start to appear in her head. There are pictures of her and pictures of other people. There is a picture of the man she saw earlier. There is a picture of him when he was younger. He looks very similar to the young version, but she can see behind her closed eyes, that it is not the same man. She can do nothing about that. She has done what she has done, there is no undoing. His looks are close enough, she decides, to justify what she has done.

Then a strange thought comes to her. She should bring him here and leave him to lie for a while, downstairs in that room; the room where he attacked her. She should leave him there and then bring others to find him. Yes that is what she will do. She doesn't have any thought about how she can manage to do that. But then she doesn't really want them to find him here. That would bring shame on her. They would know that she has been with him.

It is a few hours later that she opens her eyes again. In between these times, she has been having dreams. At least that is what she thinks she has had. She can't exactly remember the details of these dreams. She does remember that she was carrying something. The something was lighter than she thought it would be. She remembers that much.

It is daylight outside, as she stands up. She looks down at her cloak, but it is not dirty. She looks at the floor where she has been lying, but it shows no mark of her being there. She does not think about that. She goes downstairs and looks in the front room. Yes, she really must bring him here, to lie on the same floor.

She pulls her cloak over her head, as she opens the front door and steps out onto the pavement. There are several of these things that don't have horses in front of them. They are moving along all by themselves. She does not understand how this can be possible. She tries to not let it bother her.

She walks up towards the church. There are some people walking towards her. She has no desire to speak to anyone. She lowers her head as they approach. She stops by the wall, to allow them to pass. She can just see their faces as they walk by. They do not pay her any attention at all. She starts walking again and every time she is about to meet people, she moves up against the wall and stands there, with her head down under the hood. Not one person pays her any heed. In fact she feels they are acting almost as if she isn't there. It is better for her that way. She is not in the mood to speak to anyone.

She turns into Spittle Street and walks up the middle of the road. There are some of these transports parked there. She is almost getting used to them now. She decides to walk in the road, as the pavement is too narrow for her to let people just pass. They would have to talk and slow down to pass each other.

She is half way up the first section of the street, when something catches her eye. It is on her left in one of the shops. She stops and turns and then moves closer. There is no one else standing outside this shop. It has words over the door that she does not understand. It says 'Wenlock Deli'. It is not the sign that has caught her attention. It is the sight of someone standing inside the shop, by the window. The person is not looking at her, but she is already familiar with this person. Unless the floor is higher in there, then this person is taller than her. But other than that, it is as if she is looking at herself, inside this shop.

Chapter 21 Anne

Anne has to move, as two of these transport vehicles are coming towards her. She moves onto the pavement.

The windows are in small squares and the person she has seen is still not looking her way. She keeps looking through the window. The other girl is young and she has long blonde hair, hanging down in a ponytail. Anne steps right up to the window, as two people are walking along the pavement towards her. The way they are walking together, is as if she isn't there. They walk past her, but give her little thought and space.

As she is pressed against the window, the girl in the shop turns, to get something from a basket in the window bay. It is a loaf of bread that she is reaching for. Her hand stops in mid-air, as her eyes pick up Anne, pressed up against the glass, looking in at her. The girl's mouth opens slightly, as if she has seen something unexpected. Anne steps back a pace, so that she isn't quite so pressed against the window. This appears to bring the girl inside the shop back to reality. She grabs the bread and turns away, to continue serving her customer.

Anne continues to look at the girl. She is also looking at the bread. That is something she hasn't done since she came out of the cave. She hasn't eaten anything, but then funnily enough, she doesn't feel the urge, or the need, to eat. She returns her attention to the girl in the shop. She sees that she has finished serving her customer and is now looking out at Anne. She really does look like her.

She doesn't know what to do. She is intrigued by finding this girl, but she doesn't want to go in and talk to her. She is still not sure what kind of place it is she is in. Yes, it does sell bread, but what else is in there?

She has one last look at the girl, before she turns, to resume her walk along Spittle Street. She doesn't see the look on the face of the girl in the shop. She doesn't see the hand come up and gesture for her to stay and not go. She doesn't see the dark look that comes into her eyes, as she sees Anne ignore her and start to walk away. She is only a few paces along the street, when she hears a voice behind her. She knows the voice belongs to the girl, because it sounds very much like her own voice.

'Do I know you?' Tara asks.

Anne stops and turns round. Once again she has to move out of the way of other pedestrians, walking along the pavement. Tara takes a tentative step towards her.

'You look really familiar' Tara smiles as she says it. 'They say we all have a double in the world, but I never expected to see mine in the same town I work in.'

Anne doesn't know what she is talking about, with there being a double. She does know she looks like this girl. She is taller than Anne, but other than that, she looks the same. She has the same slender build, the same shape face and the same nose and eyes. She looks into her eyes, without moving closer. Oh yes, the eyes are the very same as hers. Lovely eyes, but when you look deeply into them, you can see the darkness there. It is something they always say about her eyes. They say she has a deep darkness to her eyes.

A few people in the street are looking at Tara, wondering who she is talking to. She is standing just outside the Deli and talking in a direction, where there is no one standing. Tara does not seem to be aware of this. Anne isn't aware of it either.

'Are you alright?' Tara asks; when she still does not get a reply.

Anne does not know what to say. Tara takes another step or two towards her. Anne is not sure that she wants this contact, well not yet. She makes to turn round, just as someone else comes out of the Deli.

'Tara, what are you doing?' Claire asks her. 'There are customers waiting to be served.'

Claire doesn't see the look in Tara's eyes, before she takes one last look at Anne. She turns and walks back into the Deli. Anne has started to walk away from her, along the street. By the time Tara is back behind the counter and looks out of the window, Anne is well out of her sight.

There are less people now, as she walks along to the end of Spittle Street. There are many more of these transport things for her to negotiate, when she gets to the Fox Inn and even more on the road, at the corner where the

Gaskell stands. She tries to remember the way the man walked home last night. It is different in daylight. She thinks she will have to take her life in her hands, to get across the road. They don't appear to see her. They make no attempt to let her cross to the other side. She decides that she doesn't need to. The way the man walked home was not across this road. She walks up the pavement, past the petrol station. It had been dark when she passed this in the night. She continues on her way, back to the house she went into last night. There are only one or two people walking in the other direction. Their clothes are so very different from hers.

She has to cross a road at one point. She does so, but very nearly gets hit by a very large transport vehicle. In fact she doesn't know how it missed her, but she manages to get to the safety of the other side, unscathed. It only takes her another few minutes to get to the house and walk up the front path. She remembers at this point that the door had locked itself when she left. She tries the door anyway and is surprised, when it opens to allow her in. She goes upstairs and into the bedroom. He is still there, lying as she left him, with all life drained out of him. She touches him and he is cold. She wonders how she is going to move him. She gets hold of his arm and drags him a little, just as a test to see how heavy he might be. She is surprised that he moves quite easily towards her. This might not be so hard to do as she had thought. But then what will people say, when they see her dragging a dead man along the street. Surely they would not just stand and watch. Surely they would want to stop her and then she would be in trouble. No, she doesn't want people to see her.

She sits on the edge of the bed, to try to work out what she should do. The easier option is to leave him here, but she does not want to do that. She wants him to be in the place where it happened. It will be easier to move him after dark. She will wait until then to move him. In the meantime, she will return to the house and wait out the time. But first she is going to move him off the bed. She doesn't want someone to come in and find him, before she is ready. She finds a small room that has a key in the lock. She drags him along and puts him in there, locking the door to keep him in, not that he is any position to try to escape.

It is as she is walking back down Spittle Street, that she sees another man. He too looks familiar. In fact he looks to her eyes; very similar to the man she has just left. Rather than go back to the house to wait out the day, she decides it would be a better idea to follow this man. The next thing she notices about him; is that he appears to avoid other people walking, rather like she has to do. Then he stops to talk to people. He has just been avoiding bumping into people. It is not a case that they haven't seen him, like it appears to be in her case.

He stands and talks for some minutes. Anne stands about thirty feet away, watching him. No one is taking any notice of her.

Chapter 22 Anne

Anne watches and waits. The place where she is standing makes it easy for her to keep out of people's way. No one tries to come to the place where she is. There are many of these transport things moving around. They have people in them. Sometimes there is only the one person, but often there are more than the one person in them. Every now and then a larger one comes down. These ones are obviously more respected, because people stand and look at them. She can sometimes see their lips moving, as the big vehicle comes down the street.

The man she has been watching, stands in the same place, talking to these people he has met, for ages. Anne finds it very odd that he should do this. Another thing that is puzzling her; is why there are so many people about. Surely they have work to do? Surely they cannot afford to just stand around and waste the day. Surely they need to be working, to earn what they need to keep them alive?

Eventually the man moves along again. He goes into one shop and a minute later he reappears holding some bread. The man then goes back the way he has come, before he stops behind a queue of other people, outside another shop. Anne moves a little closer, to see what he is doing there. No one takes any notice of her, as she walks past the man and the other people and looks in the window, on the left hand side of the door. There are more people inside and beyond them are four men behind a counter, busying with something. She still can't see clearly what is going on in this shop. She manages to squeeze past the people standing in the queue in the doorway. She walks along behind them, until she gets to a place where she can actually get to the counter. What she sees is an array of meats and pies and other meat products, like she has never seen before. She is slightly surprised that no one has commented on her making her way in like she has done, but thinks nothing of it, as she turns away and goes outside once more.

Her man is little further forward than when she had last seen him, a couple of minutes ago. She crosses the road and stands in a corner, just by a big red thing on the pavement. Every few minutes, men and women come up to this red thing and feed it with thin things. She is standing out of the way behind it. No one gives her a second look. She is not sure they even notice that she is there. That is fine with her. She would rather it was that way.

It takes a long time for the man she is watching, to progress and get into the meat shop. It takes as long as that again, before he emerges once more, with a bag in his hand. He turns right out of there and walks about twenty paces, before he goes into another shop. This time she follows him in. He is looking at a stand. She walks past him and tries to work out what it is that this shop might be selling. It is Mrs Ps and it sells a variety of goods. Again there are things that she hasn't seen before. In fact everything in there is new to her. She knows nothing about newspapers and magazines, let alone sweets, cards and Belgian chocolates. She is mesmerized by the things she sees, every which way she turns. The smell is attractive to her too, but she doesn't know why. She is so engrossed with what she sees in there; that she nearly fails to see her man leaving the shop. She has no idea what he may have got, but she just catches a glimpse of him, disappearing out of the doorway. She has to wait a few seconds while other people come into the shop. She gets out and turns to follow her man. Her eyes catch a glimpse of the girl, looking out of the window in the Deli, which is opposite. This is the girl who tried to speak to her earlier. She is looking out at Anne. The look on her face is odd and there is no doubt about the dark look coming from her eyes.

Anne feels that she needs to know more about this girl, but for now she knows she needs to follow her man. He is quite a distance ahead of her now. She turns away from the girl looking at her, and starts along the footpath after her man. She finds that she can move quite effortlessly. Her feet almost glide over the ground. She has no difficulty catching him up. She doesn't want to get too close though.

He crosses over at the corner and then walks on up a few hundred yards, before crossing over the main road. He has to wait for a gap in the vehicles, to cross. Anne crosses over at the same time, but maybe twenty feet away from him. He doesn't look over his shoulder once. She recognizes this area, as being the one she arrived at. She recognizes the post where the other man had stood, before turning round. It is near to this point, that the man turns towards one of the houses and lets himself in. Anne makes a mental note of which house it is, before she turns round and makes her way back into town again.

She really doesn't want to walk down the street where the shops are again. She wants to speak to the other girl, but not right now. It would be best if she didn't pass in front of that shop, until such time as she is ready to confront the other girl. Then a thought crosses her mind. Maybe if she does meet her, then this girl will help her move the body of the other man.

She is suddenly tired. She wants to meet her, but first she needs a rest. The lightness of the day is getting to her and she needs to rest her eyes for a while. She makes her way down Back Lane and where that meets Queen Street, she turns right and then left. She opens the door to her house and goes in. It is dim inside and she feels the relief straight away. She makes her way upstairs and settles down on the floor, to close her eyes for a time.

By the time she opens her eyes again, it is dark outside. She has slept for much longer than she had intended to. Gone is the opportunity to speak to the girl in the Deli, she suspects. It is unlikely she will still be there now. That is a shame, as she really wants to move the man to here, if she can. Then she intends to make sure that the man will be found here, in this house. She isn't sure why she needs him to be found, but she knows that she does.

She gets up off the floor. She doesn't look down at where she has been lying. If she had, she would have again seen that there was no mark where she has been lying down. She makes her way downstairs and out of the front door. It is so dark out there. There are long poles, which should have some lights on them, but they do not. It is dark out there. She thinks she sees something else moving. She thinks she hears the swooshing of something else move, but she doesn't see it. The building opposite is the old police station and just along from that is another really old building. She can't remember what it is called, but she remembers the tales about it. That house is said to have a ghost that moves around it. Such stories abound in the place where she lives.

She doesn't walk towards that direction. Instead, she goes in the other direction. She walks over the Bull Ring and along towards the church. She stands in the doorway for a few seconds, as she is feeling slightly apprehensive about the lack of light. She knows she has to move, or the fear will take a total grip of her. She moves among the path towards church walk. She bears off to the left, across the grass and under the big tree. There is no light at all back here. She cannot make out very much ahead of her. She stumbles on a grave and nearly falls over. That makes her turn back towards the path again. She gets there and walks along Church Walk. She comes out at the far end. There are no lights on at all, in the town. Even the ones in the shop windows are not lit tonight. She looks to her left and then to her right. There is nothing that she can see at all. She strains her eyes and even after a few minutes, she can barely make out the outline of anything at all. She feels that she may have returned to the place that she knows. That she may not still be in the place where she was, before laying down her head to sleep. This may be the place she knows again. Yes, it is certainly dark in Wenlock tonight.

Chapter 23 Anne

Anne glides her way along Barrow Street. At the far end, in the distance, she can just see a light. It isn't very bright and she doesn't know what is making it. She decides not to go along there to see what it is. She stops on the corner by The Raven and looks up that road. There is nothing to see, but the darkness along the street. She whooshes as she turns round. She likes the sound of that, so she does it again.

She knows she should be walking along the road, to where the light is. That is surely the direction she needs to go, to get to the man she has locked in the small room in his house. She should really go along there and get him and take him along to the house where she lives. That is where he needs to be. What stops her at this second; is the thought that she would like the other girl to help her. Yes, it would be good to have help. She is sure that the man will be too heavy for her to move on her own. The other girl is pretty like she is. She is sure to have been abused at the hands of this man, just like she herself has been. She will revel in the reward of getting at least some kind of revenge.

In the end, she decides that she should go to make sure he has not been discovered as yet. She hopes that he hasn't been, before she gets the opportunity to do what she wants to do.

Anne goes along Barrow Street and then turns at the end, into Hunters Gate. It doesn't take her long to find the house she needs. The door opens to her touch and she goes in and up the stairs. She is surprised when she opens the door to see, but hear more like, that there are a number of flies, already buzzing around the body. They must have been in the room that she dragged the body through to. It is nothing less than the man deserves; to have loads of flies buzzing round him. At least he hasn't been discovered.

She is slightly concerned that the front door is unlocked. That surely will make it easier for people to get in and discover his dead body. But when she leaves, she tries the door before she walks away and is pleased to find that the door appears to have locked itself now. That brings a smile to her face.

As she walks back along towards the town centre, she feels that she is not alone. She thinks she can hear the sound of other things whooshing. None of them are near her, but she stops to try to locate them. For five minutes she stands alone in the middle of the road, in the near pure darkness, trying to see who or what is making the noise. She isn't successful.

She nears the place where she lives and decides that she has to wait for the other girl to come back. She walks along Queen Street and into Back Lane, in total blackness. The other swooshing noises seem to have gone now. There is just the sound of her own whooshing coming to her ears, as she turns to walk up the car park and through the passage by the Corn Exchange.

She is just coming out of the passage into the open area of the Corn Exchange, when she hears the sound of voices. She then sees the glow of something in the dark. She stops and listens. The voices are of young men, maybe even boys. She can now hear them more clearly. They are talking about breaking into one of the shops. The glow comes again and she briefly catches sight of their faces. A puff of smoke rises into the air, after the glow. She knows that she is not back in her place. She is still in the place she arrived at. These boys are dressed like the people she saw yesterday.

She sees the glow one more time and then the glow is dropped to the floor. She then hears a voice saying

'Let's do it now.'

As she hears the voice, the light in the passage flickers. She is not expecting it, as the place is in total darkness. She doesn't know what causes it either, but the light suddenly flickers. It then crackles and sparks this time, rather than flickers. The boys turn and look in that direction. It also happens to be her direction too. A moment of panic and fear rises in her. It is not good to be out at this time of night, when she might be put in danger. It wouldn't be the first time she has been attacked and abused, in the dark of Wenlock.

The light sparks again and crackles again too. Anne takes a step backwards, in her haste to withdraw out of their sight. Her foot hits an old can that is lying on the floor. The can flies against the wall. The boys start to get up from the bench they are sitting on. Their eyes grow large, as they try to see what it is in the dark that has made the can move. They know the sound of a can being kicked. Even with the crackle and the sparks, there isn't anything like enough light, for them to see who has caused this. They think it might be one of their mates, trying to creep up on them, to give them a start.

Kicking the can has caused Anne to panic even more. Her heart is in her mouth, as she believes she has given away her position to them. In addition to that, she has seen their outlines starting to rise from the bench. She is feeling more than a little bit scared now. The last thing she needs right now, is for the light to come on. She retreats back into the passage and towards where the light is. It is crackling and sparking more now. In fact it is doing that almost continuously now. She needs to stop that from happening. She doesn't know how it works, but she thinks that if she hits it, it will stop doing what it is doing. She stops and her hand goes up to the light. It is just above her reach. She realizes she will have to jump up and hit the light, if she is going to succeed in her ambition. She gets ready to spring up into the air.

The two boys have moved across the open space towards the passageway. They still believe it is one of their friends trying to scare them. They reach the other side, where they have a view of the passage. They also have a view of the light that is sparking. They realize straight away that there isn't anyone there. But then they realize that the can has been kicked and there must be, or must have been, someone there. They are not going down the passage to investigate. They have their break in to get on and do.

They are just about to turn round to get on their way, when Anne decides that this is the moment to jump up. She has seen the silhouettes of the boys appear, beyond where the passage opens out. She whooshes into the air and touches the light. Her intention has been to bang it with her hand, but the reality is that her hand just comes into contact with it. The electricity arcs into her as she does so. It travels down her arm and into her body. It lights up every part of her, just for that fraction of a second and parts of her for much longer than that.

That fraction of a second is enough for the boys to see it too. Just the fraction of a second before they turn away, they see it. They see Anne. Anne sees that they have seen her. She pulls her hand away from the light, but her body is still lit up with the electricity. Her intention is to run away from the boys, but what she does is completely different. She is still off the ground. She is just at the point of starting to fall down to the ground, after jumping up. She lets out the most eerie long howl and wailing, as she lands and then propels herself forward towards them, whooshing as she moves. The boys, in their turn, can't prevent letting out screams themselves. Theirs are motivated by pure fear. Both of them loosen their bowels, as the figure rushes towards them. They feel the air move, as Anne comes straight at them. She looks like she is gliding and not running. Just inches before she collides with them, she turns and rushes out onto the street. The boys don't turn to see where she is. They are scared out of their wits. They know they have messed themselves, but that isn't stopping them tearing through the passage as fast as they can. They need to get away from here and back to the safety of home. They aren't going to tell anyone what they have seen. They aren't going to have their friends laugh at them for being scared. They are certainly not going to tell anyone at home about this. This will be their secret. If they are asked if they came out to do the break in, by their friends, they will say that they couldn't get out of the house without being noticed. No one is going to know they have seen a ghost.

Chapter 24 Anne

Anne keeps running along the street. She doesn't care where she is running to, as long as they aren't chasing her. As far as she is aware, they are not. But she can't be sure. The blood has rushed to her head and she is still behaving like someone in a blind panic. Of all the times to be stuck in the dark, this is the time she really wishes that the lights on the long poles would work. They aren't going to. It is the time of night when they have been turned off.

She isn't thinking about where she is running to. Her legs are just taking her wherever they choose to. Her head is not having any input at this stage. She reaches the end of High Street and turns left. She knows this corner. She has been here before, in the last day or two. She arrived in the town from straight ahead, but her legs are taking her to the left.

She runs past Waggies, the dog groomers, but it is all in darkness, as is the petrol station just up from there. She runs across St Marys Road and on up the hill. To turn left there would take her back towards the town again. She doesn't want to do that yet. She doesn't know where the boys are. Common sense is telling her that they are not following her, but the raw fear she feels in her body, is telling her that they might still be after her. She does not understand as yet, that they are not and never were.

From behind the clouds, a little bit of light enters her world, for the first time in hours. The moon is now visible and it changes the scene around her. She takes a quick look over her shoulder and the relief that she feels when she sees she is not being followed, is immense. She stops running and stands still for a minute or two. She is still nervous, but she can see that she is not in any imminent danger. The houses to her left are all in darkness. Somewhere in the distance, she hears a dog barking. That is the first sound she has heard for a while too, other than her own howl and wailing, in fear at the boys, and their screams too. For the first time the thought comes to her, that they may have been just as scared of her, as she was at them.

She recovers her poise and looks around her and then up at the sky. She can see that the clouds have rolled back and there are now stars visible in the sky, as well as the moon. She can see something over on the other side of the road. She walks over there, hoping that she might find a safe place to wait for a while. She discovers when she gets in there, that she is in a graveyard or cemetery. She can make out the outline of the chapel, but when she gets there, the door is locked.

She isn't comfortable in this place. It is not that she can remember this being here, because she can't. It is probably just because it is the place it is, a resting place for the dead.

She makes her way back across, to where the road is. Before she emerges onto the road, she checks to make sure the coast is clear. It is all clear and she can still see much more than she could earlier. She crosses the road and keeps on walking along, away from the town. This is a familiar route for her. She has used it in the past day. She knows where she will go, to spend the rest of the night.

She turns left at the edge of town and walks back past the primary school. She cuts down the path just after the school. It is dark down here. The overhanging trees are preventing much light at all, to penetrate their cover. She quickens her pace, to reach the open area at the end of the path. Once there, she cuts across the green area and walks up to the door of the man's house. She has a brief concern that the door will be locked. She tried the door when she last left and she is sure it was locked. However, she finds the door opens to her touch and she goes in. She doesn't want to turn on any lights. She doesn't want anyone to see that anyone is up, in the house.

She decides that she isn't even going to go upstairs, to see if the man is still there. To be honest she isn't that keen on the flies that she will find in there with him. Instead she settles down on the settee, in the living room. She closes her eyes and gets some well-deserved sleep.

It is light when she wakes up. It isn't a natural awakening. It is something that frightens her as she comes to. There is a knocking on the door, followed by a bell ringing, somewhere in the house. It brings her awake, in a start. She sits up, but doesn't move other than that. She hears the knocking on the door again and then the bell rings again. She looks round the room, to see if there is anywhere for her to hide, but she can't see anywhere obvious.

The knocking stops and after a few minutes, she is hopeful that whoever it was has gone away. It is time she wasn't here and she knows that she needs to move the body today. If she waits any longer than that, she is in danger of having the body found, before she has the chance to move it to her house. On that note, she knows she needs to find the other girl.

Slipping out of the house without being seen; is not as easy as she would have liked. There are people around. What she manages to do in the end, is to go out of the back door. She follows the path round and finds it comes out a little away from the front of the house. She walks towards the green area, but when she gets there, she sees that all of the people out walking are also walking in the direction of the path. She decides to go the other way. No one takes any notice of her whatsoever, as she goes through the kissing gates at the bottom and then out onto Barrow Street. She hears some dogs barking as she crosses the entrance to a small cul-de-sac, but other than that she doesn't encounter anyone else, until she reaches the centre of town. She turns up Spittle Street and makes her way to where the girl works. The shop opposite is open. That is Mrs Ps and there is a man working in there. The Deli has no one in there and when she tries the door, it does not open. She rattles the door, but it still won't open. The man in the shop on the other side of the road obviously hears her doing this, but he does not come out to her. He turns to get on with his work.

Anne moves away from the door. She doesn't want to bring any more unwanted attention onto herself than is necessary. She had thought for a minute that the man might come out and shout at her, but he hasn't. She needs to find a place where she can stand, but at the same time be out of the way. There isn't anywhere ideal for her to do that. The one place where she could sit is under The Corn Exchange, but she can't bring herself to do it. The memories of what happened there last night are still too fresh in her thoughts. She makes do with standing in the corner, behind the big red thing. Again, every now and then, people come and put something into it, feeding it. It doesn't make a noise though and it does a good job of keeping her out of the way of other pedestrians. Not one person remarks on her standing there. Not one person attempts to talk to her either. Every now and then, she steps out and walks up to the Deli, to see if the girl is there yet. The door is still locked every time she does it. The man over the road in the other shop keeps looking over, when she rattles the door, but he doesn't come out to speak with her. He is looking more puzzled every time she goes there now. She goes back to her chosen place of waiting.

Chapter 25 Anne

It is a good hour later that Anne goes once more from behind the pillar box up to the Deli. The sign is outside as she approaches and she sees someone coming out, just before she reaches the door. Rather than look through the window right outside, she crosses the road and looks in from there. At first she only sees another girl, but after a minute or two her girl appears alongside her. She isn't looking out and so hasn't seen Anne. She is pre-occupied with something and although Anne moves about and even waves at her, the girl does not look in her direction. She gives it a few minutes, but finds she is getting frustrated, by her lack of success in attracting the girl's attention.

Anne gives out a sigh of frustration, before moving off the pavement into the road. She doesn't notice the vehicle coming along the road. It isn't making the same amount of noise that the others make. The car is a hybrid. She sees it just in time and skips over the last couple of paces to the other side. It is just as well she does, as the driver has no intention of slowing down.

The girl is inside, busy with something. Anne stands directly outside the window and looks in. She hasn't got the time for this. She opens the door and steps into the Deli. There are a couple of people sitting at a table, near to the back. Other than that, the only other person in there is the girl behind the counter. She hasn't looked up yet from what she is doing. Anne isn't for waiting for her to be ready. She gives out a little cough. The girl looks up. Anne sees straight away that there is so much of a dark look in this girl's eyes.

'Hello' Anne opens with.

'It's you' comes back the reply.

'I'm Anne'

'My name is Tara. You look familiar to me. Do I know you?'

'You look exactly how I do' Anne replies.

Tara thinks that she doesn't look anywhere like she does. She is way shorter for a start and that is before you take into account the girl's looks. She may well have been pretty once upon a time, but she isn't as pretty as I am right now. But then there is something in the girl's looks that says she isn't as old as you would think, on first glance. Yes, maybe she is right. The nose is the same shape as her nose. The shape of the bones on her face is very much the same too, if you look hard enough. The hair line is the same too. Her ears are tucked the same way to the side of her head. But it is the eyes that say the most about the similarity of the two girls. Tara looks into Anne's eyes and sees a great darkness there. There are things that those eyes have seen, that a girl so young should not have seen. Or is it that the eyes hold the secret, of exactly what this girl is capable of doing. As she thinks this, Tara feels something inside her. She feels the need to do something, to release the feelings she has suppressed all of her life. This girl can maybe help her, to do some things that she has secretly longed to do. It has always felt as if she has been a prisoner to her own thoughts and a prisoner in someone else's mind. She comes back, to see that Anne is looking at her.

'Why don't you sit down and I'll get you a drink.' Tara says, as she notices the women at the other table looking at her.

Anne moves over and pulls out one of the chairs. Tara walks through to the back, to get her a drink. She brings the drink out a minute later and then puts it in front of Anne. She sits down beside her. As she sits down, so she notices how slight Anne is. She notices how pale her complexion is too. She also notices that it is hard to put an age to her. Anne, on the other hand, is thinking, now that Tara is up close, that she is beautiful, just like she herself is. She guesses that she won't have much time to ask Tara for help, before she has to carry on working.

'I need some help and I think it is something that you will want to help me with.'

'What's that?' Tara replies. She is quite surprised by Anne just coming out with this.

'I need some help moving a man's body.'

Tara had no idea what she was going to ask her to help with. But this has to be way down on the list of possibilities she would have thought of giving time to do so.

'Did I hear you right?'

Anne just nods. Tara is thinking that she should be shocked. Tara is thinking that she should be asking loads more questions about this girl. Tara is thinking that something is wrong here; if this girl is looking for that kind of help. Tara is thinking that she is not that sort of a girl. But all the time Tara is thinking, her head is nodding in agreement.

'You will?' Anne asks, but Tara is still in the middle of her thinking.

Suddenly another voice breaks into the conversation.

'I don't think you should be sitting there, drinking your coffee, Tara'

Claire has walked through from the back, only to see Tara is not behind the counter working, but sitting at the front table, with a mug of coffee there too.

'I was just talking to Anne for a minute.'

'You've got work to do' Claire replies, puzzled because she can't see Tara's mobile phone.

'I know' she says.

Anne sees that dark look come into her eyes, as she talks to this other woman. Tara starts to get up from the table.

'You will help me won't you' Anne says again.

'I will' Tara says 'when are you thinking of?'

'When it gets dark' she replies.

'Today?' she says in surprise.

'It has to be.'

Tara looks at Claire. Claire is looking over at her, now with an extremely puzzled look on her face. Claire can't see a mobile phone, so maybe she has an earpiece in and a microphone on the cord. Tara looks across at Claire and then down at Anne. She knows she needs to get back to work.

'What time and where?' she says, now feeling really under pressure.

'When it gets dark, and I'll meet you outside here if you like.'

'Alright, I have to go.'

Tara turns towards the counter and starts to walk away.

'Don't forget your coffee' Claire says to her. Tara is about to say it is Anne's coffee, but as she turns, she sees that Anne is already half way out of the door. The coffee is untouched. It is Tara's turn to be puzzled now. How did she move so fast? Why hasn't she stayed and drunk her coffee? Why hasn't she stayed, so that Tara can find out a little more about this man's body she wants her to help her move. Why is Claire looking at her in that way, as are the women at the other table? OK, maybe Anne isn't exactly dressed in the most usual of clothing, but there are others who dress oddly in this town too.

Tara reaches for the coffee and takes one last look at Anne, walking away from the Deli. Claire is looking at her, as if she is really not pleased with her. What is her problem? She was only having a few words with someone. From nowhere in her thoughts comes the picture of an icicle. Why and where has that come from?

She takes the coffee with her and goes back behind the counter, to resume her chores. She is joined shortly by Liz, carrying a fresh Coffee and Walnut cake. She places it on the shelf and remarks to Tara.

'What did you go and do that for?'

Tara doesn't know what she is on about. All she has done is get Anne a coffee and bring it to her. Then she has sat down to have a few words with her too and Claire comes breezing out, telling her to get on with her work. It is almost as if Anne wasn't there, is what she thinks in the end.

Anne walks away from the Deli. It became clear to her very quickly, that Tara is the ideal person to give her a hand. She is very pretty. She noticed that when she was close to her. Yes, she is very pretty, but not as pretty as Anne herself is, of course. And then there are her eyes. She knew as soon as she was close and looked into those deep dark eyes, that Tara will help her.

Chapter 26 Anne

Anne walks away, satisfied that she now has secured the help she needs to move the man. What she now realizes, is that she may have found someone who can help her in the future too. All she has to do now is to wait for it to get dark and they can move the man to where he needs to be, to the place where it happened. She wonders briefly where it might have happened to Tara. Maybe it is in the same place, but she doubts that somehow.

She needs to go there and make sure all is ready, for her guest who is coming this evening. She walks down Back Lane and into Queen Street, before turning into Sheinton Street and then stops outside her front door. There is someone walking along the other side of the road. She waits for them to pass and then watches them continue towards the town centre, before she turns the handle and goes in. The light of the day does little to brighten this house. She sees it as it is now, with no furniture in it and no one living in it, but it is still her house. It is where she believes she lives or lived; she isn't sure which, but it doesn't matter. She goes over the entire house, trying to decide which room she should put him in. While the upstairs appeals to her most, she decides that the living room is the best place; the place where he will be most easily found.

Ideally she will bring him in through the back door, but when she gets out there, she finds that there is only a small courtyard. There is no way in from the back. That might make things slightly difficult. She seems to remember that there used to be a way through, so you could access the back door, but it isn't there now. She slips out of the front door and round into the old yard at the back. Things have changed here now, as there are houses where there used to be old barns. At some time during the changes, they have blocked up the old access out of the back yard. Maybe she will be able to find it and use it.

Her investigations are interrupted by someone coming into the yard. She stands close to the wall and as out of sight as she can. The people in the car get out and go into one of the newly converted buildings. If they look her way, they make no sign that they have seen her there, with her back as tightly to the wall as she can get it. When they have gone in, she slips out of her hiding place and walks round quickly to her own house. She waits there patiently, until the light starts to fade.

Anne walks round and into Spittle Street. The shops are all closed now, but there is a couple of drinking houses that are still open. Nothing changes there then! She stands in her place of preference, behind the pillar box and waits for Tara to turn up.

It has been dark properly for well over half an hour, before Tara does indeed arrive, in her vehicle. She stops and gets out. She is looking around for Anne as she does so. Anne steps out from her place and that gives Tara a start.

'I thought you weren't here for a minute.'

'I am here.'

'Where are we going? Get in and I will drive us there.'

'I'm not sure' Anne replies.

'To which part?' Tara asks.

'The part about me getting in that!'

'You said we have to move a body. I've already put the back seat down, to get it in.'

Anne is not sure about this, but then she hasn't really given it a lot of thought, about how they are going to move the body. All she has been thinking; is that it would be easier with the two of them.

'Where is the body?' Tara decides that things need moving on. She has other things she wants to get done this evening. She very nearly didn't bother coming this evening. She isn't really sure about Anne. After all, she has only met her face to face today.'

'It is in his house.'

'Where is his house' Tara can feel that she is letting her impatience filter through to the tone in her voice.

'Along at the end of the street down there, and then somewhere off there.'

'Have you been there?' she is starting to wonder about Anne and this body.

'Oh yes, I have been there on more than one occasion, but I haven't been in one of these.'

'We can drive to the end of the road and then walk from there, if you like' Tara really wants to get moving.

Anne reluctantly gets in and they drive to the end of Barrow Street. Tara turns into the end of Hunter's Gate and stops the car. They both get out. Anne takes stock of their position and starts to walk up Hunter's Gate. Tara locks her car and then is at her heels. Anne walks quite fast and Tara just keeps up, even though she has the longer legs. Anne turns into a front path and strides up to the door. The house is in darkness, unlike some of its neighbours. The door opens and they walk in. Anne goes straight up the stairs. Tara, now that she is inside, slows down a little. This has turned from being a hypothetical adventure, into something of a reality. She climbs the stairs more slowly than Anne. By the time she reaches the top, Anne is already inside the small room at the end, waiting for her.

Reluctantly, Tara walks along the landing. It is reluctantly, because she can now hear the buzzing and she can smell something that isn't exactly pleasant. There is some light coming through the windows. Anne hasn't turned the lights on and she doesn't really want to, but that is the only way she is going to be able to see clearly what she is dealing with. She reaches for the light switch.

Anne is startled by the illumination of the tiny room. Tara is startled by the sight that greets her eyes. There is a dead man on the floor. He is covered in flies, as is the room. The smell is definitely coming from him.

'You really want to move a body!'

'You know I do. That is what I said.'

'Did you kill him?'

'I did. He did things to me that a man should not do to a woman. I used my hat pin' she says, taking out the pin tucked into her hair.

I'd have used an ice pick, or an ice pin, she thinks to herself. Then there would be no evidence of a murder weapon.

'Where are you thinking of moving him to, and why?'

'To my house in town.'

'Wouldn't he better being left here?'

'No, I want them to find him where he did it.'

Tara stands and thinks that she really doesn't want to touch the body, nor does she want it in her car. But on the other hand, it has an appeal to it, this task. Maybe there is another way they can move it.

'Are there any bags anywhere we can put him in to carry him?'

'I don't know. I haven't looked.'

Tara disappears out of the doorway and goes downstairs. In the kitchen she finds some loose black sacks. She knows where they have been bought. AJ's sells these black sacks. She grabs a couple of them and makes her way up the stairs again. She knows she can't waste any time, getting on with the task. It is so distasteful, that if she hesitates, she will find she can't do it. She dons the rubber gloves she has brought from work. Anne does not seem to be bothered about wearing any, but Tara is. Between them, they get the body and several hundred flies into the bag.

They start to drag it out of the room and along the landing. Tara moves to go down the stairs first, but Anne gets there first. She pulls the body towards her and pulls it onto her shoulders. She backs down the stairs and waits for Tara to open the front door for her.

Anne must be a lot stronger than she looks, Tara thinks, as she shuts the front door and walks quickly after Anne. She is thinking that it won't be very good if they bump into anyone, but then it feels darker now than when they went in. The street lights are out, which is odd. They reach Barrow Street and the lights are all off there too, even the corner sign. All the way along Barrow Street, Anne carries the body in the dark. Nobody is out on the streets. They pass the square and go into Wilmore Street, still in darkness. Once past the Bull Ring, Anne stops outside a door. She opens the door and then lets Tara push it wide open. Anne steps inside and then shuts the door in Tara's face, saying not a word as she does so. Tara tries the door, but it is locked. She knocks quietly on the door, but there is no answer. She waits a couple of minutes, before she stomps away, thinking some extremely dark thoughts, as she makes her way back to her car. The street lights have come back on, which is better, and she passes a couple of people, on the way back to the car.

Inside the house, Anne moves into the living room. The body slides off her shoulder and onto the floor. She makes no effort to soften the blow, as it falls down the last couple of feet. She arranges the body on the floor and stands back to admire her handy work. The bags are gone and the flies are back. She is happy with what she has done. She goes up to bed, knowing that she needs to be up early, so that she can open the front door. That way, someone passing is going to be sure to notice it and hopefully come in, to investigate why it is open.

Tara reaches her car and gets in. She drives home again, wondering why Anne has asked for her help, when she is so obviously capable of doing the entire deed on her own. What was the point of asking her, if she wasn't going to allow her to help? Next time will be different, she thinks.

Chapter 27 Anne

Anne doesn't really sleep at all. She lies down on the floor, in the room upstairs. She would have stayed downstairs, but to be honest with the buzzing of all the flies and the smell that is coming from the man, it is just too much for her. But she has a bit of self-satisfaction, that he is lying dead on the floor of the house.

The hours of darkness pass slowly. She tries lying on the floor and sleeping, but she is too restless to do that. She goes down and looks at the body for a few minutes. The smell is immense. She can't stand there all night. She decides to go out into the night air for a walk, to get some fresh air. She slips out of the front door, intending to just maybe stand around in the quiet of the night. She has been out there no longer than five minutes, when she hears the sounds of footsteps. She doesn't want to rush back and go into the house. She doesn't want anyone to remember that, when they find the body. She moves out of the shadow of where she is standing and crosses the road. The figure is closer than she had originally thought. She has to move away now, so she crosses the Bull Ring and walks in front of the church. She turns onto the path and stands in the church doorway. The figure comes closer. She fears that she might have been seen. When he reaches the point she turned off onto the path, she breaks cover again and walks deeper into the darkness of the church green.

Eventually the figure goes on his way and after staying well back in the deeper gloom, Anne returns to the outside of the house. She realizes that she can't stand there all night, so goes back inside.

She still can't sleep. She can't do much more than lie there and thinks about things. The one thing she isn't thinking about initially; is Tara. She doesn't for a minute think about what she did to Tara, all through the night, until just before dawn. Then the thought comes to her about what she did, by slamming the door shut in her face and also wondering why she had involved her in the first place. Was it because she looked like her that she was drawn to her, or was it because she needed help to move the body? At the time when she asked her, she did not know that she would be able to carry the body as she had done. If she had known that, would she have brought Tara along? She doesn't know the answer to that, but in the end concludes; that she brought Tara along for a reason, other than the two she has already thought of.

These thoughts are interrupted by the approach of dawn. She shakes herself into action and gets up. She looks down at the floor she has just vacated and notes she hasn't left a mark on the floor. It doesn't matter and it might just play in her favour, with the plan she has in mind.

She goes downstairs and checks on the body. It is just as she had left it. She goes through to the hallway and opens the front door. She opens it as wide as it can go. She then goes back through to the living room and waits for a while. Nothing happens. It is still dark outside, but the street lights have come on again, at some stage in the night.

She decides to wait outside. The smell in there is just too much, to just stand around and wait for who knows how long. She steps through the front door and crosses the road. She stands by the wall of the old police house opposite. There is no one around, to question why she might be standing there at this time of the morning.

A vehicle comes along the road every now and then, but none of the occupants notice the open door. It is almost an hour later, that the first person approaches on foot. When she sees the figure approach, she presses as close as she can into the wall. It is a man, walking along the pavement. He is on the right side of the street. As he gets closer, she recognizes who it is. It is a bit of a shock to her. It is the other man she followed the day before. That gives her a start, as to her eyes he looks just like the man lying on the floor inside the house. But then that is why she had followed him too. That is a most strange occurrence; that he should be the first man to come past the open door.

She watches him. He is walking slowly, as if he is thinking about something. It occurs to her that he must have been out for some time, walking like this. This is not the direction he lives in.

He comes to a stop, before he even reaches the door. It is almost as if something has come to him. Maybe he has had a premonition about what lies ahead. Anyway, he has stopped about ten feet short of the door. He looks around him, both behind and ahead. Anne is sure that he must see her against the wall. If he does, he does not intimate he has. He then tentatively takes a few more steps forward. It is as if he is expecting someone to jump out on him at any second.

He is now at the front door. He turns towards it, almost as if that was his destination. He doesn't appear to be shocked at finding it open. He knocks on the door and calls quietly in. Of course there is no response. He gingerly takes a step into the house and then another. Anne watches him, until she can't see him anymore. He is gone for maybe a minute, before he comes out again. He is definitely whiter than before. He takes something out of his pocket and looks at it, before walking quickly along the road towards High Street.

A few minutes later a car, with a blue flashing light on top, turns up. Anne decides it is time she moved from this place. Ideally she would like to be in the room and watch them look at the man. Ideally she would like to tell them, why he is there lying as he is. Ideally she would like them to know what he did to her. She realizes that that is not realistic. But she can maybe get into the house and listen to them.

A minute or two later, the man and the recently arrived one, come out of the house and move away from the door. She takes the opportunity to slip across the road and into the house. She is certain that they haven't seen her do this.

Throughout the morning many more people arrive. She can hear then talk, from her place at the top of the stairs. At one point someone comes up, to search the upstairs. She manages to hide in a cupboard and even though they open it, they do not see her in the darkest corner of it. She resumes her place of listening. She is disappointed that they do not seem to be making the connection, that he is dead and that the reason for that; is because she has punished him for abusing her.

She finds that she is getting angry about it. The other thing that is coming to her repeatedly, is that she is beginning to think that the other man is actually the man who has done this to her. If that is the case, then she has killed the wrong man. She is not certain that this is the case, but she has a nagging doubt. The niggle gets stronger as the morning progresses, to the point she finds that she wants to do something about it. There is no point in the body being here, if it is the wrong man.

She just cracks and walks down the stairs. This just happens to time with the people working inside, going outside, so that another set of people can come in to remove the body. Anne sees them go out of the front door, as she reaches the bottom of the stairs. She marches to the front door and slams it shut. She then turns and goes into the living room. She wastes no time picking up the body. It seems even lighter than before. She knows she can't go out the front way, as there are too many people there. She goes out of the back door into the yard. She sees the old gate in the corner. It opens to her touch and she is gone through it in a second.

Chapter 28 Anne

It doesn't take her long to get the man home. This will be the place they find him, eventually. When she has deposited the body back in the room, she makes her way back to the house. She needs to find this other man. She needs to find the man who found the body this morning.

She is disappointed to find that she can't see him. She stays back at a distance, well out of sight, watching the people who are near to her house. She just can't see him. She sees another man and feels for some reason that she should know him too. She can't remember seeing him before, but something inside her tells her that she knows him. She retreats a bit further away and to a position where it is unlikely that anyone will be able to spot her. It is this person she is really trying to keep out of sight of. He is not looking around particularly, it is nothing like that. She sees him walking and then it comes to her where she has seen him before. This is the man who was walking in the middle of the night, when she was standing outside her house. It is odd she could feel like this for him, but there is something about him that draws her to him.

She has had enough of standing here. She needs to find this other man. She also feels the need to see if Tara is working today. When she gets to the Deli, she cannot see her. She waits outside for well over an hour, going back every now and then to peep through the window. She isn't there today. There is a young man behind the counter today.

She decides to spend the rest of the day wandering up and down the street, looking for the other man, but he does not put in an appearance either. Frustrated by her lack of success, she walks to where he lives. He isn't there either; well at least he doesn't answer the knock at the door. She has no idea what she would say to him if he had answered the door, but she hadn't thought of that.

Over the next few days, she keeps walking the town, day and night, trying to find the other man. She also goes to the Deli each day, but there is no sign of Tara. She spends the rest of the time, resting in her house.

Then on the same day, everything changes. The first thing she sees; is the man who had found the door open. She watches him closely, before she comes to the conclusion that she was indeed right. This is the man who has done those terrible things to her. True, he is older now, but there is no mistaking that this is the right man this time. She follows him closely as he goes round the town. He also goes into the Deli. It is at this point that she sees that Tara is working today. The man has gone in and is standing at the counter. Tara is serving the man. Something about the way she is standing and looking at the man, tells Anne that Tara knows this man too. She knows what he has done and maybe even has done it to Tara too. Anne notices, even from outside the window, the look on Tara's face as she serves the man. She notices the look of disgust she gives him. She also notices the really dark hooded look that she gives him. When she puts things on top of the counter for him, she does not want any contact with him. Anne knows that this is the right man.

She steps back from the window. She does not want them both to notice her. She is surprised that Tara hasn't noticed her, but no matter. The man comes out of the shop again. He doesn't see Anne standing by the red pillar box, as he strolls by. He is whistling a happy tune. That does nothing to make Anne feel any better.

What should she do now? Should she follow him, or should she go and talk to Tara? She decides to do the latter. She already knows where the man lives, but she doesn't know where Tara lives. The only place she knows she can have contact with Tara, is here where she works.

Anne opens the door to the Deli. Tara is the only person in there.

'What did you go and slam the door in my face for the other night?' Tara wastes no time in blasting at Anne.

The wind caught the door' she replies 'I didn't mean it to happen, it just did. I'm sorry.'

'Well, you didn't come back out for me, when you put him down.' She realizes she has nearly said 'put the body down' but caught herself just in time.

'I did, but not for a while' Anne lies.

'You ask for my help, but you carry him on your own and when we get there, you just slam the door in my face and then ignore me.'

'I've said I'm sorry. I didn't realize that had happened. I really thought I needed you to help me move the body, but then when it came to it, I found that I could carry him on my own. I didn't mean to waste your time.'

'Well you did, whatever you say.'

The look on her face is an angry one. Her cheeks have gone red and she is frowning at Anne and glaring at her, with those deep dark eyes.

'I can make amends' Anne offers, after a few seconds silence.

'How?' is all she gets in response?

'Who was that man you have just served?'

Tara thinks for a second or two.

'That was Bob. I really don't like him. I find him a bit creepy, but I really don't know why.'

'Would you like to help me with Bob?'

'What do you mean by 'help you with Bob'?'

'By doing what I did, to that other man we moved.'

'But you didn't let me help you with him in the end.'

'I'll let you kill him, if you like.'

Tara can't resist the temptation to let out a huge smile at this. Anne couldn't have offered her anything better than this, to compensate for the other night.

'Shhhh' she says suddenly 'we can't talk about this here.'

'I need to get it done quickly.'

'I'll meet you after I finish then.'

'How long will that be?'

'It should be about five o'clock, depending on when the last customers leave.'

They meet after Tara has finished. They walk back to her car and then sit in it, to make their plans. Tara is bursting to tell Anne something.

'I have the perfect murder weapon. Afterwards there will be no trace of it.'

She takes out of her carrier, a cool bag. Inside the bag, she has wrapped some icicles in bubble wrap. She shows them to Anne, before quickly rewrapping them up and putting them away.

'I found them in the freezer out the back. I just saw them and got the idea that they would be great for a murder weapon. Then, when you came in and said what you did, then I just knew it was right to do it with you.'

'We need to go now' Anne says. 'We must do it now.'

'I'm up for it' Tara says 'anyway these won't stay frozen forever.'

'It is just going dark now. If we are lucky, we won't be seen. We need to walk there though and not go there in this.'

They make their way through the side streets, keeping well out of the way of anyone walking along. In that they are fortunate, in that it is quiet, helped by the fact it is now raining. They get to Bob's door and Tara rings the bell. Bob answers the door a few seconds later.

'Tara, what are you doing here?'

'I have brought you these' she replies holding up the cool bag.'

'You'd better come in then' he says, standing aside for her to come through the door. He doesn't make any comment to Anne. 'Have you got time for a cuppa?' he asks, as he closes the door.

Tara looks at Anne and she nods.

'That would be nice.'

'Come on through to the kitchen then. I'll put the kettle on.'

He walks past Tara and she follows him into the kitchen. He starts to fill the kettle with water. While he is doing that, Tara quickly opens the cool bag. Tara starts to unwrap the icicles. She grabs one and so does Anne. They lift them above their heads and then step forward, right behind Bob. Down come their hands, plunging their weapons deep into his neck and back.

Chapter 29 Anne

His death has been instantaneous. He had no idea what was coming, when he let the two of them into his house. They had no idea, that he would have a caller while they were there. Of course they hadn't cased out his house, to see who comes and goes and at what time. It has all been on the spur of the moment.

Bob has fallen to the floor in the kitchen. Anne doesn't need to check that he is dead. Tara is different. She bends down and checks for a pulse. There isn't one. His skin is still warm to the touch, but there is no pulse. She looks at the place where the two icicles are sticking out of him. She had plunged hers into his neck. Anne had plunged hers through and into his heart. Tara is slightly disappointed, as she thinks that it is probably Anne's weapon that has caused the death so quickly. She still feels some satisfaction, at having been part of his execution, which is how she sees it in her head.

She stays down beside the body. What she has just done, is so out of character for her. She is a nice girl. She has had a good upbringing. This isn't the sort of thing that nice girls do. Why has she been feeling like this recently? Why has she been having these dark feelings come over her, since she came back from Uni? It's not that she isn't feeling right about what she has just done, because she is quite at ease with it, funnily enough. It is just that she knows she is behaving differently. It is not about Anne either. She had these dark feelings, way before she even met Anne. She has known Anne a week, if that. She has had these dark feelings come on, way before that, months even.

Tara is still down beside the dead figure of Bob. Anne is standing a couple of feet away, looking down at her. She is remarkably like herself, looks wise.

Suddenly they are interrupted, by a knock at the front door. Then the doorbell rings too. Tara and Anne look at each other in surprise. Their plan, such as it was, did not include in being interrupted by anybody.

'If we don't answer it, they will go away in a minute. It is probably just someone cold calling at every door.' Tara stands up as she says this.

She looks round the kitchen for somewhere to hide, should that be necessary. There really isn't anywhere suitable. Anne is looking out of the kitchen window. She is wondering what whoever it might be would be able to see, if they came round to the back door. The answer to that one is quite simple. They will see them and probably at least part of Bob, lying prostrate on the kitchen floor. This is not good. It is definitely not a good situation. She can only hope that whoever it is will just turn round and go away, when no one comes to answer the door.

The door is knocked again and the bell rung again too. Tara is holding her breath. She can feel her heartrate has gone up. It is kind of exciting, being on the possible verge of being discovered. But then the consequences of that are too terrible to dwell on. She has only just started.

What happens next, takes the entire situation to a different level. It is one thing which neither of them could have anticipated. The front door opens and they hear a woman's voice calling out. They had shut the front door, but not made sure it was locked. It is too late to do anything about that now.

'Bob! Are you there Bob? I have just brought round those things I promised you earlier.'

Tara and Anne do not reply. Tara is backing away, towards the back door. She looks for the key and sees it on the shelf to one side. She grabs it and then fumbles, as she puts it in the lock.

From the sound of it, the woman who has just come in the house must be standing just inside the door. Her voice comes again and it is no louder than it had been the first time.

'Are you there Bob? I said I'd be round.' There is a tinge of concern, audible in her voice now.

They hear her move forward, well Anne does. Tara has now got the back door open and is about to step outside. It is probably a wise decision. However Anne has no intention of leaving the house. She moves towards the door between the kitchen and the hall. She opens the door, just as the woman takes her first step on the stairs. She has decided that Bob must be having a lie down. He is, but not in the way she is thinking about it. She doesn't see the door open. Her eyes are fixed on the stairs and the landing at the top.

'Are you in bed Bob?' she asks, as she climbs the stairs.

She keeps climbing, even though she is not getting an answer. She reaches the landing and turns towards his bedroom. She obviously knows the layout of the house. Anne is now at the bottom of the stairs. Tara has turned round from going out of the back door and has followed Anne into the hall.

'What are you doing?' she mouths quietly to her.

'She's obviously someone connected with him. Look at the way she has gone straight up the stairs. She must know what he has done and she has done nothing about it.'

Tara recognizes the look in Anne's eyes. It is the same look she gets in hers sometimes. It is something it is really hard to get out of, when you have the darkness descend on your thoughts. There is nothing and no argument which is going to change you, from your chosen dark path.

'Shut the front door and lock it' Anne says to her.

Tara moves to do what Anne has asked her too. By the time she turns round from doing this, Anne is almost at the top of the stairs. The woman has gone into the bedroom and stopped. Bob isn't in there, but she has just heard the front door getting shut and locked. A little spike of fear enters her. She feels her heart start to race. There is someone in the house, but she isn't convinced it is Bob. Bob would have answered her by now, unless he is out in the garden.

She turns round to leave the bedroom. There is no one on the landing, but she can hear someone coming up the stairs. She takes a step forward, to see if she can see who it is. She peers over the bannister and sees someone she recognizes, coming slowly up the stairs.

'Tara, what are you doing here?'

Tara looks up at her and wonders why she is looking over the bannister at her, but obviously ignoring Anne, who is standing less than two feet in front of her.

'I came to see Bob, but he wasn't here. He asked me to bring some things up from the Deli. The door was unlocked when I got here. I thought he was maybe out back, but I have just checked and he isn't in the garden. Just as I came back in, I thought I heard someone calling out.'

'That was me' she says 'I wonder where Bob is?'

She stands up and turns to move forwards. Anne is right in front of her. She lifts her hand up and pulls out the pin she has in her hair. She thrusts it forward and into the woman's heart. She doesn't see it coming. She hasn't seen Anne!

'You could have waited' Tara says, as she gets to the top of the stairs.

'There wasn't time. We need to move her somewhere. Do you know her?'

'I think her name is Joan. She lives somewhere in the town.'

'She can't stay here. We need to wrap her in something, to move her. If we can find out where she lives, we can take her home for a while, before she goes to my house.'

'I'll look in her bag. She might have some ID in there.'

'What is ID?'

'It tells about you, never mind. You look for something to wrap her in and I'll look through her things.'

Anne goes away and comes back with a sheet, a minute later. In the meantime Tara has found her driving license.

'Joan Potts is her name and she lives in Swan Meadow.'

'Is that far?'

'No, we have been past it nearly. It is near where that other man was.'

'Oh, alright. We can take her back there, but first we have to get Bob up the stairs into his room.

Chapter 30 Me

Tara moves through to the back of the Deli. The kitchens are out there. I sip at my coffee, wondering where I fit into all this. I have found myself in the middle of something that I truly do not understand. All this has happened to me, because I walked home in the middle of the night, when it is truly dark in Much Wenlock.

But of course it is not going to be because of that. This was happening anyway. I just happen to be the one person who has been involved, in some way, in all three findings of a dead body. I don't believe for a second, that the police think I have anything to do with it all. I do think that they think I know some things that they can't find an explanation of.

That thought brings me back to Tara. She has come through and is working behind the counter. She is getting some things out of the cool cupboards, under the counter. She is refilling the cheeses and the other merchandise which is displayed there. I can't see her face, as she is keeping her head down, due to the work she is doing. I continue to drink my coffee.

A few other people come in and take their places, at the other table in the front. There are more tables round the corner. Tara stops what she is doing and serves these people. I watch her as she goes about this. She is definitely subdued today, compared to how she is normally.

The question in my head is do I want, or is it need, to pursue this thing any further, or should I retreat back into my usual daily life. Something is going on in Wenlock. There is something about this figure I have seen. In my eyes, the figure is definitely involved in the finding of the bodies at least, maybe more. Then there is the tenuous link that she and Tara look the same. That is either by relation, or by pure chance. I am not a great believer in pure chance, so it is probably by the former, relation. The other question in my head is, can I walk away from it all, or will my natural inquisitiveness make that impossible.

I don't resolve anything there and my coffee is finished. I can't sit around here all day. I have writing to get on with at home and the other things that need to be done, in the mundane daily routines. I pay up and leave the Deli, trying to put these things out of my head, at least for the moment.

I get a good night's sleep that night. I have done a few jobs that needed doing round the house and the garden. We've been to the Bilash for a meal. The place was quite busy and there was a lot of talk, about the latest finding of a body in the town. I noticed that I was getting a lot of looks. I could feel that people wanted to ask me what I know, but not quite being able to ask me. That was probably because I may have known some of them by sight, but not to talk to.

I am banned from going out for a midnight, or later, stroll, by my better half. To be honest I am tired and have to go to bed early, to catch up on my sleep anyway. When we take the dogs for a walk in the morning, all is quiet in the town. There aren't any more cars outside the house in Sheinton Street. There aren't any unexplained sightings, although to be fair, I think I am the only one to have seen this whooshing figure.

The bodies are still the talk of the town, when we go down later to do some shopping. I get asked a few questions, but I keep my answers strictly to my part in finding the bodies. I make no mention of the whooshing figure. To be fair, I am not asked about that either.

All is well and we stop for a coffee in Tea on the Square. Another round of talk about things, but that is all. It is when I get home, that I find I have a visitor.

'I have been trying to ring you' Andy says, as we turn into the drive.

'There's no signal in town, if you've been trying my mobile.'

'I guessed as much. The dogs have been barking at me. I saw your car was here, so I guessed you weren't far away.'

'Are you coming in for a coffee? I take it you want to talk to me?'

'I have one or two things to go through with you, I have to admit.'

We go in and over a cup of coffee he tells me what is on his mind. Of course it is about the figure. She seems to be the common thread, but no one else has seen her. He doesn't doubt that I have. He would like me to sit with a police artist and try to get a picture of her. I don't know whether to bring it up, about her similarity to Tara, at this stage. It is a dilemma. I don't have anything concrete to link them together, other than they look similar. The dark look in her eyes is hardly a crime in itself. Even though I do think there is a connection between the two of them, I keep it to myself for now. They will see when they get the picture drawn from my description, that there is a similarity. At least, I expect that will happen, when the picture gets circulated.

I know that some people already know about the figure. There has been a bit of talk, so Andy tells me. That makes me a little surprised, as well as him, that no one seems to have come out and related her to something in the history of Much Wenlock, or surrounding areas. Surely someone knows a story about figures like this. The ghost of Bastard Hall, which isn't that far along Sheinton Street from the house where the bodies have been found, has been mentioned. This figure though is different, is the consensus of police opinion.

What Andy really wants to know, is if I have ever come across this figure before. In that he does not just mean since I have lived here, but wherever I have lived. I can honestly say that I haven't seen her, or anything like her before. From the look on his face, I think he believes me.

'Why is it happening now?' is the next thing he asks me.

'I have got no idea. Something has obviously triggered it. Something somewhere has brought her out into the open again. I assume she is not from the here and now.'

I get a strange feeling come over me, about how she rushed straight at me and initially I thought she had gone through me. I have gone through what happened next, numerous times since and I come up with the same conclusion every time. That is, that she actually came into me and stayed there, until we were in the house and she came out and removed Joan's body. I don't tell Andy this, as I think that is taking things a bit too far. It is one thing telling them about the figure. I did for the first body, because I had seen a figure on my way past there, on my way home. At that time I really didn't think it was anything, other than someone dressed in a cloak. It is only in what has happened since that time; that I now see this figure in a different light. Light is probably the wrong word, because she is only out in the dark, as far as I know.

'We've tried to find out if there is any old folklore, but there has been little come back to us yet. I don't think it is a line of enquiry either. These three people haven't just died. They have been murdered.'

This is the first time they have told me this. I am shocked, as it brings home how close I have been at times. Andy continues:

'What is quite strange and I would prefer you don't talk about this to anyone, is that two people were killed with the same weapon. The other one was killed with something different. It was the same shape of weapon as the other two, but definitely different. Not only that, but they think that the second person was killed by two different hands. It is not that clear, but that is the best guess at this stage. I am not sure where that leaves us in the investigation. Are you free now, to get this artist's picture drawn?'

Chapter 31 Me

It is only as I am sitting there, trying to give the artist as much information as I have, that I realize how little of her I have seen. I haven't seen a clear picture in a good light. I have only seen a fleeting glance of her and never in the best light. The other thing I am struggling with; is that my mind keeps jumping to Tara. I know Tara, as I have seen her often in the Deli. We go in there a lot, to buy stuff and for coffee. The artist can see that I am having trouble, giving him something to go on. He doesn't ask me what the trouble is and I'm certainly not going to tell him. I go back in my mind and try to erase all thoughts of how Tara looks. I start again with the artist, but this time I start with the first impression I got of her. That is the sight of her crossing the road in front of me. That helps me to concentrate my mind on her and not Tara. He goes along with me and we have two pictures now going on. One is the outline of her, with her height being the main factor in that, and the way she was dressed being to the fore too. Only when I have completed that picture, do I let him move on to her face. As hard as I try, I am unable to keep how Tara looks out of my mind and out of my description. He has done this job many times, I am sure. He knows I am struggling and he ends up asking me if I am having difficulty isolating her looks from someone I know. I admit to him, that that is exactly the problem I am having. He asks if it is a relative of mine, or someone close to me. The answer to that is of course a no. He then asks if it is someone I have known from the past, or if it is someone I have seen recently. Then, of course, the question comes if it is someone local. I have to admit to him that it is, but only facially. I see his stance change enough, for me to know I am going to have to spill the beans, if only to name who it is. I feel bad naming Tara, but I don't really have any choice.

It isn't long before we stop for a break. By the time I am back in the room, Andy is there too. He asks me about Tara. I say that it is only that the figure I am trying to describe, looks like her. I don't go into the dark looks and what Claire has said. That is only second hand information anyway. I know they are going to go and have a talk with her. After all, they are investigating 3 murders in our small town.

They leave the picture we are trying to create for now. They have a lead which needs to be followed and my description of the whooshing character is being influenced by her looks. Andy runs me back into town. We stop and park up behind the Corn Exchange. I have a funny feeling, walking through the passage to the High Street, as the thought of her there, comes to me again. We walk up to the Deli and go in. Tara isn't there when we go in. When we ask Liz behind the counter if she is in today, she tells us that it is not her day in today. She directs us to Paul, Claire's husband. He is out the back in the kitchen. I am surprised that I am still with Andy. For some reason he seems to want me to tag along with him.

We find out her address from Paul. He gives me some questioning looks, about why we are there, but I can't do anything to enlighten him, as Andy wants us to go now. That still includes me for some reason.

Tara lives about two miles out of Wenlock. We pull up outside her house. There is a car there. I try to remember whether this is the car she described, that she bought recently. I can't be sure. Andy is out of the car before me and is knocking at the door of the house, before I am fully out of the car. Tara answers his knock. I see her look at Andy and then across at me. I am now out of the car.

'I wonder if we can come in and have a word' Andy says, showing his warrant card. He indicates for me to follow him in.

Tara is very cool in answering his questions. She isn't flustered by his presence and sounds genuinely shocked about what he is asking her. No, she isn't aware that she has any other family round here. Her family isn't from round here anyway. They only moved to the town a few years ago. I sit and look at her, as she answers the questions Andy fires at her. What strikes me most is that this is the old Tara I know, sitting there answering the questions in all innocence. There isn't any trace of the dark look in her, not even in her eyes. She looks young and refreshed, as she has always done, up to a short time ago. She can't shed any light on what we need to know. She also can't give any answers to what Paul has told us about her behaviour recently. She doesn't know what we are talking about and is genuinely puzzled about that part of Andy's questioning.

His questions go on and he approaches things from some different angles, but her answers don't waver in the slightest. There is no sign of a dark look in her eyes, as a sign of frustration, even though he is persistent in his questioning. She looks and sounds as if butter wouldn't melt in her mouth. If I were to judge her replies, bearing in mind that I am a total amateur to this questioning lark, I would say that we are asking the wrong person the questions. I can't tell from looking at Andy, if he is thinking the same as me. Maybe he will tell me in the car, on the way back, and maybe he won't. I would be interested to hear his take on this.

Andy asks her is he can take a photo of her, to assist in the drawing I am trying to give the police artist. She has no objection to this. In fact she seems to be flattered that she might be helping us get the right drawing of the figure in the cloak.

We leave her, after Andy has asked a couple of final questions. She remains as solid in her answers as she has been all along. As we drive away, I ask him what he thinks of her answers. He tells me that he doesn't have any reason not to believe what she has told him. She has given him no reason to suspect that she is involved, in any other way than by looking similar. There is of course the part that Claire and Paul have described about her behaviour of late, but he says there is no evidence of any of that just now. I get the feeling his experience might be telling him things that he isn't passing onto me, but I can understand that. What I don't understand, is why I am accompanying him.

We don't go back into Wenlock, but go straight back to where the police artist is waiting for me to finish my picture. Andy downloads the picture he has taken and the police artist pulls that picture up in front of him on the screen. He then approaches how we draw the picture of the figure from a different angle. He coaxes out of me the differences I can remember, about the figure in the cloak and the picture of Tara. Slowly but surely, we build up a picture of the figure I have seen. Exactly how accurate it is I can't be sure, but when I look at the finished picture, I do get a turn in my stomach. I tell the artist that and he seems to be pleased about it. He believes that is because I have got it right, or rather he has translated what I have described correctly.

With that done, I am returned to Wenlock. Andy isn't around when I leave. It is a patrol car that drops me back at my house. I need to get out and get some fresh air. We take the dogs for a walk, along the old railway line and up onto Windmill Hill. We sit on the bench and look down over the town. I can't help wondering what is going on in this town of ours.

Chapter 32 Me

I don't hear anything else for the rest of the day, not that I am expecting to. I don't know why all this has come at me so suddenly. All because of a night-time walk through the dark in Wenlock, to get home.

I find my night's sleep is interrupted by a strong dream. It is strong enough to wake me up, but I am not sure what part of it actually did wake me up. As is the way with dreams, it is hard to get an accurate timeline and thread with it. Sometimes it is clearer a bit later. And sometimes if you do leave it, then you lose the majority of it and are only left with the bare bones. In the light of my recent experiences, I have a feeling that this was the cause of the dream in the first place. I can't say I have had as many close liaisons with the dead, as I have had here recently.

Luckily I sleep with a pad and paper by the bed. I do this, to jot down ideas that I have in bed, about things I write about. I have to switch the light on and hope that I don't disturb Kate. I write as much as I can remember, hoping that it might be enough for me to fill out more as it comes to me.

The first part of the dream that comes to me, is basically a replay of what has happened to me so far, starting with my walk home in the dark. I find it interesting, as it confirms the actions to me, on my first sighting of the whooshing figure. The dream only concentrates on the part I played in finding the three bodies. That part finishes with the figure rushing across the road into me. For a second or two, I think it may have been that action that caused me to wake up. Of course I know immediately that is wrong, because that is not the point where I have found the third body. Also it is wrong, because I already have more of the dream to write down. It would have been an understandable event, capable of waking me up. I concentrate on finishing the writing, before the content disappears. Thankfully, I seem to be able to keep it in the zone.

I finish writing the first section and then move on to where the dream went next.

I am in the middle of town. I have just appeared there. The lights are off. It is absolutely pouring with rain. I hear a crack of thunder and then the scene is illuminated, by an awesome flash of lightning. I look around me, to see if I am alone. I might have thought I wasn't. I am alone. I walk from the square and walk slowly up High Street. I am walking up the middle of the road. For some reason, I don't want to walk on either of the pavements. I am hoping there will be another flash of lightning. I need to see what is lying ahead of me. I think there must be a power cut, because even the shop windows that usually have lights on all night; are bathed in darkness. Well they would be, if I could make them out.

I am about level with the Corn Exchange, when the next flash of lightning comes along, to assist my vision. I think I see something, out of the corner of my eye. It is not to my right in the Corn Exchange, but in the window of the book shop, on my left. I don't get enough of it to know what it is, but I get the feeling that there is something moving inside the bookshop.

I stop writing for a few seconds, to give it some thought. It is hard, because I am trying to interpret something I might have seen in a dream. It is not as if I can take a closer look at will, or review it again. I try to think what it is I saw in my dream. I can't quite get that close to it, without imposing my conscious thought. What I am trying to work out, is if it is in the book shop, or a reflection of something from my right. I'm not getting anywhere, so I go with it actually being in the bookshop.

What I saw was a figure, but not the one in the cloak. That is what has been causing me to try to confirm where it really was. In the bookshop would be a much bigger issue. I turn to look in the window of the bookshop, but it is too dark to see anything. I wait there for a few minutes, in the hope of another flash. When it comes, there is nothing to see, either in the shop, or anywhere around me.

The storm is getting closer and the thunderclaps are getting much louder. I hear a terrific crash; somewhere back down from the direction I have walked from. It is enough to make me jump. It is also enough to make my heart beat faster, even in a dream. Why haven't I got a torch with me, is a conscious thought I have, while writing it down. But I haven't, so I have to follow the dream.

I decide to investigate the bang. The thought behind that, being that with a noise as loud as this one has been, then there is the probability that it will have woken other people up. That way I won't be alone. I remember this thought in the dream funnily enough. I am getting the idea that I am not exactly comfortable, being out there in the dark, in the storm.

I reach the bottom of the High Street. I know the sound was from this direction, but I can't be sure which way it would be from here. It could be from along Barrow Street, towards the Raven, but it could be from the other direction, towards the church and Sheinton Street. Obviously it is still totally dark, so I am not getting any visual information to help me. Yet again, I find myself waiting for a lightning flash, to help me make a decision. The wind has come up since I reached this place, as if the driving rain, thunder and lightning isn't enough. I am getting absolutely soaked. As a thought, I try to think what I am wearing, but that information just isn't there. I don't think it is important, so don't waste any more time thinking about it. I am not sure if it is the wind I can hear while standing there, or if there is some whooshing involved in it too. I can't see her. I look around, trying to separate the sounds of the wind and the storm, from anything else that might be there.

I can't see a thing. More to the point there are no signs of light coming from any of the houses, in either direction.

Even if the power is off, there are other forms of light that people can use, to see what made the big bang. But there are no beams of light from a torch, or the flickering of candle lights behind glass. Just when I want it quickly, there is a long time since the last lightning flash. I have already decided that I am going to be looking down past the church first. This is purely based on the history of my recent saga being centred in that direction.

I am standing in the middle of the road, waiting for the flash. I am confident that I would be able to hear a car coming, should one decide to come past. It would be a welcome sight I have to say. I know I am not comfortable standing here. It is as if I am waiting for something, other than the long awaited flash of lightning. I think I am too, as I write it down. I am expecting someone to appear. But I am also intrigued about the bang I heard. I am also intrigued why no one has come out to investigate. Maybe the sound has carried from further away. It is sometimes hard to pinpoint exactly where a sound comes from, particularly if you are in an enclosed place like I was, in High Street. I didn't hear the sound come through the passage from the back of the Corn Exchange though, so it won't be from further over that way. The seconds tick by rather more slowly than I would have liked. The thunder continues to rumble and clap around me, but I have to wait a further few minutes more, before I am rewarded with the most illuminating flash of lightning.

Chapter 33 Me

I am facing the right direction. I can't believe that with what I can see while the lightning is there, there aren't any other people out on the street. What does surprise me is, that the sound of the bang I remember; wasn't as loud as I think the damage I am seeing in front of me would warrant.

The road by the church is covered in masonry. The stone is in large chunks, much bigger than the individual stones that make up the church tower. They have come down in blocks of three or four blocks together. At least half of the church tower has come down. A couple of cars parked opposite, are pretty well crushed. One has the blocks of stone still sitting on the roof. The roof is closer to the ground than the car manufacturer ever intended it to be.

The flash is long enough, for me to be able to see that there isn't another soul out there ahead of me. I can also see that the rest of the tower looks quite stable for now. That is just the thought that goes through my head. I have nothing solid to make me think that, but I obviously make that observation, as I start to walk forwards towards the debris on the road.

The thought goes through my head again, about the fact that there isn't anyone out here investigating this. The sound of the bang along here must have been huge. I don't care how sound a sleeper you are, this would have been more than sufficient to wake up the dead. A glance across at the graveyard by the church accompanies that thought, but it is too dark to see anything again. The lightning flash has long gone now and I am back in my world of darkness.

There is no doubt in my head, now that I am close to these fallen stones, that it is not the wind noise that is coming to my ears more pronounced. It is the sound of whooshing. I also think that she is coming close to me. It is the whooshing as she passes me that I hear and not the sound of the wind. Another flash of lightning helps me confirm this. Well it confirms that she is here, but not whooshing around me. She is standing in the doorway to the church. She is looking directly at me. She has her cloak flapping in the wind. The hood is pulled up over her head, but the brief light of the lightning flash allows me to see that it is her and not someone else. Just as the flash of light plunges me back into darkness again, I hear another crash behind me. It is not directly behind me. I am not in danger of having falling masonry crashing on top of me. No, the sound I am hearing is coming from back where I was before, if I am not mistaken. I also have the thought, as I am writing this all down, that at the last second of light, just before this crash, the figure had moved away from the church door. When I say move away, what I really mean, is that one fraction of a second she is still there and then in another fraction of a second, she has gone. I replay this part of the dream as best as I can and I am sure I am right in what I have written.

What I really had wanted to do was to walk on past the church and walk towards the house in Sheinton Street. I have half a thought that the sound from behind is a direct distraction, to stop me in my dreams from doing just that. There is no competition in the dream. There is in my conscious world, writing this down. I really want to carry on in the direction I am walking in; to see Sheinton Street, but that just isn't going to happen. Well not at this stage of the dream anyway.

Another flash of lightning follows quickly. I can confirm she isn't there. Nor is anyone else for that matter. I am getting the feeling that this dream is just for me. I start to walk back towards the square. I reach there, still in the dark. I can't think what might be waiting for my eyes to see, when the next burst of light appears. I don't have long to wait. I see straight away that the front of the Corn Exchange is lying on the street. Exactly how much of it has come down is hard for me to see from here. I need to get closer. I am not happy, as this street is narrower than the point in Wilmore Street, where the church tower has come down. I am a little more exposed, if I get too close. Also, having seen my figure and being on my own out here, I am getting the impression that this whole show is for my benefit alone. It may be a little extreme, but I am getting the idea that there must be a point to it all.

I get another flash of lightning, to help me assess the scene. I am outside Twenty-Twenty when this one arrives. It stops me in my tracks. Well almost, as I dare to step a bit further forward and stop outside the florist, Colours. The top floors have collapsed into the space under the Corn Exchange. I hear a rumbling from that direction and instinctively move away. I am in the dark again, but I don't need light, to know that something else is about to fall down.

The ground shakes viciously beneath my feet. It continues to do so for well over a minute. I hear the sound of masonry falling and it is accompanied by the sound of breaking glass. I keep stepping backwards, as long as the ground shakes beneath me and the sound of falling masonry continues. I find I am back in the square, before the noise stops coming from the area of the Corn Exchange. All I am waiting for is another flash of lightning, to allow me to go up there and see what this latest piece of damage is. I don't get that far though, before another sound comes to me. This time, it is more the creaking of wood that comes to my ears. This sound is from my right and definitely not that far away. I turn in that direction and move backwards into the square, where I feel I might be on slightly safer ground.

This time the lightning obliges, by coming at the same time as some of the action. In front of my eyes, I see the Guildhall twist, as if some great hand is turning it round. It then folds, in a tremendously loud creak, into a pile of broken wood and masonry, onto the street in front of it. The debris doesn't reach as far as the other side of the road. It is more like it has been held back by the twisting and dumped on its own footprint, maybe just encroaching the edge of the road.

The area around me goes quiet again. There is only the sound of the wind and the thunder being there, to keep me company. The lightning does not oblige me again, so I can't get a good look at the damage, or to see if she is standing watching. There is one last violent clap of thunder, from what I feel is directly overhead. Then that is that. There is no more thunder and there is no more lightning. Even the wind abates almost immediately. There is no sound of whooshing either.

Five minutes later, some lights come on. Not street lights, but the lights that are left on in the shop windows. There aren't any down Wilmore Street, but some of the ones in High Street have come back on. I walk up there, to look at the damage to the Corn Exchange. It has totally collapsed. The library isn't even visible. There is just one huge pile of rubble. Blocks of masonry, delicately balanced on top of each other.

The moon appears in the sky, so I take the opportunity to look at the Guildhall. When I said before it had twisted and then dropped; that is not correct. It is not as pretty as that. It looks as if it has been torn from the ground and shredded. There isn't one part that I could look at and say that it is recognizable as being part of the Guildhall.

I make my way gingerly past this demolition site and stand in front of the church. The tower is as it was a few minutes ago. Half of it still standing and half of it spread out on the ground. I turn my gaze towards the end of Sheinton Street. The moonlight continues to shine down on the town. She is standing there on the corner. There is no doubt, in my head, that she is looking directly at me. She has been waiting for me to inspect the damage. She has been waiting for me to reach the point I am at. She has been waiting for me. I am not sure if I thought this in the dream, or I am thinking of this as I am writing down the contents of the dream. She is definitely waiting for me!

Chapter 34 Me

I am still surprised that I am alone on the street. With all the noise that has gone on, surely other people should or would have been woken by it. I am thinking this in my dream I think, as well as now that I am still writing it down. There appears to be so much of this dream to write down. Of course it is slower to write it and I am probably using descriptions that weren't necessary in the dream itself. Then I realize that it is because it is in a dream; that no one else is there. They aren't needed for the purpose of the dream. I am needed for the purpose of the dream, obviously.

In my dream, I try to ignore the fact that she is there for a minute or two. I wander back up, to inspect the damage at the Guildhall again. I then walk up High Street and look at what used to be the Corn Exchange, once more. What comes to me; is that the three building have all been dealt with, is that what I should call this event, differently. The church tower has had the top half taken off it, almost as if it has been swiped off by a giant hand. The break is quite clean. Yes, there is a mess on the ground, where the masonry has fallen, but the style of building and destruction of this part, has led to this. I can almost imagine that you could put that back together without too much difficulty, using the masonry that has fallen to the ground. The Guildhall has been destroyed in a completely different fashion. It is of a different structure, true, but even then it has been again, as if the same giant hand, or hands maybe, has lifted it and twisted it and then plonked it down on its own footprint. If you could untwist everything, the Guildhall too could be put back to its original shape and restored quite easily. At least that is the thought I am writing down, as an observation within my dream.

Ah, but then you have the Corn Exchange. Now that is a different matter altogether. The first thing that comes to me is that the Corn Exchange had two attempts to get it into the state that I am looking at now. First of all the front part was brought down and then a while later, the second part at the back was also brought down. As I stand there and have a look at it, I can see that there has been more anger in the destruction of this building. Whereas as I have looked at it with the other two buildings, as being a hand or two hands doing the destruction, in the case of the Corn Exchange there has been more than that. Then it comes to me. On the first attempt the same method was used as for the other two buildings, but when they came back to inspect the damage, they were not satisfied with the extent of the damage, so they came back, possibly with some other giant tool in the hand this time, and demolished the rear section.

Why am I having this kind of thought in my dream? I really don't know, but I am. I am definitely writing this down as thoughts from the dream, while I am purposely not looking at where she was standing, or where she might be standing, watching me now I am in the High Street. I am satisfied that there is a difference and I am also satisfied that there is a reason why this building has been attacked so differently. I'd like to go round to the back of the Corn Exchange to have a look at that side, but I don't think it will make any difference.

I am interrupted in my thought of this, by the sound of whooshing. I am standing in the middle of the High Street when I hear it. It is coming from my right; that is from the bottom of the street. I can make her out in the moonlight and with the help of the faint light provided by the odd shop or two that has its display lights on. I turn towards her. She runs straight at me. I think I should maybe move out of her way, but there isn't time. I don't need to, as she slows down suddenly, about six feet from me, and comes to an abrupt stop. Her hood is over her head, but I can see part of her face. She pulls the hood back and the first thing I notice is that she has been crying. I also see a bruise under one of her eyes and another on her left cheekbone. It is hard to tell properly, as the light really isn't that good, but they look recent.

She stands, looking at me, for maybe a minute. I am not concerned by her coming up to me like this. As before, I know automatically that she wants me here for a reason. What I don't know as yet, is what that reason is. I get the feeling though, that this evening is a step closer to that. But then as I write this, I am questioning why this is all being done as a dream.

I don't make any attempt to speak to her, nor her to me. Then, after maybe another minute more of standing looking at each other, she turns and starts to walk back down High Street. I don't follow straight away. She stops maybe fifteen feet away from me, when she has looked over her shoulder and seen that I am not following. She turns away and continues to walk away from me. I know I am expected to follow and I feel my feet starting to work beneath me. I don't try to make up the gap between us, which is now about twenty feet. She turns every few steps, to make sure I am still following her. She maintains the same pace and I maintain the gap between us. She stops outside the Guildhall and waits for me to get a bit closer. She turns and looks at it for a few seconds, but then just as I get close, she resumes her walking away from me. She carefully picks her way through the debris that is lying in the road by the church. I follow her path through, maybe now only six or seven paces behind. Once she is through the debris, she picks up her pace and opens the gap quite quickly. I don't make any attempt to close it again. Somehow I am thinking that I am not meant to. In fact I think I am in the same position I was when I first saw her, so I stop walking. I am just past the last of the fallen masonry from the church tower. She stops on the corner of Sheinton Street. That is where I first saw her, just a few minutes ago.

She looks back towards me and smiles. I am obviously now in the right place and she can continue with what she has wanted to do. She stands there for a couple of minutes, not moving a muscle. I stand where I am, watching and waiting; waiting for the next part of this to happen. I have a quick thought, that maybe some more of the church tower will be brought down on top of me, but I discard that thought almost immediately. I really don't believe that is why I am here.

She pushes off the wall and turns away from me. I don't move as I watch her. She walks over the road, breaking into a run by the other side. She stops outside the door of the old police station and starts banging on the door. She is beating her hands against the really solid door. I can hear it clearly from where I am standing. She keeps this up for fully a minute, before rushing away from me, to the next house. That is Bastard Hall. It is an older building, like the Guildhall. She stops at that front door and bangs furiously on that door too. Again nothing happens, so she comes back towards me and stops once more outside the old police station front door. She knocks on that, if possibly, louder than she did before. It is definitely more frantically than she had before. But she does not bang the door this time for so long.

It is as if something has got hold of her arm. She suddenly moves across the road towards the house. It is as if she is being pulled by someone, but I cannot see anyone or anything, other than her. She disappears through the door into the house. I wait for a couple of minutes, but she doesn't come back out.

Chapter 35 Me

Just as I think I am getting to the interesting stage, the moon decides to hide behind the clouds again. That coincides with what few lights that have been on, going off again. I stand where I am, as it takes a few minutes for my eyes to adjust to the much lower level of light that there is again. It is dark, really dark and I am standing by the debris of the church tower. The thought of not being safe, is heightened by the wind picking up again and the rain starting to fall. In addition to that, I can hear faint sounds of thunder again. A few minutes ago in this dream of mine, I was feeling that she wanted to show me something and not do me any harm. I am in the process of reviewing that and am not so happy with where I find myself, albeit in the dream. This could however, be me thinking this as I am writing the dream and not something I am thinking as part of the dream. It doesn't really matter and doesn't change the dream I am writing down.

I know, in the dream, I start to move and it isn't towards the house. It may not be a smart move, to walk back past the church and the Guildhall, but that is the way I go. I suspect it is because I think there is more danger ahead of me than behind. I find myself in the dark, in the middle of the square. It is dark again up High Street. I position myself in the middle of the square, as prepared as I can be for any unexpected occurrence.

The thunder draws closer and the lightning returns to the sky, but only in the distance. The moon remains stubbornly behind the clouds and the lights that were on; remain off. Nothing is moving around me; at least I am not aware of anything that is. Other than the thunder rumbling around, there is only silence around me too. I can feel I am waiting for something to happen, but it doesn't. I am just standing there all alone in the middle of town, in the dark, in the middle of the night. I need to do something, so I move up High Street. I walk on past the Corn Exchange, or what is left of it rather, and past the Deli and Mrs P's, the Book Shop, the Talbot, the Pharmacy and the Candle Shop. I stop at the junction of Back Lane. Nothing has happened to me so far in this episode.

It is maybe not the best decision I have made, but there is the need to know what all this has been about. The thunder doesn't appear to be getting any closer. It is just going round and round, in the distance, as is the lightning. It is even darker down Back Lane, if that is possible, as I start my way down there. I keep to the right at the fork and stop by the car park, at the back of the Corn Exchange. I knew it already from the view at the front, but I can confirm it now from the back. This building has been demolished entirely. There is nothing standing of what used to be the Corn Exchange. I am sure there is a significance in this, but I have no idea what that might be, yet.

Now I know I am getting back to nearly being at the house. I walk down to the corner, where Back Lane meets Queen Street. I stand on the corner and try to make out if there is anything to be seen ahead of me. What I am looking for is someone I guess; her even. She is not there. I walk carefully and quietly the forty yards or so to the corner by the Bull Ring. The corner where she stood is on my left, the corner of Sheinton Street. It is dark, even darker than it had been before, but I am pretty certain that she isn't there.

I know this is a dream, but how have I managed to find myself down here in the dark, without having brought a torch with me. It is not as if this is the first time! But then I remember that this is a dream. Certain things don't necessarily work to logic in a dream. I have made it this far, without more mishap to the town, and without any to me so far. I feel the confidence returning. That the thunder and lightning returning, coupled with the loss of power again, are not something that she has any control over, even in my dream.

I pluck up the courage and walk over to the corner where she had stood. She is definitely not there. I can't hear her whooshing either, not that I would if she was standing still. I listen intently for a few seconds, but there is nothing close by to listen to. The wind has even dropped to almost nothing again. The door to her house is only several yards along from where I am standing, but I don't approach it directly. I walk across the road to the old police station, keeping one eye turned towards where the door is, as I go.

It is almost as if I am in the right place once more. The moon emerges from the clouds and illuminates my world once more. It is a great improvement on the lack of light I have had to cope with for the past few minutes.

The first thing that I notice is that the front door is not closed properly. It isn't wide open, as it has been on past occasions, but it is not closed either. It is maybe three or four inches open. I just know that I am meant to go and investigate. I just know I am going to have to do this on my own too. There still isn't any other person come out, to investigate the goings on in town. It is my dream and apparently I am the only one to have a role in it, other than her of course.

I step nervously off the pavement, onto the road. Any second I am expecting her to jump out of the door and run towards me. That doesn't happen. I get to the other side. I am now only three or four feet from the door. I feel in my pocket for something. I have done this before in this dream, but not pulled anything out of my pocket. This time I do though. It is a small torch. Why didn't I find that there before? I guess because I wasn't meant to. Obviously I am going to need it in the house. I switch on the torch and an inadequate beam of light shines ahead of me. It could be a lot better, but it could be a lot worse too.

I step towards the door and push it with one hand. It does not open. Something appears to be stopping it open. I try a bit harder and it moves grudgingly, under this pressure. It doesn't swing fully open. It hardly swings at all, to be honest. It is like the door has swollen and it is rubbing against the floor. It is at this moment that I realize the door has changed. This is not the door that has been on the house in the last few days. This is an older door. This is a less well fitting door. This door has no glass in it. This door is a put together, but heavy, wooden door.

The door scrapes open enough, to enable me to get through the gap. I shine my meagre light into the hall ahead of me. There is nothing that I can make out. The beam of light barely reaches the stairs ahead of me, but that is not where I am going to look first. I come through the gap and stand in the hall. I listen to nothing, because that is what there is to hear. I take a tentative step forward towards the door of the living room. This has been the room of preference up to now. I am not expecting it to be any different now.

Like the front door, this is not the same door. It is also not standing open fully. It is set at about the same gap as the front door had been, when I approached it. I build myself up to whatever it is I am going to find behind this door. I'm guessing I am going to find another body. I push the door open and shine the torchlight in there ahead of me. I am not to be disappointed, as the feeble light does indeed pick out a body lying on the floor.

Chapter 36 Me

What I can't see from where I am standing; is what sort of a body is it, lying on the floor in front of me? My dismal light will not illuminate anything, other than a vague outline lying on the floor. If I am going to establish any more than I already know, then I am going to have to advance into the room. I can feel, in my dream, that for some reason, I have quite a high level of resistance in doing that. I can understand that. This has all been so controlled and contrived so far. Now I am in an enclosed place and indeed, in a very vulnerable place too at that. I listen for even the quietest of sounds coming from in the room, but there aren't any. I am expecting she is going to make an appearance though. What would be the point of bringing me here, if she wasn't going to?

I push the door as far back as it will open. It is heavy and won't go all the way back, before it rubs on the floor. That is not the result I was hoping for. It still leaves room behind the door, where someone could be standing, waiting for me to enter the room. I can feel it in the dream, that I take a big breath and step into the room. The first thing I do is to look behind the door. There isn't anyone there. I walk round the room, shining the light into all of the corners, to check if I am alone. I am, except for the body on the floor.

The body is dressed in black and now I am looking, more relaxed, at it. I can see it is in fact her, my whooshing girl. She isn't moving at all. Is she going to spring round when I bend down and touch her? I am going to find out!

I bend down beside her and touch her, where I think her arm is under the cloak. It isn't moving, when I touch it through the material. On one hand I know I shouldn't be disturbing the body, but on the other, that doesn't matter. This is here in my dream. I move round to the other side of the body, to see if I can see more from that side, before I move her. I can't, so I gently turn her body over. I know this is the girl who has been watching me tonight. What I don't understand, is why she is here on the floor and if I am not mistaken, she is dead. The first thing I see is the bruise under her eye and the one on her cheek that I had seen earlier. They are much nastier, under my feeble torchlight, than I imagined they were earlier. There are also some more recent marks on her face, that haven't developed like the other ones yet. I put my hand to her neck, but there is no pulse and her skin is stone cold to the touch. Her lips have received some assault too, from the looks of it. I shine my torch closely to her face. I am surprised that I can see the trace of the tears I saw earlier. At least I am thinking it is those tears, but it may just be of tears. Her face is set in an expression of fear, which I haven't seen before, not that I have had the opportunity up to now, to have this close a look at it.

I let my light move down over her cloak. I can see that it is torn and shredded in places. I can see her body in places, between the shredded cloak! I am sure it wasn't like this when I turned her over, but it is now. I notice some blood on some of the shreds and keep my hand back. I really don't need to get that on me. It really wouldn't be a good move.

I fail to achieve that, as I inspect her body. The blood is wet and is still appearing. There is an area of blood on her chest and another area is appearing lower down. It makes me pull back a little, but I am too late. I have her blood on my hands. The clothes are disappearing in front of my eyes. It is as if this scene is playing out, now I am in the audience. Her head is now not covered. Her top half is revealed only a few seconds later. Her hands are crossed over her breasts and I can see the blood creeping out beneath them. Further down, there is a little cloth left. It is as if her cloak has been torn from her, whilst being physically attacked. Below that, her legs are bare and cold to the touch. I sit back from her again, trying to think what may have happened here. Well it is obvious she has been attacked, but the question I am finding myself asking is when? This, on one hand, has happened recently, because of the state of the blood. But on the other hand, it hasn't just happened. I know that much. The other question, which is really the one that I need an answer to, is why is she showing me this? I am thinking she has brought me here to show me this. I am thinking that because of that, she is expecting me to be doing something. That part has not come to me as yet, but I am sure it will.

I think in my dream that I need to do something at this moment. I move back from her, but that is not enough. I take off my jacket and place it over her, as she lies there on the floor. I know as I do so, that some of the blood from her, spreads onto it, but this girl needs some dignity. I stand up and try to think what I should do. She had no luck banging on the doors over the road. No one has come out to see what the noise has been, on the destruction of the three buildings either. How am I going to raise the alarm and get people here to help?

One part of me does not want to leave her alone in here, but I know that unless I leave her and go outside, I will not be able to raise the alarm. I have to do something, but I also need to satisfy my need to protect this girl. That sounds stupid, because she is lying dead, on the floor in front of me. But there is something in me, that knows she still needs protecting, or helping, or something like that.

I kneel down beside her and say to her battered face.

'I will do what I can. I will do what I can, about what you are trying to lead me to. I need to get help, but I am not walking away from you. I will try my hardest to achieve what you need me to.'

At that, I get up and turn towards the door. Even as I walk into the hall, the living room door is starting to close on its own. I see the front door start to move too and dart forward, to make it through the gap, before it gets too narrow. I don't stop when I get outside, but walk straight over the road and then turn round. By the time I'm there, the front door has closed, but more than that; it has changed back to the door I have known in the past few days.

Just then the moonlight reappears and I turn towards the centre of town. My mouth drops open, as I see that there is no debris on the road from the church tower. I look upwards and see that the tower is exactly where it should be. It is still standing, as part of the church again. I walk forward, guessing what I am likely to find after that, and I do. The Guildhall has untwisted itself from the mess that it had been lying in. It has reformed as the Guildhall I have known, since I moved to the town. I touch the walls and the bars, but they are real. It is as if what I saw earlier has never happened. I need to walk up High Street. There is no doubt in my head, that the Corn Exchange will be in one piece again, rather than the thousands of pieces when I had last seen it. Sure enough, when I get there, it is standing again. It is only when I get close to it and stand over the road from it, that I see something that hasn't quite been corrected. Just above where the flower baskets hang, maybe two feet up into the masonry section of the building, there are some horizontal cracks, running the width of the building. They are not particularly deep, but they are there nevertheless. I am almost certain that these weren't visible, the last time I walked past the building in daylight. I dare to walk through the passage and look at the back of the building. It too is untouched, in that it is still standing too.

As I move back to the front, the lights in the shop windows come back on followed, surprisingly, by some of the street lights. It is at this point I wake up from my dream.

Chapter 37 Me

I am surprised how long it has taken me to write this dream down. Despite my attempts not to wake Kate, it happened about half way through. She didn't need to say anything to me when she woke. She could see that I was deeply engrossed by what I was writing. A mug of coffee appeared shortly after. That disappeared at some point of the writing. She settled in beside me, doing stuff on her iPad.

I wait until the appropriate moment and run through what I have just written, about my dream. She asks me what I make of it. I have to say it is a puzzle, as well as being weird of course. Even for me and my imagination, this is something that is quite far-fetched. Well it would be, if it was a dream in isolation. But it isn't, as I have been involved in goings on in the town of late. And of course, my cloaked figure has featured heavily too.

I am not going to sleep any more tonight. Even if it wasn't that near to morning time, I would struggle to get back to sleep, with what I have written going through my head. I keep the light on and lie down, to think through what has happened in the dream. My first thought is that it will be interesting to find out what I feel, when I go down town later, with the dogs. It will be more interesting to see if the door of the house has been left open again. It closed in the dream, but part of me says that there is a good chance that the door might well be open now. I am not going to rush down there now.

The other thing that is going through my head; is whether I should mention any of this to the police, well Andy I mean. Does it have any relevance to what has been going on? I am not sure. I have obviously dreamed this, because of the murders and everything else, but whether it has any real relevance is another matter. I ask Kate about it, but she says that at this point, she thinks it probably wiser not to do it. If we find things different when we go down town with the dogs, then that might change of course.

I get up just before seven and have some breakfast, before we venture out with the dogs. It is a drizzly morning, but otherwise calm, unlike the weather in my dream last night. I have to admit to being slightly apprehensive, as we near the town centre. We detour, to walk up High Street. We can see straight away that the Corn Exchange is, of course, there as usual. I look up at the front, wondering if the cracks that were there at the end of the dream will still be there. However hard I look, I can't see any evidence of them at all. I scrutinize the front of the building and even go through to the back and check there too, but there is nothing amiss. It is comforting on one hand, but on the other, it leaves something a little bit unfinished from the dream.

The dogs are keen to get to the park for their run. We walk back down High Street and past the Guildhall and the Church. Neither of them is showing any negative effects from the damage they received in the dream last night. They are as I have always known them to be. I admit that I am slightly more apprehensive, as we approach the front of the house. We are walking on the opposite side of the road. My eyes are firmly fixed on the door, even before we are in sight of it. I needn't have got so worked up about it. It is closed.

I breathe a sigh of relief. Kate tuts at me and smiles a knowing smile. We walk on and the dogs are at last on the last stretch, before they get let off their leads.

Forty five minutes later, we are home and the rest of the day begins. We don't get a phone call from the police, or from Andy, in particular. In fact the phone doesn't go at all that day, or for the next few. I sleep well at nights and I don't get any more dreams. I don't for a second think that anything has changed, either in me or in the town, to be the cause of that, but I am not complaining.

In fact it is way more than a week after I had the dream that anything comes to light, about any of the incidences. It has been released that all three deaths have been declared as suspicious, or rather that the victims did not die of natural causes. Two of the victims died by way of, very likely, the same weapon. The third victim, Joan, died from a different weapon. In fact the weapon is very much a mystery still. The other two were killed by some form of sharp weapon. That is not a knife, but something that has a point at one end at least. None of the weapons have been discovered, despite lengthy searches in the vicinity. Nor has there been any progress in finding out who the perpetrator, or perpetrators, might be. In fact there has been no progress or advance, been made in the investigation. There is work being done, but no progress.

We walk down, as is our want, and visit one or two of the shops, to do our shopping. With that done, we go to the Deli for a coffee. I am not consciously thinking whether Tara is working or not. It is only when we get in there and we are served by Liz, that I have a thought about it. It isn't unusual, because Claire and Paul have several different members of staff they use over the week. The people and the days they work changes too in term time, as a couple of them have either college or university to fit in. One goes locally to college and another goes away to University. It is that time of year now, so it no surprise not to see any of them for a while.

I don't even mention it to Liz. We have our coffee and walk home. It is when we get there that I see a familiar vehicle, parked in the drive, waiting on our return. A familiar man gets out of the car, as we approach the front door. Andy smiles and for some reason, I feel a small pit in my stomach. I don't think he is here for social reasons. The look on his face tells me that this feeling is well founded. Before he says anything to us, I ask him in for a coffee.

Thankfully, he does not say anything, until we have drunk our coffee. Then he gets down to the business of why he is paying me another visit. The reason is quite simple. They need to speak to Tara, but for some reason she can't be found. He doesn't tell me why he needs to speak to Tara, but he does say that they have been trying to speak to her for well over a week now. I feel the pit in my stomach deepen. I wait for him to tell me a little bit more, about why they haven't found Tara.

They had gone to her house over a week ago. Initially there was no one at home. Later in the day they returned and Tara's mother was home. She told them that Tara had returned to University. She gave them the address where her digs are. They asked another force to go to see her. One thing or another got in the way and it turns out that they did not go straight round, to see her for them. When they eventually did go round and it took a couple of visits, before they even managed to find anyone in at the address, they found that no one has seen Tara since before the break and she went home. It has then taken more investigations, to try to see where Tara may have gone, when she left home. Her car is not there and to this point has not been found. It would appear that Tara has disappeared off the face of the earth. He ends with the statement; that they really need to speak to her.

I ask him why he is telling me all this. He says he just wondered if I have any thoughts on the situation. I have, but I am not sure that I am ready to tell him about the dream. It is different from the other times the door was open, but I have a feeling the result might just be the same.

Chapter 38 Me

Andy leaves us, but is back less than a day later. I don't know why he keeps coming back to see me. I'm guessing he knows that I have a slightly different angle on things. Also, to date, I have been involved in everything that has happened so far.

His investigations into the whereabouts of Tara, have progressed somewhat. He has established for certain that she has not gone back to University. Her car has been found here in Shropshire. In fact it has been found in the town. He has talked to Claire and Paul at the Deli, also the other staff, to see if they know where she parked her car, on the days she brought it in to work. They don't know for sure, but generally it is in the roads behind the shop, as close as a space can be found. Her car was found not a million miles away from where it might have been parked, if she had been going to work. The theory they are working on, is that she parked it where it has been found, at a different time of day than normal. I can understand that. The parking is different in the morning when people have gone to work and when they come home again in the evening.

Andy and co are working on the theory that she had come into town, after the shop had closed. She had parked a bit further away than she normally did. Why has no one reported the car being left there? Well that is quite simple. The road it was found on is a residential street, but where the cars park, is below the level of the houses. It wasn't the only car there and it also isn't unusual for cars to be parked there long term.

Andy says they have talked to Tara's mother about it. She can't remember exactly what day she would have done that. She knows the date that Tara said she was going back to University. She says the car wasn't loaded very much, but Tara had said she was going to be back in a couple of weeks. Anyway, most of her stuff was already at her digs. She had only brought some clothes back with her. These were found in a bag, in the boot of her car.

What CCTV there is in the town, failed to pick her up at all. That in itself isn't surprising though, as it is only in central parts. For example, it hadn't picked up anything in Wilmore Street or Sheinton Street, with the events that went on there, because there isn't a camera pointing that way. Of course the camera doesn't work either, when there is a power outage. There is another one at the petrol station, but she hadn't been there either.

The point being that they can only assume that she parked the car there, on the day she left for University. And so far, though it is early days as they have only just found the car, they haven't found anyone who might have met with her. Andy is thinking of putting out a public appeal. He needs to speak with her about something. He hasn't indicated what, but I can guess it is something to do with the murders. He is now also worried about her being missing. Yesterday I wasn't keen to tell him about the dream. Today I am of the mind that maybe, crazy as it may sound, I should tell him about it.

Over a cup of coffee, I do just that. He receives it well, considering, and then I get him the transcript I have done of the entire dream. He asks if he can have a copy, so I go upstairs and photocopy the lot for him.

Do I think Tara has any involvement in my dream? That is what he asks me. On a straightforward basis, no I don't. But taken in with the current situation and the fact that she is missing, along with the fact that she and the girl look the same, then who knows?

Andy is obviously taking some of it seriously, as he asks me to show him round to the places where I had been in the dream. I do that willingly. Of course the place we end up at; is right outside the house in Sheinton Street. This door has been replaced more times in the recent weeks, than probably in its entire lifetime of being a doorway. To that end Andy still has a key, albeit not with him. It is still technically a crime scene, he tells me. On the basis of the content of my dream, he feels that we have no choice, but to have a look inside the house. It is not that we are expecting anything to be there, but we can't afford not to take a look.

The key is brought to us. Andy is really interested in the content of the dream. While we are waiting for the key to arrive, he asks me to go through this part of the dream. We need to find out more about the door that was on the house and the one in the living room. We need to find out what age they are from? Then he asks me a strange question.

'I'd like to ask you about this figure that you keep seeing around the town?'

'That's alright' I reply 'ask away.'

'Well, you more than anybody appear to, how shall I put this, have seen her around' is all he can say about her?

'I think that is fair' I reply.

'Well, is she from now, or is she from sometime in the past?'

'She is definitely not from now' I reply, without taking any time to think about it.

'I agree' he replies 'but from when in the past do you think she is from?'

'I've thought a little about this. I am not sure basically, because I don't have anything concrete to go on. My first thought was that she was from several hundreds of years ago. I don't know why. It is probably influenced by things I have seen and read throughout my life. But then as I have thought about it more, I have adjusted that thinking somewhat. There is something Victorian about her. Again there is nothing to actually point me there. It is more of a gut feeling. Why are you asking me this?'

'I'm just trying to get a handle on her. Something is going on and she is trying to tell us something. I don't understand for one second what has happened to the bodies in here; here one second and gone the next. They are not figments of our imaginations. They actually existed. Our guys touched the bodies, so they are real. I'd love to know how she moved them, but I don't think I'm ever going to get to know that.'

'I suppose if we know what era she is from then, we can start digging into the history of this place. See if we can discover any events that might coincide with the sort of thing we are finding at the moment. It is harder than trying to find a needle in a haystack though.'

'Detective work is often like that, but when you start digging, you quite often unearth some little nugget of information, which on its own means nothing. But when you slot it into the bigger picture, it can often lead to a new line of enquiry.'

'Is that what you are trying to do?'

'We need a new line of enquiry. All we have at the moment; is someone we can't find to talk to.'

'I can think of a couple of people who know about the general history of the town. Whether they will know about any specific events of the nature we are thinking of, is another matter. I can only ask and see what comes out.'

'Maybe they will know of people you can speak to.'

'I'm doing this, I take it?'

'I think it will be easier for you to do than me. Also it might stop the situation getting out of my hands. If I start asking about the figure and long time ago, then the word will get out and we will have the press from who knows where, poking their noses in and commenting on police practice in Shropshire.'

'I see where you are coming from.' I reply. 'With me doing it, people aren't necessarily going to associate it with these events. I take it I approach it from just a personal historical interest angle?'

'That is what I have been thinking, if you don't mind doing this for me. The problem I have is; that I do believe that she is a ghost or whatever, from the past. You can imagine how that would go down in certain places.'

Chapter 39 Me

The key arrives and our conversation on that matter ceases, at least for the time being. The key bringer stays with us, to look inside the house. Andy hands me the key and asks me to unlock it and open the door, to the point at which I found it open. He knows it is not the same door, but I see what he wants me to do it for. I do that and then we push on from there. In the hall, we stop and listen. I know what he is listening for; the flies. Luckily, we don't hear any. We move on to the living room next. Again I put the door at the right point, before we venture in. I open the door back, as far as the one in the dream went. That is not as far back as this one goes. The door in the dream stuck on the floor. The room is of course empty. While the key bringer goes off to get some takeaway coffees from The Smoothie for us all, Andy asks me to describe what I saw in the house the other night. I tell him as closely as I can, word for word, bearing in mind that I haven't got my transcript with me. I describe the girl and how she was lying. I describe the injuries I could see that she has. He asks me if I think the figure had been murdered. With injuries like those, there is little doubt in my mind that that is the case. In fact I go further than that and say that the entire dream was designed, to lead up to me finding the body in this house.

'What was the other stuff about, with the buildings collapsing then?'

'I have absolutely no idea. There must be a reason to it though, otherwise why didn't she just lead me here to the house. No, it was quite elaborate and very detailed in some ways, but in others it was not.'

'Well, as usual, there is no sign that it ever happened here, what you saw in your dream.'

'No, but it does sort of lead me to the fact, that this girl was connected to this house somehow.'

'I think you are right in that. Maybe that is where your search should begin.'

'The only problem with that; is that it then will be directly connected to the case. They will wonder why I am looking at this house, when I am asking about supposedly general history of the town.'

'That is a good point. We need to know the answer to that one though. I will have to get someone digging back at the station, to get some of the history of the house.'

'I can always ask about the street in general. There is always the old police station over the road and then there is

Bastard Hall too. I have heard talk about there being a ghost there.'

I stop in mid conversation. Something has come to me about those two buildings. It is something from the dream.

'I remember from the dream now. She ran across the road and then banged on those two doors for a while. It was frantic banging on the doors. No one came out of course. She did the old police station twice too.'

We go outside, to wait for our coffees to come. That takes a few more minutes. In the meantime, we have wandered over the road and looked at the house from there. It is nondescript really. It is narrow, even narrower than its neighbors. I have no idea looking at it, how old it may be. I am fairly certain that looking back through its history will reveal something about the house. Whether it will reveal anything about her is another matter. But that isn't for me to do. He is going to get one of his detectives to do it.

The coffees arrive and we drink them out on the street. For some reason neither of us are particularly keen on standing in there to drink it. It is not like the other occasions, at least we don't think that it is, but events previously have left an indelible mark in our brains, about the house.

When we have finished, we get ready to lock the house up.

'I guess we should just take a quick look at the rest of the house, while we have the keys here and it is open. It wouldn't look good if I didn't and we missed something.'

The key bringer stays by the front door, while we go back in. A quick search of the rest of the downstairs doesn't reveal anything at all, nor does the back yard for that matter. Andy climbs the stairs first. He checks the back bedroom and the bathroom, while I remain on the landing. They aren't the biggest of rooms and it really doesn't take two people to check whether they are empty or not. They are empty, as it turns out, which isn't a surprise. Something draws me into the front room; right after Andy has walked in. I didn't have any intention of going in, until my feet started taking me there.

Andy is literally one step ahead of me into the room. He is walking straight in and it looks like he is going over to the window. I come in the door literally, as I said, right on his heels. At first I think he must see it, but it becomes obvious a microsecond later to me that he hasn't seen it.

'Stop, Andy!' I say in a loud voice.

He does so, with one foot still in the air. He doesn't know yet why I have said it, but the tone of my voice has indicated that something is very wrong.

'What's the matter?' he asks, still with his foot raised to take the next step.

'Come back. Don't put your foot down in front of you.' I move to one side, to allow him to step backwards to where I was standing. 'Alright you can step back now.'

He does that and looks around the room, before turning in my direction and looking at me.

'What have I just stopped for?'

'There on the floor.'

I point to the middle of the room, where I can see that someone is lying on the floor.

'There's nothing there.'

'There is' I reply and then I know who it must be. 'Can't you see her?'

'Can't I see who?' is all he replies.

'She's lying on the floor, right in front of you.'

'I can't see anything there.'

I move forward, maybe half a pace. I move my hands, to show him where I am seeing her. He isn't seeing anything.

'Can you touch her?'

'I'll try' I say, without too much enthusiasm in my voice; or within me for that matter.

I edge forward and kneel down on the floor beside her. I can see the gentle up and down movement as she breathes.

This is not something I am keen on doing. I decide that before I touch her, I will talk to her, but then she has just slept through me telling Andy to stop and that wasn't exactly said in a quiet voice.

'Hello, can you hear me.'

I say it softly to start with and then I say it a bit louder. Nothing changes in her breathing. I naturally put my hand forward, to give her a gentle shake. I don't come in contact with her. My hand just disappears into her, unlike in the dream where I was able to turn her over. I tell Andy what has just happened.

'So if I had carried on walking, I wouldn't have felt anything?'

'I'm guessing you wouldn't.'

I try again, but my hand cannot feel anything. But my eyes are telling me she is there.

'Have you got your phone?'

I nod that I have.

'Try taking a photo of her.'

I take my phone out of my pocket and do as he has suggested. I look at the picture I have taken. So does Andy. There is nothing to see in the photo, but for the bare floorboards.

'But you can still see her now?'

'I can, but that is all. I have to say that this is weird.'

'I believe you, in that I believe you can see her. It would be great if you could stay and watch what she does when she wakes up. I am presuming she is going to wake up at some point.'

'You want me to do that?'

'Part of me wants to say yes, but then it is asking a lot. I would have to get someone to be with you, for your own safety and to be in the house, but I think I might have trouble convincing someone why.'

Chapter 40 Me

I am not sure about it either. It is not that I am afraid of her as such, because I am not. It is the weirdness of something I think I already knew. That is that I can see her, but other people can't. Then there is the part about what people are going to say. There is little doubt that this is going to get out into the public domain.

I am thinking that she could sleep here for a long time. In my head, I am probably thinking that she will stay asleep until it gets dark, as she appears to favour the dark to move in.

Andy says he is going to go and have a chat with his senior officer. Could I stay here with her, just in case she gets up while he is away? The officer who brought the key will be downstairs by the door, in case I have to leave in the meantime.

As Andy leaves me, I look at the figure on the floor. She appears to be sleeping peacefully enough, which is more than she was the last time I saw her, albeit that was in my dream. She certainly hasn't got the wounds that she had then. Her clothes are back in reasonable condition too. On the surface of it, there doesn't seem to be any lasting consequence of what was happening in the dream. Was the dream my own interpretation of the events that have happened so far here? Or were they something that was planted into my subconscious by her? I have no way of knowing the answer to that one at this point. I may never know the answer to it.

I step round her and have a look out of the window. The glass is dirty and my vision is obscured somewhat by that. There are one or two people out there on the street, just walking by. Heads are turned towards the door, as they walk past the house on the other side of the road. I can hear someone talking close by. Maybe it is Andy down below, talking to the man who brought the key. I can't hear what they are saying from where I am.

I am distracted by a noise behind me. I turn round to find that she is awake. She has sat up and is looking at me. There isn't a look of surprise or anything like that, on her face. She is just looking at me standing by the window.

'I saw you in my dream' I open with.

I know she hears me, because the next thing is, I see her nod her head fractionally.

'Are you alright now? I saw you with some terrible wounds.'

The nod is just perceptible this time. I am not sure if that means it is not such a definite yes.

'What is your name?' I ask her next.

I don't get any response to this. I give her the opportunity to answer. I am trying not to spook her too much. I am also quite keen to get an answer to my question. I try again.

'Will you tell me your name please?'

Again I am unsuccessful in getting her to tell me. If she wants me to help her with something, and that is why I believe I am involved in all this, then knowing her name will be a great help, to enable me to dig into local history. She is just sitting there looking at me. I am loathing to move from where I am. I don't want it to look in any way that I could be intimidating her. I try a slightly different tack.

'My name is Bill. Did you know that?'

I get a miniscule nod to that. Then for the first time, she breaks the silence.

'Anne' is all she says to me, but that is enough. It is a breakthrough of sorts for me.

'You are trying to show me something aren't you, Anne?'

The nod I get is the most forceful one yet, but even that is not greatly strong. I am hoping that she will take the opportunity to tell me more, but I am to be disappointed in that. I give her time to say something, but her lips remain closed. It takes me a few minutes before the thought comes to me, that maybe just maybe, she can't tell me that. Did I think that, or did she put that thought into me. It doesn't matter which, I ask her anyway.

'Am I correct in saying that you can't actually tell me what it is you are trying to get me to help you with?'

I can see her struggling to interpret the sentence I have just delivered. I try to rephrase it in an easier way.

'You can't tell me about it, can you?'

She shakes her head.

'So you have to show me things, either when I am there, or in my dreams.'

She actually smiles, as she nods at me this time.

'I can see you, but no one else can.'

I don't get the expected nod to this one. She is shaking her head.

'I am not the only person who can see you?'

She shakes her head. I am getting a little confused with my own questioning, but what I am getting from this, is that there are others who can see her. I try to confirm this.

'There are other people who can see you?'

She nods at this. That makes it clear for me too.

'Are there other people here in Wenlock that can see you?'

I get a nod for this question too.

'Can you tell me who they are?'

She shakes her head at this. That is a shame, but not a total surprise. I might try to narrow it down a bit, from a different direction.

'Do you know how many people, other than me, who can see you?'

She nods at that too.

'Is it just one other person?'

She shakes her head.

'Is it two other people?'

She nods her head at that.

'Are they both alive, like I am?'

She nods again. I don't know where to go with this. I would like to know who else can see her, but I don't think she is going to tell me who they are, or even give me a clue as to their identity. I try to think of something that I can ask that will help me with this dilemma. She just sits there watching me. I would say she is quite relaxed as she sits watching me. I am not getting anywhere with locating a good enough question to ask her. Then one springs into my mind from nowhere.

'Are you showing anyone else the things you have showed me?'

She shakes her head. Now that is very interesting. She isn't showing anyone else what she is showing me. If that is the case, then what are the other two people who can see her doing? Another angle pops into my head.

'Are you related to either of them?'

A puzzled look appears on her face. She isn't nodding, or shaking her head. I try to work out why that may have puzzled her.

'You are not sure if they are related, is what I take from that.'

She nods at me.

'Is that both of them?'

I get a shake of the head.

'So you are not sure if one of them is related to you? You think they might be, but you aren't sure.' I am just saying this and she is watching me intently. 'You think that you know them for some reason.'

I stop as a thought comes to me. I want to go down this route, as it is the one that makes sense to me. It will be interesting if I make the call, whether she will agree with what I am about to say and suggest.

'I think that you recognize something in one of the two other people who can see you. I think that is because you look like them; or them like you.'

I get a reaction in her face, which is enough to tell me I am on the right track with this one.

'I'm going to have a guess that this person does look like you. You saw them and they saw you.'

She isn't making any movement with her head. She is listening to what I am saying. I guess I am still within the rules.

'This one is a woman or a girl.'

Again I can see I am right, without her having to do anything.

'I think I know who this person is. Your face reminds me of someone who works here in Wenlock. I think that one of the other people, who can see you, is Tara?'

She lowers her head when I say this. I am a little confused as to why she does this.

Chapter 41 Me

Anne keeps her head lowered for quite a long time. I am not sure why she is doing this. She hasn't told me. I have guessed who one of the other people is. I hope I have not caused a problem with what I have done. I look up, as something catches my eye. It is someone who has just climbed the stairs. I really don't need to be interrupted at this time. I look up and see it is the key bringer.

'You need to go back downstairs now.'

I say the words quietly, but firmly. I don't want to spook Anne. I don't want him to come into the room.

'I've got a message from Andy.'

'OK'

'He says he has got to go back to the station. I will be downstairs by the door if you need me.'

I take it that Andy has told him something of what is going on up here. Otherwise I don't think he would have taken my request for him to not come in so easily. Thankfully he turns round. I see him disappear down the stairs again. When I return my gaze to Anne again, she has brought her head up again and has been listening to me talking. I need to get back on track again.

'Have you talked to Tara?'

She nods at me.

'You know she has gone missing?'

She looks a bit puzzled, but she still manages a nod in reply.

'Do you know where she is?'

I get a shake of the head with this one.

'Has Tara helped you?'

I don't get an answer to that one. What I do get is a tear on her cheek. I see another one starting to fall from her eyes.

'Has Tara got involved in what you have been doing?'

Again I don't get a reply from her. I do get some more tears starting to fall. I take a clean tissue out of my pocket and lean forward to hand it to her. She looks at it for a second, before drying up her tears. I am guessing that she has had contact with Tara. I am not going to find out what sort of contact she has had, at least I don't think I am. It makes sense to me that Tara could be related, by the fact that she can see Anne. What is worrying me, are a couple of things. Has Tara somehow got herself involved in what has been going on in Wenlock and secondly, has that involvement somehow got something to do with her disappearance.

I am unsure of what may have happened, or how things may have progressed to this point. I can't do anything about that and I am not going to get any straightforward answers to questions I'd like to ask Anne. I don't think she is going to be able to answer them, even if I could think of pertinent ones to ask. I do know that Andy wants to speak with Tara, so I can guess that she may well have some involvement with one of the murders that have come to light recently. Something has led him to the need to question her again.

I need to put that on one side if I can and not pursue it any further at this stage. I would like to have a guess or two at who the second person is, if she will let me. I think she might be more resistant in allowing me to do that, now I have discovered the identity of one of them.

'So can I ask about the second person, who is here in Wenlock and can see you?

I don't wait for a response. I don't want to see a nod, or a shake of the head, yet. It isn't a relative, of that I can be pretty certain. It also isn't someone who she is trying to get to help her in her quest.

'Have you seen this other person and talked to them?'

I get a shake of the head, but I asked two questions, so I don't know what she is saying no to.

'Have you seen them?'

I get a shake.

'Have you talked to them?'

I get another shake.

Now that is a bit of a surprise to me. I fully expected her to have either seen or talked to this person. If she hasn't, then how does she know that they can see her? I don't know the answer to that one. There are a couple of scenarios going around my head. None of them are realistic, so I move on again. I think of something else I can ask. It is equally odd, but may be interesting.

'Does this other person know they can see you?'

She shakes her head. We are in the realms of things I don't understand, about this situation. Somehow she knows that the person can see her, but they probably don't know it yet, is what I am making of this.

'Is it a man?

I am not expecting to get an answer, but I do. I get a nod from Anne. I also a get a look from her; that tells me the door is now closed on answering any more questions. Maybe she is putting this straight into my head, but any which way, I am getting that as a clear message. I haven't done that badly, so I will have to go with that. To make sure that this isn't going to happen, Anne starts to get up from the floor. She does so in a very smooth way. She does so, effortlessly and gracefully.

She turns away from me and starts towards the door.

'Am I supposed to follow you now?'

She stops and turns her head towards me and smiles. I take that to be a yes. Something inside me isn't totally happy about this, but I am here and I am going to do it. It is a shame that Andy isn't here. I would like him to come with me.

She walks along the landing and starts to descend the stairs. She turns her head briefly, to make sure I am following her; I am. When she reaches the bottom of the stairs, she stops and looks in the living room. I move closer to her and have a look in there too.

At first I can see nothing, but then right there in front of my eyes, for a brief second, I see the scene I saw in my dream. She turns her head, to make sure I have seen it; I certainly have. I blink and the scene has gone. She glides past me, brushing her cape against me as she passes me. She stops when she sees the man standing, just outside the front door. She looks at me. I shrug and say.

'He brought the key, so I could get in.'

She turns round and brushes past me again, making towards the back of the house. I take a step towards the front door.

'She's on the move. You'd better let Andy know.'

'OK, I'll lock up after you leave and keep you in sight, until he gets back.'

By the time I turn round, Anne is moving out of sight, towards the back. I quickly take steps in that direction. I am in time to see her open the back door. She steps out into the back courtyard. I am a few seconds behind her. When I reach the doorway, she is standing in the middle of the back courtyard. I stop in the doorway. Part of the reason for that is that I can't see a way out of the courtyard. I don't understand why she has come out here. Maybe she doesn't know the courtyard is enclosed.

I think that I need to get the man at the front door to move away, so that we can leave by the front door. I am about to turn away and walk through to ask him to do just that, when she starts to walk towards the wall. As she starts to move, I notice in the wall a place where it looks like there used to be a doorway, but it looks bricked up to me. As she nears the wall, she looks over her shoulder at me. Her eyes are telling me to follow her. I don't see how I can at the moment. As she reaches the wall, she pushes open the door. I see a space, easily big enough for her to go through. I speed up, so I don't get too far behind her. The doorway is still open as I go through it too. I glance over my shoulder when I am through to the other side. All I can see is a bricked up space. I have just come through that!

Chapter 42 Anne

I know Tara was with me when I went to Bob's house. I know Tara was with me when Joan interrupted us. I know that Tara brought along something with her and wanted to be part of what I am doing. What I can't remember, is what happened. I can't remember anything, after Joan came into the house. I can't remember what we did, or where we might have gone after that moment.

What I do remember, is that I woke up on the floor of the house. It was dark and cold. It was raining and the wind was howling outside the window. I lay there, listening to the sound of the wind and the rain, trying to place where I was in time. It is not quite like the time I woke up in the cave, but I do feel that I have missed something. Something and some time has elapsed since I can last remember anything. I am thinking that Tara has been a distraction somehow. I need to find her, to try to fill in some of the gaps I know that are there.

I try to get back to sleep, as I know that Tara will not be in town during the night. It is surely night-time now, as it is dark outside and in here. I can't sleep, so I just lie here and think about things. Tara has been a distraction. Her involvement, whatever it may be, is only to satisfy some need in her. That is what I think. She is not the answer to why I am here. The answer lies with the man who has seen me already. He is the one who will help me, I hope.

Although I have just thought that, I can't help my thoughts from returning to Tara. Is she related to me somehow? Is she someone who is descended from me? How long is it since I was here? I don't know, but maybe it isn't as long as I think it is. When I first saw the lights on the poles, they were strange to me, as were the things that moved along on their own with people inside them.

Now I have had some time and they are not so strange to me. In fact, what is strange to me; is the attire I find I am dressed in. I don't think I dressed like this, when I lived in this place. These clothes are the ones people used to describe people of old as having dressed in. I have a black cape, dress and hood. I am dressed for the dark. Why is that?

I can't find the answer for that one in my head. I don't have the concentration, or the thoughts, to be able to delve deeper into my own mind for the answers. What I do find coming to me, is the extreme need to get this man to help me. I want to be able to go up to him and talk to him, but I am told this is not allowed. I have to do this in a different way. I don't know how I am expected to do this.

To that end, I lie down on the floor and close my eyes. I am not going to get the answer by thinking too much. I am hoping that it will come to me while I am resting. I am pleased to say that something does indeed come to me. There are things I have to do, to make things go forward. I need to find this man in the daylight. I then need to find out where he lives. I had thought that I might already know this, but I don't appear to.

The light is in the room, when I open my eyes again. All is quiet outside. The rain has stopped and the wind has abated. I get up from the floor and go downstairs. All is quiet in the house. I am going to have to go into the street and see if the man comes by. At the same time, I can also go to see if I can find Tara too.

I manage to slip out of the front door, without anyone taking any notice of me. I am getting the idea that not everyone wants to take any notice of me, as I move around. They certainly do not make any effort to get out of my way, as I walk along the street. I find myself in the square. There is a place where I can stand, beside another red box thing. Occasionally someone will come near me and stand in this box, but they pay me no attention. I see many people come and go, around this part of town. I am reluctant to leave, even for a short time, to go and see if Tara is at work today. But in the end I do so, just to relieve the boredom of watching all the people, except for the one I want to see, walk by.

When I get up to the Deli, I look through the window. I can see that Tara is not there at the front. It is another girl. I get brave and open the door to go in. They do not take any notice of me. I walk past the counter and towards the back. I go up the step and have to sidestep someone walking the other way. I do a left and a right and find that I am in the kitchen. There is a girl in there, but it isn't Tara. Obviously she isn't working today. I make my way back through to the front, again having to sidestep the same person, coming back. It is as if I am not here.

It is when I walk through the front door, out onto the street, that I see the man I am looking for, in the shop over the road, Mrs P's. He is working behind the counter.

I don't want him to see me. That is the whole point of what I am doing today. I need to find him, and I have. I also need him not to see me. I think I have achieved that so far, but I need to move somewhere where he won't see me, when he comes out. That is not quite so easy to achieve, as I know that he is someone who definitely can see me.

I find a place where I can see the door, but not him. It is the best I can do. It is two or three hours before he comes out of the door and starts to walk down the street. I follow him at a distance, but as best I can, keeping out of sight if he should look over his shoulder behind him. He does this on a couple of occasions, but I manage to get cover both times.

It is harder when he gets to his house. He goes in, but when I try to follow, he has two dogs and they bark at me. I remain outside, keeping an eye on the house from my hiding place, besides the building in front of it. It is some hours later that the lights go off downstairs and lights going on in a room at the front upstairs. Shortly after that this light goes off too.

I give him some time to fall asleep, before I try to get into the house again. The first time I do so, one dog barks at me. I try another place round the back, after leaving it for a while. This time, as I walk through the house, I can see a dog fast asleep in the hall. I climb the stairs and creep quietly past the other dog, which is asleep at the top of the stairs.

I move into the bedroom and I can see that he is asleep, on the side of the bed nearest to me. I move noiselessly to his side. His breathing is relaxed and slow. I know what I have to do. He does not know I am here and he will never know I have been this close. I reach out my hand and gently place it on his forehead. Thankfully, he is facing towards me. He reacts momentarily to my touch, but it is nothing more than a slight movement. I move my other hand over and place that on his forehead too. This time there is no movement. I can feel the activity going on in his head. I close my eyes and then start to transmit the images I want and need him to see. I see them as a story; he will see them in a dream.

Chapter 43 Anne

He nearly catches me out. I am not there long, as he dreams of a journey in Wenlock. Suddenly he stirs and comes out of the dream. I am not quite finished yet, but I have no option other than to take my hands off his head and retreat out of the room. The dog on the landing stirs as I move past it. The one at the bottom of the stairs is looking up at me. They stay quiet thankfully. I am thinking that I may be able to go back in and finish what I have started. But as time goes by and the light is still on in the bedroom, I realize that what I have put there; is all he is going to see.

Eventually it gets light. Every time I try to make it down the stairs, I can hear one or other of the dogs starting to growl at me. I decide to leave it until later, to leave this house. I am not in any hurry. In the meantime, I stand behind the door in one of the other rooms. Thankfully the dogs do not come to investigate. It is only when they see me that they growl.

Later in the day, I make it back to my house. I stop on the way, to see if Tara is at work, but she is not. Once again I venture into the shop and all the way through to the kitchen, but she isn't there. I wait around for a while outside, behind the red box, but she doesn't come. I go to my house and go to sleep on the floor, in the front room upstairs.

I don't know how long I have been lying here on the floor. It could be a minute, an hour, a day, a week or even longer; I just don't have any idea how long I have been here. I open my eyes and I see him standing there, by the window. It is a surprise to see him here. I wonder why I did not wake, when he came into the room. That thought worries me a little. He does not mean me harm though, but I do wonder why he has come here. Was he looking for me? Then he starts to talk to me. He is asking my name. I would normally have answered this straight away, but I find that there is something that is stopping me doing that. He persists in his questions and when he gives me his name, I find I can then give him mine, Anne.

He asks more than just that, but I am not able to tell him things. Despite that, he finds out more than I think he is meant to. He seems to believe that everyone cannot see me. At first I am puzzled at this, but as I think about my recent times, I find that the knowledge comes to me that this does indeed make sense. Then for some reason, I find that only three people here can see me. I know two of them. One of them is Tara; another is this Bill in front of me. Then there is one other. I realize that I have not seen this person yet. I do not have a name, or a picture of his face. But I do feel, when I think about this person, that he is different. He is not like Tara and he is certainly not like Bill. This is the man I have come back about. This is the man I will need the help with, before I get the help I really need. That will be the help that will allow me to rest.

Someone else approaches us, but Bill manages to stop them coming nearer. I think that is a good thing. I know that we need to move. They are watching Bill and I can't allow them to do that. If they do, I will not be able to get the help I need.

I get up off the floor and walk out of the room. I am hoping that Bill knows he has to follow me. There is no real reason why he should. The things I have shown him in his dream were not the entire story. I had not got to the part which would have showed him what I need him to do. I feel that the opportunity to do that is lost. I don't feel that I will be able to go back and finish that.

I walk down the stairs and turn into the living room. I am not expecting what appears in front of me. I see myself lying on the floor, with body wounds and my clothes in tatters, what there is of them. It only appears for a brief second. I turn to see if Bill has seen this scene too. I can tell from his face that he has indeed seen that.

I turn to go out of the front door, but the man who came up the stairs briefly, is standing there. I know he cannot see me, but for some reason I feel I can't go out of the house that way. I brush past Bill and make my way to the back of the house. I hear Bill say something to this man, before he follows me out of the house into the back courtyard. I know he will be thinking that we cannot get out this way, but I will show him that he is wrong in that thought.

I walk towards the place where the doorway out of here is. I know that all he can see is the wall, but he is wrong. To me and for a few seconds for him, there will be a way through the wall. This is where the way out was, in my time.

As I step through the gate, I feel the light starts to leave us. As soon as Bill is through the gate, it disappears back into the solid wall again. It is not that dark yet, but the change in the light is quite dramatic. It is not because it is night-time; it is because of the dark cloud that has come overhead of us.

The path that we are on is rough and full of holes. It is not easy to walk along here, without sufficient light to see ones way safely. By the time we reach the lane at the end of the path, there is thunder in the air. It has come upon us very quickly. Such people as there are about, are scuttling away to try to find cover. I have no intention of seeking out cover. I only hope that Bill will stay with me. We walk along, until we are behind the Corn Exchange. There are a few people running down, just as the first drops of rain start to fall. These drops of rain are large and strike us with quite a force. I turn to see that Bill is looking at me, wondering what is going on. I am not sure myself yet. I just knew that we could not stay there in the house, with the other people around. I needed to be out here in the open.

A flash of lightning gives me a start and brings me back to the here and now. I look up at the building in front of me. I see a face looking out of the window towards us. It is a woman, but I do not know her. She cannot see me, but of course she can see Bill. She is probably wondering why he would be standing there, in the now heavy rain. He has no coat on and he is very quickly, getting very wet. Why would he do that? That is probably what she is asking herself.

Bill looks up, as he sees the woman at the window too. He does not seem to mind the fact that he is getting absolutely soaked. She looks at him out there and then turns away for a few seconds. A moment later, she is joined by someone else. She is joined by a man. I cannot see his face clearly, as the rain is now driving down and into us as we stand there. I notice that Bill too has seen this other person at the window. We need to move from here, as this is not doing us any good. I do not need people to take notice of us, just standing in the pouring rain. That will not have any purpose in our cause. Maybe, hopefully even, they will not be able to make out who Bill is, with the force of the rain masking their view. Hopefully, all they will be able to see is that there is a man standing out there in the rain.

Chapter 44 Anne

Just as I turn away from the window, there is a bright flash of lightning. That has followed almost instantaneously after a huge clap of thunder. I turn back as quickly as I can, but I am only in time to see the man stagger backwards out of sight. I know he hasn't turned away or anything like that; he has definitely staggered backwards. I catch sight of the woman turning, to see what has happened to him. Bill is still standing, looking up at the window. I am not sure if he saw exactly what happened, as the lightning illuminated the scene. I do know that I will not be able to ask him. The need for us to move is greater, now that whatever this is has happened.

The rain is lashing down now, even harder than it was a minute ago. Another clap of thunder booms out over our heads, but it is not followed this time by any lightning. I start to carry on walking along the lane. At first I was thinking I might go up and through the passage of the Corn Exchange, but I can't do that. I will carry on along the lane for now. I see, when I glance over my shoulder; that Bill has started to walk after me. I do wonder what he saw, when the lightning came.

When we reach the end of the lane, I turn to the right. I am not going to go back down Spittle Street into the town. I am going towards the corner, where the coaching inn lies. When we reach the corner, there is water all across the road. There aren't any people out walking, but that is not a surprise. The first thing that strikes me, after seeing the water, is that things are different from the last time I was here. The surface we are walking on is different. Only a minute ago, it had been hard and smooth. Now the surface is rough and muddy. I turn to see how Bill is coping with this. I can just make out his face. He is indeed puzzled. The lights on long poles have gone. There aren't any of the vehicles I have seen around, anymore.

The rain is still coming down as hard as I have ever known it. The thunder, which had been moving away, comes back with a vengeance. A loud clap over our heads, results in any light that was there in the windows of some of the houses disappearing. I stop, as I feel a sudden fear coursing through me. I know Bill is somewhere close, but I think that maybe he is not near enough to me. A brilliantly bright bolt of lightning shows up the scene around me. Suddenly I am lost. I knew where I was, but suddenly I do not. Where there were houses before me, there are not. Even the coaching inn is not there. I swing round quickly, but Bill is not there anymore. He has gone. The lightning does not last long enough for me to search in every direction for him, with my eyes. I feel frightened. I can't remember when I last felt this frightened, and then I do. It is not a good feeling.

I can't hear anything over the sound of the rain falling on the ground. I can't see much more than a few feet ahead of me. I am not sure where I am. It is dark where I am and that is all that matters. I can feel the water slushing around my feet. As I move, the mud claws at me, trying to stop me moving. There are deep ruts in the road and the water is gathering in there. I can't see where I need to walk. I don't know what direction I should be walking. I had felt I was being led here for some reason. I had come this way, because I thought I was meant to be showing Bill something. That appears not to be the case.

Am I still on the corner? I really don't know. Should I keep walking in the same direction I was? I don't know if I should. There is nothing that I can see in that direction, but then to be honest, there is nothing I can see in any direction.

Out of the dark, someone appears just a few feet away from me. My first thought is that it is Bill, who has come back to be with me. I am wrong. It is not Bill. I can't see who it is though. He has obviously seen me, because he has stopped suddenly. The movement of doing that sprays water onto my legs. We stand there for a few seconds, knowing that we are close. I have a thought who this might be. It would not be my choice to be out here alone with him, if it is indeed who I think it is. I have heard many things spoken about this man.

'Is that you Anne?'

He has recognized me. My heart goes into a flutter. I would not say it is a panic, but it is close to that. I don't answer him. I am hoping that will put some doubt in his head. I pull my soaked hood further over my head and attempt to move slightly further away from him. The fact that I haven't answered him does not please him.

As I take a half step backwards, he makes a grab for my cloak. He would have got some sort of a hold on it, had I not put my foot in a deeper bit of the rut I am standing in. I almost fall to the ground, but I manage to put out a hand, to stop me falling totally into the water. Then he would have no problem in getting hold of me.

My semi falling has put him off a bit. He steps forward, but his foot too goes deeper in the rut, than he knew was there. But as his hand was still reaching out for me and he continued to do that, he did not have anything to stop him falling down into the water. I feel an inward smile at the sound of that happening. It does not delay my reactions though. I know I have been given an opportunity to escape his clutches, if I have the speed to do so.

At the same moment as all this has been happening, someone else has come along. Initially I am relieved by this fact. It should help me with my escape. That is until I hear a man's voice.

'Have you been assaulted?'

'She tried to rob me' the man replies, from his position in the water.

'I did not.' I reply, but am not going to wait around for the resulting accusations. There is only one thing worse than coming across the man in the puddle, at night and when you are alone, and that is coming across these two men together. It is worse when they have been drinking. These men are known for being partial to more than a drop of beer. They drink during the day and in the evenings. Once they have had more than they should, then it is no place to be, in their path on their journey home, or on their travels to the next drinking house.

I scrabble away from them, trying to get out of this bit of a rut I am in. I don't know which way to run, but I do know that I must be still in Wenlock. I also know that the darkness in Wenlock may just prove to be my friend, on this occasion.

The man in the water is now being helped to his feet, by the other man. I may be lucky, in that I think they are both a little worse for wear, having drunk plenty already. While they are getting themselves together, I make a run for it as best that I can. I run back the way I think I must have come from. I don't know for sure, because it is pitch black and the rain is falling heavily still. The road is muddy and my progress is slower than I would have liked. I can hear them running after me. I don't think the gap is closing, but if I don't find somewhere to hide from them, then they are going to catch me. I know they will. They have caught me before. They will part and one will go one way and the other one will loop round and try to work out where I run to. I do not want them to catch me. They hurt me and do things a man should not do to a woman, against her will.

Suddenly I know where I am. Spittle Street is ahead of me and the lane goes down to my left. I take the turn to the left. I am just a few steps down the lane, when the rain lets up considerably. There is flickering of lights in the houses I am running past. The lane beneath my feet becomes more solid. The skies lighten, in just a matter of a few seconds. The sounds of feet running behind me are no longer there to be heard. I am out of breath, so I stop. I turn around; to look in the direction I have been running from. The men are not to be seen. Then I nearly jump out of my skin, as a voice behind me talks to me.

'I thought I'd lost you there for a minute!'

Chapter 45 Anne

Anne is about to set sail again and run for her life. That is until she realizes that she knows this voice. This isn't the voice of the man who had fallen into the water, while trying to make a grab for her. This is the voice of someone else entirely. This is the voice of someone from a different era. It is Bill. She relaxes, as she turns towards him.

She sees that she is right. She just wants to throw herself into his arms and burst into tears. The relief that she feels from being safe again is almost overwhelming her. Something about the two men she has just escaped from is making extreme pressures on her. She knows she would not have been safe, if they had managed to catch up with her. Something deep inside her stirs, as she knows they have done so before. But this time could easily have had a different outcome.

Why has she been brought back here? She is not meaning this very second, but about why is she back here, with Bill helping her? She doesn't get an answer to that one. Some things are not to be explained, or so it is becoming clear to her that they are not.

Bill steps closer to her. She remembers that on one occasion she had run out of the house and straight towards him. She thinks that she remembers that she actually ran straight through him. She didn't feel anything at all as she did so. Did she run straight through him, or did she actually stop within him? Try as she can, she cannot remember which it was. What she does remember, is that she did not feel anything as she got to him. Whether she went through him or stopped inside him, there was no feeling of touch at that time. But things have moved on a bit. She thinks about when they had passed each other in the house. Twice she had cause to brush past him in the house. Both times she had felt the brushing sensation. She knows that he had felt it too.

Now she is here, suddenly transported from one era to another, so she thinks. And she is thinking of throwing herself into his arms and getting him to hold her safe. Would he be able to do that? She doesn't know the answer and anyway, now that she has been standing thinking here for a minute or so, has the moment gone for her?

She looks up, to see that Bill is watching her. He has a kind face. He is looking concerned. It is as if he knows that she has just been through an ordeal. What happened to Bill, when she walked along the street? What happened to Bill when the lights went off and the houses disappeared and she didn't know where she was? He takes a small step towards her. That is all it takes for her to know that she has to step forward. She doesn't rush, but steps slowly forward. He stops as she does so, so that the decision will be hers alone, to make any contact. She steps right up to him and then she comes into contact with him. He heaps his arms round her, as she tucks her head into his chest, with it resting just under his chin.

He doesn't say anything. He doesn't hold her too tightly. He just holds her enough, so that she knows she is safe. They stay that way for a good five minutes. If there had been any other people come along, then they would have thought it a strange sight. But I notice that there isn't anyone about. Even though the rain has stopped, as has the thunder and lightning, no one has ventured back out again. I venture out from my safe position. I don't think I have ever been held safe like this ever before. It is a nice feeling, something that makes a difference.

I let my eyes wander up towards the windows of the building. Before, there had been the woman standing there, looking out at us. Then briefly there was a man who had staggered out of view, before I got to see him. But then with the vision possible in that light and the driving rain, I doubt I would have been able to make out much more than the fact it was a man.

'I thought I'd lost you there for a minute' Bill talks to me again, with the same words he used when I got back.

I find that I am able to talk to him, at least for the moment.

'What do you mean?'

'We had moved away from here. We walked up the lane and then along High Street to the corner. Then all the lights went off and I lost sight of you. You were only a few feet ahead of me, but suddenly you weren't there. When the lightning came you had gone. You were nowhere to be seen. I shouted for you, but I doubt you would have heard me, above the rain that was falling on the ground. I thought I heard some voices, but I couldn't see anything.'

I am wondering as he says this whether he was actually there, although he was not. When he says that he heard some voices, was it the voices of the two men in the water? Bill is still talking.

'I shouted some more. I couldn't see much and there was no one about. I thought that you might return here. If it hadn't been here, then I was going to go back to the house and wait for you there. Anyway, as I moved away from the corner, the thunder became less violent. The lightning hardly came at all and the rain even started to slow down. By the time I got back here, the day had brightened up once more. I looked down the lane and then up towards the back of the Corn Exchange. Then, when I turned round, well there you are right in front of me, but facing away.'

It is strange that I can feel him. I can hear him talk to me. I don't want to use up everything straight away. It has been most comforting being held by him. I feel I am back down to earth now. I ease back from him. His arms part and I edge half a step away.

Is this what was supposed to happen, when I got him to follow me? I am supposing that it is. Is this all that I am supposed to do today? I don't know yet if that is the case. I let my eyes fall on the window again. There isn't anyone standing there looking this time. Bill notices me doing this. He asks me another question. As he does so, I feel quite uncomfortable inside.

'Is there something about this building that is important in all this?'

It is just a question. He hasn't put any great emphasis on it. I find I cannot answer him. That is disappointing because I feel the stirrings of things inside that I want to tell him. I don't know what they are, but I know that I have things to be told. I think they will be told to Bill sometime, but not just now or yet. He isn't being pushy. I can tell that, but he does try to get some sort of answer out of me. I hope he doesn't take my not answering in the wrong way. Somehow I don't think he does. I think he understands that things have to be taken slowly. More importantly than that, that there is an order of things and when they can be told.

'The Corn Exchange and also the Guildhall; I think they are important to you. The church is too, I believe, but not in the same way. They were all buildings that featured in my dream.'

He waits for me to answer him, but I am not going to do so. Instead, I walk forward, up towards the Corn Exchange. When I am there, I turn left through the passage and out the other side. Surprisingly, there is still no one out on the streets. I turn to my right and walk across to the far wall. I know it is here somewhere. I just can't remember exactly where it is. It has been a long time. Maybe it is not here anymore. I used to be able to walk straight up to it, when I first came back. Now I need to find it, I am struggling. Then I find it. My fingers feel over the single little mark in the wall. I glance over my shoulder and Bill is there, watching my finger. I lift it, so he can see what I am feeling: A.

Chapter 46 Anne

I know he has seen it and I move away a few feet. There is something else on this wall that might still be here too. Until we moved through from the back of this building, I had not remembered about my initial carved into the wall. Now I am looking for another one. I have only a vague recollection as to where it might be, if it is still here. It wasn't as deep as mine was. I get the feeling I am not going to find it. Anyway, I do not want to dilute what I am doing. Bill is watching me, as I move along the wall, hunting for this other mark. I stop looking!

I have to get this back on track. I want to make my way towards the end of the street. That is to the corner where the coaching inn lies. I walk to the right, coming out from the Corn Exchange. I notice that still there are no people back out on the streets again. To a degree I find that a bit concerning. It means that there is still something going on. Even though the thunder, lightning and the rain has gone, for now at least, there is something that has not been concluded.

Everything is alright, until we walk past an establishment called the Fox. In fact we are in front of Salon Ten when things change again. The change is sudden. It is almost as if I have tripped over something as I walked along, that has triggered this change. I glance at Bill and I note that he has seen it too. He indicates that I should stop. I do as he says.

'I think you need to step back a few paces.' He says to me.

I don't answer him, but I do as he suggests.

It stops getting dark, almost as soon as I retrace my steps. The thunder, which had sounded a warning, remains silent. Bill then signals to me that he is going to walk forward. He lets me know that he wants me to stay where I am. Once again the change is immediate, when he gets just a few paces ahead of me. He retreats and he then gets me to do the same. The same thing happens when I go forward on my own.

'Have you any idea what this means' he asks me.

I do not and I tell him so.

'Something does not want us to go forward beyond this point. I am assuming that something similar to what happened last time will occur if we do. I had relatively little happen to me, but for you it was worse. I don't think we are meant to go here, well not yet.'

It is the "not yet" that makes sense to me. Everything appears to have an order and if I go in the wrong order, then I am not going to achieve what I need to. I step back a few more paces and the scene around us comes back to normal. It is still not back to where the people come out again, but it is calm and quiet again now.

'Is there something in this direction that you need to get to?'

I hear the question and I find that I can't answer him. I can't think of what it is that I was coming here for. I try not to look at him. I don't want him to see the slight confusion that I am feeling at this second.

'Let's try walking in another direction. There are a limited number of ways we can go.'

I don't answer him verbally, but I do take some action. I start to walk back down the street, towards the main area of the town. At the junction with the lane, I keep going straight on. Bill has caught me up and is almost walking by my side. I like him walking this close to me. He makes me feel safer.

I stop when we reach the bottom of the street, by the square. I look to my left, where I can see the Guildhall, the church and beyond that is where my house is. I know it is none of these ways that I need to be going to now. If I had, then I would have gone a different way when we came out the back way of the courtyard. I am trying to think if there is anything beyond that that I might go. There is nothing beyond my house. The only other place in that direction would be the old priory. That is certainly a possibility, but there are other ways that you can get to the old priory, other than going via the Bull Ring.

It is the other direction that holds more draw for me. Something inside her tells her that at least that is the direction she should try next.

Bill is remaining quiet which is good. He is giving me the room to decide the next direction. I make up my mind. I start to walk in that direction.

We have walked about a hundred yards, when I stop again. I have another decision to make. There is a road going off to our right. I am drawn up that way, although I can think of no reason why I would be. We make it only a few yards, when I realize that once again the powers that be make it known that we are not meant to come up here. We aren't expecting it, so it comes as a bit of a surprise when we are plunged into darkness. The clouds come across from literally nowhere. The thunder claps right over our heads and the lightning starts a second later, along with the driving rain. I am too late to make a grab for Bill. He is just out of my reach. Then he has gone again. He is nowhere to be seen. I spin around, but I don't know where I am again. The ground beneath my feet becomes rough and wet. This time I know I need to move back in the direction I came from, to stop this. I really do not want to experience what I did last time.

Suddenly I am pulled on my arm. I had started to move in what I hoped was the right direction to stop this and then someone grips my arm. I feel extremely frightened. This time there hasn't been a voice, but I am thinking it is them again. If so, I am really in deep trouble. I try to break the grip on my arm, but it is strong and resistant. I need to get away from them, or I am in grave danger. The rain increases by the second and the thunder claps overhead.

It is only when the lightning strikes a bolt near to me, that I see that it is not them who have hold of my arm. I relax for just a fraction of a second and that is enough for them to pull me towards them. I allow myself to be pulled. I have relaxed and they have got the upper hand. I am not sure how it can be, that he can pull me back from this, but my eyes tell me he is. Bill pulls me harder, almost to the degree that I lose my balance in the water and on the uneven ground I am on. My fear is that maybe he cannot pull me back far enough and fast enough, to stop all this. My other fear is that he will be dragged into this world and then what happens? I can feel him pulling me and in normal circumstances it should be enough, to move us in the direction he is pulling us.

It is at this point, that I hear the voice I have been dreading. It is not by me, but it is close. I see from Bill's face that he has heard this voice too. Then the man is beside me. His hand is reaching out, to try to take hold of my other arm. I squirm to escape his grasp, but I am fearful that I don't want to shake off Bill's grip on me.

The man steps so close to me and I know he is going to try to get hold of my clothes. His hands are almost touching them, when I hear the most almighty roar. It is enough for him to stop in his tracks. Whatever it is makes the difference and I can suddenly feel my feet moving across the ground. The movement is so sudden, that it makes me lose my balance. Bill loses his balance too. We both fall to the ground, but thankfully our momentum has taken us out of the dark and onto the firm surface, where we had been just a minute ago.

Chapter 47 Anne

We aren't quite out of the mire yet. We may have landed on our backs on the ground out of the darkness, but for some reason it is still there. We are literally just out of it. We are absolutely drenched, although the ground we are on is dry, as it was when we turned into St Mary's Lane. I try to move further away, but there is some force that isn't letting me do so. Bill is a fraction further away from the dark, but I can see that he isn't able to move away either. Well it is either that, or he isn't trying.

Suddenly a hand appears out of the darkness and grips my leg, well my ankle really. It is quite a surreal moment. The grip tightens on my ankle, before he then starts to pull me. At first I move, but then I stop. I do that, because Bill has climbed over me. It appears he can move towards the dark, but not away from it. As he does this though, the dark creeps towards me. I only just notice it doing so. It has moved a fraction. It is almost as if it is trying to envelope the man's hand, as he holds my ankle. The problem I have with that, is that it will envelope my foot too. What will happen then?

Bill leaps to his feet and jumps up in the air, coming down firmly on the man's wrist. I don't know how he judges it, that he wouldn't hit my foot, but he does so. I hear the bone crack and a roar from within the dark. The grip has gone from my ankle. The hand is pulled back into the dark, as the roar still continues. Bill has landed and is now trying to regain his balance. I manage to grab his clothes and pull with all my might, to stop him from falling into the dark. Who knows what might happen to him, now he has injured and angered the man in there? He falls in my direction. I try to roll out of the way, but feel I may not be able to do so, if the force is still stopping us move away from the dark.

I find that I can move though. I scramble out of his way, as he falls to the ground beside me. I am scrambling away and he is rolling away. The dark allows us to do this. We keep moving away in this unfashionable fashion, until we come to a stop, maybe twenty feet away from it. I look at where the dark meets the ground. I stare intently at the ground, trying to see if it is still creeping towards us. As far as I can make out, it has stopped. We stand up and back away a bit further. Our clothes are dirty from rolling on the ground. This is not helped by the fact that we are still drenched. The water is literally dripping off our clothes as we stand there. As we are standing there, a face appears at the edge of the darkness. It is as if someone is standing at a window. We can't see him properly, as we can now see the rain falling between us and him, on the edge of the darkness. The street, the firm street, we are on, is getting wet from this rain.

I know Bill can see him there too, as he is leaning forward trying to get a look at the face of the man. From what I can see through the driving rain in front of him, it is not one of the men I encountered earlier. This is a different man. It is hard to make him out. We are standing in the dry, but there is a sheet of rain between him and us. Neither of us has any intention of being drawn back closer to the darkness. It is so unpredictable, that we may be in danger of being enveloped by it, if we do go closer.

It is hard to say whether the man is looking at us, or just looking out of the darkness. I say that, because from what I can see, he is not looking directly at us. Then another person comes and stands beside him. I can make out that this person is a woman. She stands beside him and points to us. His head turns directly towards us and then I make out that he staggers backwards out of view. The woman turns to him and both disappear from our view. Then in the matter of a few seconds, the darkness lifts. The road in front of us dries up, in a matter of seconds. Our clothes dry too, in the same time span. They feel as if they have been wet, but they are now dry. They are still a bit dirty of course.

We can see straight up the road again, but we are not going to try walking up there. We know what will happen.

There are no words spoken between us. I think Bill is finding this all a bit too bizarre. I admit that it is all strange to me too.

Bill brushes the dust from his clothes. I do the same on mine. He still doesn't talk, but points that we should maybe try to walk along towards Broseley. I nod in response and we carefully take the first steps in that direction. We reach the corner at the end of the straight, without further mishap. There is no point in going further out of town. I can feel no need to do so. The only thing I know about this part, is that I came here recently. It is in this area that two of the people live. I stop to think if I should be going back there, but feel nothing. This is not what I am looking for. It must be something else.

Bill is standing watching me. There is still no one around, so I know this has not finished yet. I am guessing that he is thinking the same. What is it that I need to find? It cannot be anywhere new. There are buildings here that were not here in my day. It must be something back in town, but not where I have walked so far. That doesn't leave much.

We walk more confidently back along to the Raven and then continue towards the square. For a second I think I may be close, but then that feeling goes again. I am not sure if I have missed something, or if it wasn't really there in the first place. We veer off onto Church Walk. The green is on our right and the church is ahead of us. I am feeling nothing. We turn right and skirt round the church and out beside the old tower. The school is on my right. We are only a few paces along the road to the Priory, when I know that this is not the right place.

I stop and put my hand to my head. It is not easy trying to do something, when you don't know what it is. I get the thought that it is something I should know. More precisely it is somewhere I should know. Where could that be? Bill puts his hands on my shoulders. I feel the warmth and a second later, I can also feel his mind calming mine.

'Where else could it be?' is all he says, when he breaks our long silence.

'I am not sure. I don't know what I am looking for.'

'I can see that. Do you feel something that might guide you? I mean, you seem to know what it is not and the darkness stops us from going places it does not want us to.'

I think deeply for a second.

'The only place I have had a different feeling, is the other side of the church, on the road we were on.'

'Let's go back there then.'

We retrace our steps and come out of Church Walk onto the street. I stop and gather myself, before I take one step at a time along the street. I step and then I stop. Nothing! I do it again and again and then I get it again. I get the feeling of being close.

'What about the well?' Bill says quietly to me.

'The old well.' She looks around her. 'It is so different here, that I struggle to get my bearings.'

'The old well is down this lane' he says, but stands still.

I start walking down the lane. With every step I take, the feeling gets better. About twenty yards down the lane the feeling is at its strongest. I almost miss it, but Bill touches my arm and points down to the right. There is a small depression in the ground, guarded by a metal fence. Bill opens the gate and I walk slowly down the steps and look into the hole in the stone wall that is the old well, St Milburga's Well.

Chapter 48 Me

I am standing in the dark. I don't know how long I have been standing here. I just become aware that I am here. There is no light around me whatsoever. I could be standing there with my eyes closed. In fact, just to make sure I am not, I reach up to my eyes with one hand, to check that my eyes are indeed open; they are. I literally can't see my hand in front of my face. It is an odd feeling. I am almost as unnerved by that fact, as I am by the fact I know I have only just become conscious of the fact I am standing here.

I try to remember the last thing I can remember. At first it doesn't come to me, but as I stand there, forcing myself to be calm, I manage to trawl the memories from somewhere in the depths of my brain. I remember, bit by bit, the recent events that I have witnessed and been through. Eventually I actually remember the last thing that happened and where I was at the time. We had just climbed down the few steps, into the pit by St Milburga's Well. The very last thing we did, well actually I remember it as what Anne did, was to look into the hole that is the well. The next thing I am here. Maybe I am in the same place, but somehow I don't believe I am.

I wonder how long it has been since I was by the well. I have no answer for that. Is it dark because of where I am? I mean by that, am I in an enclosed space, in something or somewhere? I suppose what I am really asking, is whether somehow I am deep down inside the well? Is the well that deep? I really don't know.

If I am not in the well, have I somehow fallen foul of the darkness that tried to envelope us, while we were out and about round the town? The only thing wrong with thinking that; is that this darkness is just that. There aren't, at this second anyway, any of the accompaniments that were with the darkness before, namely rain, thunder, lightning and wind, as well as the darkness. No, I don't think I am in that darkness right now. Surely I would have experienced the start of it, before finding myself like this?

I am brought swiftly back to the here and now, by a noise. It is coming from behind me. It is like someone is banging on a door. I turn round, but still I can't see anything. The noise is coming from in front of me now. Yes, definitely someone is banging on a door, somewhere in front of me. I want to step forward and investigate this, but my feet are rooted to the spot since I have turned round. It appears that I can't even turn back round to the way I was facing before.

The banging gets a bit louder and then it is accompanied by someone shouting as well. I sort of recognize the voice and then I don't. I place it a few seconds later. I think it is the man who brought the keys. That would make it that I am back in the house in Sheinton Street. Which door would he be banging? Well the last door of the house I went through was the back door.

Then I hear my name being called. Then the banging resumes once more. It is a bit more frantic each time it is being banged. I can't answer back. I can't move my feet and I can't use my voice; wonderful. I wonder where Anne is. Why isn't she with me, to help me, or at least to shed some light on what is happening?

The banging stops and the man shouts one more thing before that stops too. I can't make out the words that are being said to me. I give myself a few seconds to think about things more. The last time I was at the house, I went out the back door and then through the doorway in the wall in the courtyard, that isn't there. Great! Am I to presume that I am back in the courtyard?

I don't get time for another thought, as another sound invades the air around me. It is not close, but I can hear it clearly enough. It is the sound of fire engines, well one at least. Yet again they are coming to this house, to open a door. This time, I am presuming it is the back door they are going to attend to. I listen as the sound stops getting any closer. It is close enough, I think, to be somewhere out the front of the house.

Another couple of minutes pass, before I hear the banging on the back door resume once more. It is different voices trying this time and they aren't just knocking to try to get an answer. This is the sort of an effort that gets doors to open. Sure enough, a few seconds later the door splinters. I hear it give way. Then I hear some words being spoken.

'It's pitch black out here. You can't see a thing. I mean, not a single thing, it is so dark. Someone bring the flashlight.'

I wait in my dark cocoon for another minute, before the next thing happens. The voice is back. He isn't that far away from me, but he might as well be miles away. I can't see him, or anything, still.

'It doesn't penetrate this darkness one bit. Someone get me a rope.'

Once again the silence envelopes the place where I am standing. I know he is standing not many feet away from me. I hear my name being called, but I still am not able to answer him. I gather that the rope has been brought.

'I'm going to take the first step into this. If I don't answer you, you are going to have to pull me out. I don't know what this is.'

'Shouldn't you put breathing gear on, before you go in?'

'Good point' is the reply. There is another short period, before he indicates he is ready to join me in here. I am not sure if they know I am here, or are just presuming I must be, because there is no other way out.

'Bill' I hear my name being called again. I try to respond, but am still not able.

'Alright I am one step in and it is still the same. I can't feel anything around me.'

'Shine your light back at us.'

'I am doing it now.'

'We can't see it. This is really weird stuff. What is it?'

'I have no idea. I'm going to take the next step. I can't feel anything around me.'

He does this a few times with the commentary being kept up. I can hear that he is getting closer to me. I am encouraged by this. A thought goes through my head, that he might not be able to feel me, even if he gets to me. From the sound of his voice, I think he is less than four or five feet away from me. Another step, two at the most and he will be in touching distance of me. I feel a burst of excitement, that my rescue is possibly that close.

'This courtyard isn't that big. I must be reaching the back wall soon. Hang on, I've got something.'

I feel him touch my arm and then my body.

'Bill?' he says to me.

'Yes' I find that at last I am able to utter a word.

'Why are you here? Are you alright?'

'I think so. Until now I haven't been able to speak and since I turned round, I haven't been able to move.'

'Can you move now?'

I try to move my feet. I find I can. I tell him this.

'I'm going to hang onto you. They are going to pull us back. Can you grab my arm?'

I do so immediately.

'Whatever you do, don't let go. Let me know if you feel you are going to stop, or be stopped.'

'Ok, I'm ready when you are.'

'Pull us back slowly. I have a hold on him and he is gripping my arm.'

'Will do' comes back the reply and we start to edge slowly towards the back door.

Fifteen seconds is all it takes. We step out of the darkness. He does before I do. As soon as I step out of the darkness it just disappears, in less than a second. There is nothing else in the courtyard and there isn't anyone else there either. By that, I mean that Anne has not been with me.

Chapter 49 Me

It takes a few minutes to realize fully, that whatever the darkness that had enveloped the courtyard has gone. Hopefully it is not coming back, well not for now. I have a feeling that it probably isn't the end of it all.

I thank the fireman who has rescued me. He is looking at me. I think he is waiting for me to explain what it was he has just pulled me out of. That isn't going to happen.

I hear another siren coming over the roof top, from the street outside to the front. Less than a minute later, we are joined by the back door, by Andy. The firemen have all been looking at me for an explanation. I have been resisting saying anything, other than the thank you I issued, soon after I was dragged out of the blackness and darkness.

'Are you alright?' Andy asks, as he pushes his way through.

'I'm fine, if a bit confused.' I reply.

The firemen gather in to listen, as if I am about to reveal what this is all about. They have already been here to break a few doors down, without explanation. Andy nods at me, to say a bit more. I reckon he wants me to speak, but I am also guessing he only wants me to say enough to let them leave us alone.

'I came out of the back door, after I came down the stairs. Next thing I knew was that the back door slammed shut on me, pretty much the same way that the front door had done in the past. Before I got the opportunity to turn and try the door, even though I already knew it would be pointless as it would be jammed, this darkness came down on me. I lost my bearings almost immediately. It was quite strange this darkness. Anyway I found a wall, which was the back wall as it turned out. Then as I moved away from it, suddenly I was unable to move. I tried to shout out, but nothing would come out, or if it did, it got swallowed up by the density of the darkness. It was only when he got hold of me that I could move and be heard again.'

They all look at me, as if I am a bit mad. If the firemen had not experienced it for themselves, then I think they might have been calling for the men in white coats. As it is, they start to collect their things together. Andy ushers me through into the kitchen, while he sees the firemen out of the house. He re-joins me a few seconds later.

'Do you want to talk here, or somewhere else?'

'I think I need to get out of here for a while. It is too weird what is happening?'

'Is what you said out there what happened?'

'It is the truth, but only in part. I went out of the back door and they had to break it down. They found me by the back wall. It is the bit in the middle I didn't tell them.'

'Tell me!'

'I will, but we need to go out of here first.'

He leads me out of the front door. The man with the key looks at me, before he secures the front door. He is going to hang around, as the carpenter is on the way to fix the back door, at least enough to secure it.

'Where do you want to go?'

'I'd love a cup of coffee, but I don't think what I have to say is for anyone else's ears. We'll go back to my place, if that is alright with you?'

His car is parked right in the middle of the road. There is more than a small crowd of people looking on. Yet again, I am going to be the topic of conversation in the town over the next few hours. It is that sort of place. I get into the passenger seat and Andy jumps into the driving seat. Rather than take him the direct route to my house, I tell him to turn right. We go to the top of Queen Street and take a left. At the junction we go left and again left at the petrol station. That brings us out at the Raven, where we take a right and along to my house. It is not that I think they will tramp along to my door to get answers. It is just that it stops them seeing where we are going.

Kate puts the kettle on, the second we come through the door. I go up to her and give her a kiss.

'Something has happened!'

It isn't a question. It is a statement.

'I can tell' she continues 'it's your bottom lip.'

I smile. She often says that when I don't tell her how things are with me. There is no point in trying to hide things. She will know anyway.

She makes the coffees and we settle down in the living room, for me to tell the tale as it is. I go through everything that I can, from the moment I followed Anne out of the back door through the garden wall, to the point where I last remember being with her. That last memory was being at the well.

There is a brief silence, when I have finished talking. I bury my face in my coffee mug. It isn't as hot as it was, as I have told my story without stopping to drink it. Kate and Andy have finished theirs. Kate looks across at me. I can tell she is worried about what is going on. I can't say that I am totally comfortable with it all. But I have been chosen, for whatever reason, to be a part of this and I don't believe I have any option to sit out the rest of it. I firmly believe there is more to come.

Andy is the first one to speak. Kate gets up to make us all another coffee, as I put my mug down.

'It is very odd. I know that sounds weak, but you know what I mean. I was there talking to the Chief Inspector and I get this call come in. I had to continue my talk on my way here. He doesn't want any of this to get out, if we can help it. It will lead to hysteria on one hand and a load of people heading for here, on the other. We need to try to control it, without causing a stir.'

'That is rather easier said than done. I don't think we are in control of this. From the beginning, we have been manipulated. This latest episode epitomizes that. How or why I got from the well to the back courtyard again, I have no clue. Nor did I have any say or influence on the matter. It just happened!'

'We are getting concerned about the whereabouts of Tara' he says, changing the subject a fraction. 'There is still no sign of her, either here, or where she goes to University. We need to speak to her, about her involvement with Anne, if she has one that is. We are not even sure that she is involved. It is just that her fingerprints are at one of the houses. We know that she knows him, but we need to speak to her, to eliminate her from the enquiry, or not for that matter.'

'She looks like Anne, or maybe it is the other way round. She can also see Anne, I believe.'

'Now that is interesting! It also makes a bit of sense. It might mean she is more involved than not though.'

He stops to have a think about something.

'Did Anne mention her?'

'No, not really, I don't think she did.'

I try to think back. It is hard to differentiate between my thoughts and what Anne said. I can't be sure if Anne did actually mention her, or whether it was just me saying that she could see Anne. Another thought swims across my mind, as I think of that. Anne reckons that someone else can see her, but she didn't say who it was. I decide to keep that bit of information to myself for now. I can't see it being helpful, when I do not know who the other character is. I know it is a male, but beyond that I don't have enough information, to start pointing fingers at anyone in particular. I am not sure if they might have picked up anything from when I told my story. I hope not, is what goes through my head.

'Do you think she could have been with Anne and then something similar to what happened to you then happened? She was there one minute and then somewhere else the next.'

'I have no idea. But if she did, then where would she have gone to or returned to? I went back to the courtyard, which is where I started with her. Where did Tara start with her, if she did?'

'I don't know the answer to that one either. It was just a thought anyway.'

Chapter 50 Me

Andy's phone goes. He steps outside, to take the call. He is gone for maybe five minutes, before he comes back inside.

'I need to go. The boss wants to go through things with me. I don't suppose there is any chance you could spare the time to come with me. He might understand a little better, if he hears the words directly from your mouth.'

I look across at Kate.

'You are not going to be able to get away from it. Best that you go now and hopefully this whole thing might reach its natural conclusion.'

'Alright' I say.

'I'll drop you back afterwards.'

It is three hours later that I get dropped off at the front door. His boss is pretty sceptical about everything and I suppose I can understand that. What I do gather, is that they are getting quite concerned about the whereabouts of Tara. She hasn't been seen since leaving work many days ago. Her mother is frantic with worry. It doesn't help that she knows the police want to speak with her about something. It is possible that she has gone off without her car, but no one she knows has been able to say that they have seen her.

The next morning, we gather in the centre of town, to start the search for her. There are many who have turned up to help for the search. The enquiries door to door started last night, but to date, nothing has emerged from that. While one team, the police, concentrate on the door to door enquiry, the rest of us, guided by more police, start to search the land around the town. It is a large area to search. There are a good number of volunteers. The search starts out in the area around the Stretton Road, not for any other reason than the police think she may have been at Bob's house. The walks up to The Edge can be accessed from there. There are also some old quarries. There are plenty of places that a body could be found, not that they have any evidence to say that Tara is not still alive and well. It is just they are checking to make sure, at this stage.

The search reveals nothing out of the usual and they swing round, some going in one direction and the others in the other direction. They extend the search to other areas, a similar distance from the edge of town. By the end of the afternoon, the two teams meet up at the other side of town. The search has been exhaustive, in the limited breadth of the search area. That is not to say there could be other places they could search, if they want to widen the net some. That may well happen tomorrow. Tara's mobile is switched off and has been since she disappeared. The last known trace of it puts her as being in the town, very likely at work in the Deli.

I have been beside Andy for most parts of the day. His mind has been on other things for the majority of the time. I have been concentrating on the job in hand, searching for Tara. My own thought is that this search is going to be fruitless. I am not saying that she wasn't at Bob's, or even possibly with Anne. I am just saying that I don't think that we are going to find Tara lying in the trees, or in a shallow grave for that matter. I don't believe she is dead. I can't see Anne wanting that either, not that I really know her.

Something has been bugging me about Anne and my episode with her and all the buildings falling down. But I haven't been able to put my finger on it. It is close to becoming recalled, but not yet.

'I need to get back on track' Andy announces, as we walk back to Sheinton Street.

He wants to go and have another look in there before he finishes for the day. Obviously he wants me along, as I am the only one that he knows who can see Anne. He has had another key cut. We let ourselves in through the front door. I have to say, I am getting less comfortable coming in here, the more I do it. I let Andy go first and I stick to him like glue. I don't mean that literally of course, but I am only a pace behind him as we walk through the hall. Downstairs is clear, so we make our way up the stairs and onto the landing. A quick search of the bedrooms reveals that she is not here, or at least I can't see her if she is. We make our way back down the stairs and exit the house, before any of its quirky habits manage to exert them upon us; or me in particular. We lock up and go for a pint in the George. I still can't recall what it is that is on the edge of revealing itself to me.

'I meant to ask you, to show me where the well is.'

'There is more than one well.'

'Which one did you go to with Anne?' he asks me as quietly as he can.

It is not that easy to talk quietly, as the George is busy and there is a general buzz of conversations going on. I don't answer him directly straight away. Something else is buzzing at my memory now.

'There is one in Back Lane, not that you would notice it that easily. That is St Owen's Well. Owen was said to be a French monk who visited the area in the 6th century.'

I stop for a few seconds. I know what it is now that I have been trying to recall. It is about Anne and something she showed me and something she did and looked for. Andy is waiting for me to continue. I store away the thought I have just had. I will go and check it out later. Now I have remembered it, I am sure it will stay with me now. Andy gives a quiet cough, to get my attention back. I can see that he knows I have just thought of something, but I am not going to tell him, before I have checked it out for myself. That I will do, when we leave the pub.

'Where was I? I know; there is St Owen's Well, and then there is the other one. She didn't go straight there. In fact it was pretty much the last place that she tried to go, before she knew that was where she needed or wanted to go. It was the last place I was at, before I ended up in the darkness in the courtyard.'

'Is it far from here, the other well?'

'No, it will only take a couple of minutes to walk there. I'll take you when we have finished our drinks. It is St Milburga's Well.'

We don't talk a lot, until we have finished our drinks. Part of the reason for that is a number of people have just crammed in. There is standing room only now in here and not a lot of that to be honest. We make our way out onto the street. To be honest, I would like to go to my left to check out what I have thought of, but for now I have to go right with Andy. A right at the bottom of the street and then a left about fifty yards later; takes us into the lane where the well is. We walk down about 20 yards, until we come across the place. On our right there is a small depression, like a pit, behind some iron railings. We go down the few steps and stand in front of it.

'I think we should get this checked out' he says as soon as he sees it. 'Does it go far?'

'What you are seeing is the extent of my knowledge' is my reply. 'I may live here, but the first time I saw this, was when I came down here with Anne.'

I don't have any inclination to step too close. My last memory of being here was a bit odd, to say the least.

Andy takes a step closer. I retreat back up the steps and stand by the railings. Andy bends down, to have a look inside. I don't think he sees much, as he stands up pretty quickly and turns to me.

'We have people who will know what to look for. Are there other places like this in Much Wenlock?'

I am sure there are. In fact it is something I have been asking myself about, since Anne and I came here.

'I don't know, but I will do some digging. There are a couple of things I want to look up.'

Andy just looks at me.

Chapter 51 Me

I make my way into High Street. Andy has gone off to do what he has to. I walk halfway up and stop outside the Corn Exchange. I have remembered what I need to, but there are still a couple of questions to be asked. The real puzzle is the date. I am also struggling to think whether I saw this in the dream, or if I was actually there. That is, of course, if any of this is actually happening to me. I walk over to the wall and try to find the place where Anne touched first. It takes me a few minutes and it is old and not particularly clear, but it is there. I put my finger against it and feel the letter A. Now I need to check the next thing that might shed a different light on things. Is the wall a shared wall, or is it the wall of the Corn Exchange solely.

I can't tell you how many times I have been by the Corn Exchange and through it even, but I couldn't tell you off the top of my head, if it shares a wall or not. It only takes a second or two to confirm that the Corn Exchange is a stand-alone building, on that side at least and that is the side I am interested in.

So now I have established that much, I can think about when she could have done it. The cynic in me thinks there is always the possibility that she could have done it recently. My head is telling me that is not the case. If I go with my head, it tells me that the clothes she wears look as if they are from hundreds of years back, but in fact they are going to turn out to be from the Victorian era, with the Corn Exchange having been built in 1852. Then another thought comes to me. Is she from more than one era? I don't think I can deal with that. It is hard enough coping with her not being from the here and now.

So with keeping with the Victorian time frame, I can do a little bit of investigating. What I need, is to find the newspaper of the day and then start hunting through it. That could prove to be a long job, unless I can get a better idea of when Anne lived here. I am always assuming that she lived here. The other thing I need to do; is to talk to some true locals. I need to talk to someone who will have an insight into local history, from the locals' viewpoint, not necessarily what has been written down for prosperity. I will have to give that some thought, as to who that could be, later.

I make my way home and start my search of the internet. To actually find that there was a local paper of the day is the easiest part of the task. It takes less than a second for the results to be shown. I don't get, pretty much as expected, a paper for Much Wenlock, but I do get a newspaper for Bridgnorth and surrounds, which is hopefully going to be good enough. It will be a good place to start. The newspaper is called: Bridgnorth Journal and South Shropshire Advertiser. I look up the British Newspaper Archive and I see it was a weekly paper, or at least that is what it suggests to me to be. But it is only showing the paper for the year of 1856. I do a bit more hunting around, but I can't see evidence of there being any more years in the archive. It is a possibility that the Bridgnorth journal archives will go back all the way. I try that avenue next. I see that it says they are kept by the Shropshire Archives and not the national archive. Okay, that is probably easier, but it would still be a long job, hunting my way through it, looking for a single missing person or death, in a period of say 50 years. I don't think I need to be at that stage at the moment. Maybe Anne will provide me with a simpler solution to my quest.

I turn my thoughts to someone I could speak to about local things. There are some obvious choices, historian wise, but I don't want to go down that path.

For some reason my thought are tuned in to tunnels. Why am I thinking this way? My initial search throws up Ippikin and the cave on Wenlock Edge. Somehow this is not the sort of cave I was thinking of. I am thinking small. I am thinking the sort of cave that people wouldn't know is there. I am thinking the sort of cave that has been left undiscovered for a hundred years. Am I being unrealistic? There is a possibility that I am. I don't get any hits on tunnels, other than railway ones of course. I keep trying and changing the search words, but I don't get any answers that I think are right, whatever that is. I get the feeling that I am not going to find the sort of thing I am looking for on the internet. I need a dose of local myth and legend, that's what I need. Then I get the idea of someone I can talk to. I send him a message on messenger and then stop for the day. Kate is pleased to have me downstairs, as are the dogs.

Early the next morning, I get a reply to my message. He is busy in the morning, but has some spare time in the afternoon. He asks why I thought he would have some information that is not widely available. I don't tell him what I am thinking; I just send a smiley face back at him and agree a time we can meet at his house.

My thoughts are that in a town where there is an old priory, dating back more than a thousand years and then a number of other buildings dating from the 1200s onward, that there are going to be things about these houses that may not be written down, but will be known about, by certain individuals. I know that a lot of the buildings have cellars and that is always an encouraging sign, at least in the area I am looking at.

I take the dogs for a long walk, before getting back to find, that for a change, there isn't anyone waiting for me. I see plenty of activity still in the town, as we walk through it. There is still a search going on. While there are people out on the edges of town, where the search area has been extended a bit further out, the main concentration is on the buildings in the town itself. I note as we pass the door, that a policeman has been posted to stand guard on the house in Sheinton Street. I am surprised that I haven't been asked back, to check whether Anne has returned. The reason I haven't, is probably because Andy's boss does not want this whole thing to be lost in something he isn't convinced on, despite listening to my narrative on my involvement to date. It makes little odds to me. Technically I am not involved, other than I have seen some things. They know it really does not have anything to do with me. Maybe that is why I have been edged out a bit. I can't say that I am unhappy about that, as it had been getting a bit on the weird side, the longer it went on. Do I believe I have heard the last of it? Certainly not, I'm afraid. My time will come again I feel, whether I want it to or not. In the meantime, I make the best of what time I have to myself. I also try not to think what will be the manner of my re-involvement, when it comes.

We take a light lunch in town, before we part. Kate comes back along Barrow Street to our house, while I go the other way along, to see my man. We have a cup of coffee downstairs, before I am led upstairs to the sanctuary of his study. I have a good feeling about this. Before I get the opportunity to ask what I want of him, he wants me to bring him up to speed, with what I know about what has been going on in the town. I give him a brief update, but certainly not the whole story. I need to keep a lot of it to myself for now. I do give him enough though, to be able to ask the questions I want to, about the history of the people in the town.

Chapter 52 Me

He knows a lot about the town. How much of it is fact I am not sure, but then what is fact anyway? At first all I get is bits and pieces, about how the town is today. I get quite a bit on how the town is run. In the modern era, it is still trading on the fact it is a town, but in real terms it is only a village. Many things have moved on since it was declared a town. Many things have moved on in general and not just in Wenlock.

At last we start to encroach on the edge of the area I am interested in. I want to know about the people of the town. I want to know about happenings of the past. I want to specifically know about happenings regarding a girl or a woman, but in a time frame that I am totally unsure about. We dance around the subject for several minutes. Most of what he says is way too recent for me; well I am assuming it is well too recent for me, but I don't know for sure. Anyway the contents are not juicy enough for what I am searching for.

I move the conversation onwards. Much as I would like to get some real advance on my search, I can see that is not going to happen. So I then turn the conversation to the buildings of the town, rather than the people of the past. I am of course looking for some history on the buildings that might be pertinent to me, but I will only know that when I hear it, I hope.

We start quite predictably with the old priory. It was built in the 12th century on the site of St Milburga's 7th century abbey. On one side of the site is a private house, well it is these days, which was part of the Prior's lodging originally. The priory is open to the public. The priory of course was dissolved by Henry VIII. After that the Guildhall was built, to hold a court room etc. These days it is still the council chamber. My thoughts immediately go to the last place I saw Anne. That was at St Milburga's well. I bring myself back to this moment. I push him to see if he can shed any light on the Guildhall, without me telling him I want to know why it collapsed in front of me, but he can't, or doesn't know anything which is pertinent to me.

We talk about the other buildings in the town, particularly the older ones, but there is nothing that stands out to me of being of specific interest, regarding what has been happening in the town and with my involvement. We wind it up and I leave, a little disappointed. Well I say that, but as I am ready to leave, he throws in something that catches my interest for a second or two.

'Of course I haven't said anything about the tunnels.'

He knows he has my interest. I am at the gate when I hear these words. I start to edge back towards where he is still standing by the front door.

'Which ones do you want to know about?'

'There is more than one?'

'There are quite a few, if you count the ones in the Edge itself.'

I know about the Edge. I know there are caves and I guess I expect I know that there would be tunnels there too.

'They blocked off the entrances to some of them, sometime in the 1800s.'

I find that my interest peaks at that comment. I don't know why that is the case. I try not to ask any questions. I want him to continue on his own.

'I think I read something about they were dangerous or something. You'll find it in the old journal. I'm not sure when it was, but sometime in the nineteenth century.'

It is still going to be a long shot, trying to look through the archives for a non-specific decade, let alone year and week. I have a feeling it isn't really that important.

'And then there are the tunnels in the town. As you know, a lot of the older properties in the centre have basements. It is said that there are tunnels running away from some of them.'

I need to ask a question. I have to open my mouth.

'Are there any buildings in particular that have tunnels?'

He thinks for a few seconds before answering me. I can see him eyeing me up. Am I worthy of being passed this knowledge? He comes to a decision. It looks like I may have passed the test.

'There may be some leading away from some of the very old houses in town. I don't know about them. No one who has lived in the houses has ever mentioned that they have come across any tunnels. I guess they would have, if they knew about them. I mean that over the years they have all had work done on them, so I would think if there were any to be discovered, they would have been. But then saying that, the ones I am about to tell you about, now come under the same category. They are talked about, but no one knows where the entrance is.'

'Is this worth another coffee to talk about them?'

'I suppose it is' he replies, smiling at me. I think he is pleased that he has found something that I need to know about.

We go back inside and sit in the living room this time. I think that means he doesn't expect the telling of this information to take too long. Probably long enough for a coffee, but not much longer than that. With coffee to hand, he continues:

'There are two that may be of interest to you. They are both connected to public buildings in the town, if you like.'

I don't mean to, but I edge forward a fraction on my seat. I can't help it, but I believe what I am about to hear may be important for me to hear correctly.

'Holy Trinity Church is on the site of the nun's church of the old Saxon Abbey, Milburga's. The monk's church was where the priory, or what remains of it, is now. It is said that there was a tunnel that ran from the church, or maybe before that, the nun's church, to somewhere, possibly the monk's church. It was said to be tall enough to walk through. As far as I know it has not been come across. I suspect the entrance would have been found and filled in, when they built the Holy Trinity Church.'

That makes sense to me too. I wait for him to continue.

'It may be the same tunnel, or it may be a different one. It was said that another tunnel ran from the Holy Trinity Church towards the town. Some say it went to the Milburga's well area. Others say it didn't go that far, maybe only as far as the Guildhall. It is said it was constructed when the Guildhall was built in the 1600s. No one has found any entrance or tunnel.'

I admit to being interested in that one. But the next one interests me more.

'When they built the Corn Exchange in 1852, it is said they dug a tunnel back towards the church. It isn't known why they built it, or if they did anything other than start it. It was either going to the church, or the Guildhall. There isn't any sign of an entrance to it under there, or round it anywhere. It may be just an old tale, but it has stuck around.'

Then he puts his chin up in the air. It is obvious he has just thought of something else. I let him take his time, to bring what he has remembered forward. Eventually he does.

'I was just remembering something. The story is that the monk's always had an escape tunnel. I was thinking about the one between their church and the nun's church, but there was another one. It was said that it ran all the way from the Abbey down to Buildwas Abbey. Of course, no one knows where the entrance would have been. It has been covered over, or filled in, over the years probably. I remember something from when I was much younger. I'm not going to tell you where this happened. It wouldn't be great if people started tramping round where it was, to look for it. Anyway, a hole appeared in the ground. It was part of the water tunnel from' he stops himself from saying where, just in time. 'Anyway, the strange thing is, when we climbed down into this hole, just along a bit at a slightly different level, we came across another tunnel. It was obviously so much older and quite a bit bigger. It was running across it at 90 degrees in both directions, which made no sense in relationship to this pipe by the hole, but it was in line with both abbeys. None of us had the guts to go down any further and along the tunnels, to see where they went. We didn't have lights or torches with us. By the time we did go back some days later, the hole had been filled in. No doubt I could take you there and show you pretty much exactly where it was. I'd have to ask G...' he stops himself again, almost in time.

'Now that is a good story I say.' I don't need to press him for more at this second. I will bear it in mind, if I think there is a need to investigate this any further, in the interests of what has been going on. Maybe when this is all over, I will press him further, out of interest. If there is such a tunnel, it would be good to see where it does go. Wenlock to Buildwas is a fair distance.

Chapter 53 Me

I make my way back towards town. As I stop at the first junction, to check if it is safe to cross, I get a strange feeling come over me. At first it throws me off completely. I know I have a feeling, but I can't place what it is. Then I recognize the feeling for what it is. I think I am being watched. The question obviously is going to be, who is watching me?

I look around me, but to be honest I can't see anyone on foot. There are people in vehicles that I can see, but the vehicles are travelling as normal along the road. I wouldn't say that any of the occupants are watching me. I feel my back tingle and this just backs up what I am already feeling. I decide I should start walking again. I am not getting anywhere by standing here. If anything, I will just get more uncomfortable.

The feeling doesn't go away as I walk along Sheinton Street. I stop opposite the house and turn to look towards it. I am half expecting for Anne to be standing at the window, looking out and down on me. She isn't there! I don't know if I am surprised by that.

This is not the place to stand and think about things. I already have people wondering about me. I don't need any more things to be said about me. But on the other hand, the feeling is strong. I need to stop somewhere and that somewhere needs to be somewhere where I will feel safe, but at the same time have a good view of the town. I settle on The Smoothie being the ideal place, particularly if I can manage to sit in one of the comfy chairs, to the right as you go in. It must be my lucky day. The table is empty. I order my coffee and sit there, looking out of the window. There are quite a few people walking around the town. Some of them I recognize and quite a few I don't. There is nothing unusual in that. I scan the area carefully, looking for signs that someone might be paying too much attention in my direction. I just can't pick anyone out, but the feeling is still with me. I finish my coffee quickly and order another. I look in different places, but still can't see anyone. I find it all a bit unsettling.

I am just about to empty my cup, when something catches my attention, out of the corner of my eye. I had been watching someone using the telephone box on the square. You don't see people using them much these days, now most of us have a mobile telephone. So, out of the corner of my eye, I see something. I sit back in my chair and actually wish I was sitting in a less exposed place now. My attention has been caught by someone moving just into view, in the alley between the Guildhall and the Ecclesiastical Outfitters. I can't see much of them as yet, but from the way they are standing, it feels to me as if they are reluctant to come fully into view. But what has caught my attention is that, if I am right, I have seen this person before. The vision of it springs straight into my mind. The last time I saw them was when I was with Anne, at the back of the Corn Exchange, looking up at the window. It isn't the woman, but the man who appeared to fall backwards, out of our view.

I am 99% certain that this is the same person. I drain what is left of my coffee, while keeping an eye on him. He has retreated a half step into the alleyway. I thought I saw him look over in my direction, just before he did so. The tingle in my back, is telling me that this is connected. I take my empty cup up to the counter and say my goodbyes. Then with a glance over in his direction, I slip out of the door and dive up to my left and through the arch. I am hoping he is standing too far back to be able to see me do this. I am also hoping that I can get into position, before he realizes that I am not sitting in the Smoothie any longer.

I turn left into the Mutton Shutt and walk over the cobbles down to the bottom, where it meets Barrow Street. I don't step straight out, but carefully edge forward, looking to my left, to see if I can see him. He is not in view. I cross over the road and then cut onto the path, which leads me onto Church Walk. I walk quickly along the back of the building, until I am almost at the far end of the alleyway where he was standing. I am not sure how I am going to play this. If I walk into the alleyway and he is still there, then I am going to lose my advantage. If I look round the corner and he has gone, then I will have to try to work out which way he has gone. Maybe he is coming along behind me. Hopefully though, he will still be standing there.

I stop just before the alleyway. I edge forward and peek round the corner. I feel a sigh of relief. He is still there, but he is not alone. That may have saved me from being followed any more. I am not in the ideal place to see what happens. I need to find a better place to watch and wait for him to move off again. I walk past the alleyway, only briefly checking that they are still there. They don't turn towards me as I do that. I get to the church and turn to go onto the pavement. I find a place to sit on the wall, which gives me a view of part of the square and the bottom of High Street. I won't be able to see if he is still there, but I will be able to see him if he moves forward onto the street.

I don't have long to wait for him to appear. He steps into my vision and then stops to have a look around. His first look is a long one, in the direction of the Smoothie. He then looks in every direction, except for the one I am in. Clearly he isn't seeing what he needs to. I can almost hear the sigh of frustration he lets out, when his search reveals nothing. He stomps off, walking up High Street. I push myself up off the wall and walk quickly past the Guildhall and then turn into High Street. I can't really contemplate jumping into doorways, if he turns back in my direction. I can see him, not as far up the High Street as I would have imagined he would be. That puzzles me a little. Maybe he hasn't given up on the idea of finding where I am. I stop to look in a shop window. It has to be a bit further up than I would like. I am quite close to him now. He is standing opposite the Corn Exchange. He is looking up at the front of the building. I am looking in one of the windows of Twenty-Twenty gallery. I am using the reflection of the glass, to keep an eye on him. It is a wonder that, the way he is looking up at it, that there aren't others stopping, to see what it is that he is looking at. I think I probably would, if I was walking past him.

I must have stood there for more than five minutes and so has he, before he moves. It is almost as if he has been in a trance. Either that or he has been thinking about something and has come to a decision. Anyway, he snaps out of it and marches forward, across the road and into the offices above the open space. He slams the door shut behind him. I see him disappear, just as I reach the place opposite. I am just in time to see him disappear through the doorway and watch the door slam shut.

I wonder what he was looking at. He has to come out the way he has gone in. I take a step to the edge of the pavement, to look up at what he has been looking at. I see what I saw before, after the building rebuilt itself, if you know what I mean. Along the top edges, above where the hanging baskets are, there is a line of cracks in the stone. They are bigger than they were before. I almost think that they are getting a bit bigger too, as I look at them.

Chapter 54 Me

I know I take a step or two closer. My thoughts are only with what I can see in front of my eyes. I can understand now, why the man I was watching kept his eyes on the cracks (I am assuming that is what he was looking at). As I watch, at least one of them visibly changes. It doesn't cross my mind, even for a second; that I should be concerned at what the consequences might be. You would think I would after what I witnessed before, but I don't.

I must have taken more steps forward than I knew about. Almost simultaneously three things happen. Above the cracks, I hear a noise. It is not the sound of the building getting ready to collapse, as you might think. It is the sound of breaking glass. My eyes switch immediately upwards, at the first sound of the glass breaking. What I see are shards of glass breaking away from the window pane, as something comes flying through it. My hand comes up automatically, to shield my eyes from what is starting to fall in my direction. I just have time, to also take note that something is coming right through the glass. This is what has broken the glass I presume. The first thought I have about what this is, is that someone has jumped through the window. That's what my first glimpse of it tells me. I don't have time to work out for sure, what it is that is flying out. That is because the second thing comes to my attention.

My ears pick up the sound of a vehicle approaching from my left. It is a one way street and that is from the correct direction, so it isn't a great surprise that a vehicle is coming down the street. What is a surprise; is the sound of the engine and the speed at which the vehicle is approaching. I hear a crash, as I turn my head in that direction. The crash is from the car hitting the car that is parked at the end of the line of cars. It is the first car in the parking bay. Even by the time I have turned to see that, the car has moved so much closer. It has only clipped the parked car. It is already almost upon me.

It is at this moment, that I realize just how many steps forward I have taken, to look up at the cracks on the front of the Corn Exchange. I am standing in the road. More to the point, I am out in the lane where the traffic comes down. Even more to the point, I am right in the path of this vehicle that is travelling straight at me. Yet even more to the point, is that it is obvious that the driver has no intention of slowing down. I am going to be mown down in a fraction of a second. I have not had time yet to react to what is happening around me. I just about get my eyes to lock on the driver of the car, when the third thing happens.

I have turned to look at the car hurtling towards me. I have just locked my eyes onto the driver and that has frozen me to the spot, for just that extra fraction of a second that might have made the difference, in how I end up after all this. I hear a shout coming from by the Corn Exchange. In that split second, I don't have the time to put a face to the shout. What I do hear is my name being shouted, but that isn't the third thing. The third thing is that before I can respond to the shout, I am suddenly thrust backwards, as someone collides with me. I have to say that the collision is absolutely intentional and if they hadn't, I would have been killed by the car. As it is, as we fall back between two parked cars, I feel the speeding car brush against my foot. It is nothing more than that thankfully.

I land on my side, with my saviour landing awkwardly on top of me. Before we have even begun to compose ourselves, the car has raced off to the bottom of the street, clipping another two or three cars on its way. It turns left and shoots down Wilmore Street. We can hear the sound of the engine roaring for a few seconds, before it goes beyond our hearing.

But we aren't out of the woods yet. The thing that has come through the window, has now landed, more or less where I had been standing. It is not, as I had first thought, a person who has come through the window. It is a manikin, dressed like a man. It is not just any old manikin though. It would look like this one has been specifically prepared for the purpose. At least looking at it, that is my first thought. The reason for thinking this; is that the manikin is covered in spikes. Spikes would have done a lot of damage to me, if then the manikin had landed on me, or anyone else for that matter. I don't think it was aimed at anyone else though. I get the feeling I was the intended target, for the manikin and the speeding car.

The manikin is lying smashed on the ground. Bits of it hit us as we are lying there. It must have hit the ground, literally the second the car had passed us. I am not sure how this thing could have been coordinated, but it seems that the two must be connected, in my eyes.

My saviour is recovering from the position we have landed in. I am feeling a bit sore from the way we landed on the ground, but I am still alive thanks to Ryan. Ryan stands up and bends down, to see if I am alright.

'Thanks for that, Ryan' are the first words that come out of my mouth.

'Are you alright, Bill?' are his first words.

'I am thanks to you. You risked your life to save me.'

'I didn't think of that. I just heard the car and knew that something was wrong. By the sound of the engine, there is no way it was going to stop.'

He helps me up to my feet. There are a few people who have gathered around us now. We move over to the bench under the Corn Exchange. I am still recovering from the effects of hitting the ground so hard. Don't get me wrong. That is so much more preferable than being dead. That is what I would be now, if Ryan hadn't leapt out and pushed me to safety. What is more remarkable; is that Ryan isn't that big. Part of that is his stature, but the main part of it is that he is only a teenager and a young one at that. His mates have gathered round him, as others have come round me. He appears to be unharmed by his heroics. I am probably suffering more from shock now.

It takes me a few minutes to regain my composure. In that time some people have drifted off. Others have gone to inspect the damage done to the cars that had been clipped. I have had a good feel around my body. It would appear that nothing is broken, thankfully. I expect I will have a few bruises to show for it.

Out of the corner of my eye, I see someone coming out of the offices door, at the back of the Corn Exchange. I get a shock, because it is the person who I believe was watching me. He looks over at me very briefly, as he turns and darts down the passageway that takes you out to the back car park and beyond. I try to get up, but my body protests and a couple of people tell me to take my time. I know that he will already be well away and out of sight, even if I did manage to get through there now.

The reason I got a shock at seeing him, is because it was his face that I believe I saw behind the wheel of the car. It can't have been, because here he was coming back out of where I had seen him go in. The question I have now though is; was he responsible for the manikin coming out of the window?

The people around me are too much concerned about how I am, to be able to explain that I need to find out who he was. My mind is taken off that temporarily, as I hear the sound of a siren approaching. The police car pulls up further up the street, a few seconds later.

Chapter 55 Me

The police officer comes to see me, briefly. As soon as he sees that I am alright, he leaves me to sort out the other things that have been going on. There are people ready to make a complaint, at how the car was being driven down the High Street. There are those who have had their cars clipped by the speeding car too. Then there is the case of the manikin coming through the window, onto the street below. That is not to mention the chap who has had his car stolen; his being the speeding car. That does not come to light before one of Ryan's friends steps forward, with a photo of the speeding car, as it nears the bottom of the street. The number plate is clear to see. That gets reported in first.

From what I can gather from the ones still gathered around me, not one of them thinks that I was actually being targeted here. In their eyes it was just that I happened to be standing in the street, looking up at the front of the building. I do pick up the odd comment a little away from me; that I was a bit stupid standing in the road like that. What did I expect? There is always one or two willing to offer their opinions, whether needed or not. What I find interesting, is that the episode of the manikin appears to be the one that is being left on the back burner, so to speak. That one, as far as I am concerned, is right up there at the top, beside the speeding car, if not ahead of it. There has to have been quite a degree of planning for that. You don't just have a manikin, with spikes sticking out of it, ready at any moment.

I don't voice these thoughts. I don't need to change this into a personal victimization. Somehow I don't believe anyone thinks it is that way.

The lone officer is joined by a couple more, within a few minutes. In my opinion, at long last, one of them starts to take an interest in the manikin. I am almost recovered now. Ryan and his friends are in a small group by the library door. I step over and once again thank him for his brave and alert action. He brushes it off, as if it is an everyday occurrence. I don't think he understands the magnitude of what he has done. Few would have done it, even if their reactions were fast enough in the first place. One of the officers comes over to talk to him and me. By the time we are done, the officer who had gone in the offices about the manikin is coming out again.

No one knows where the manikin came from. No one knows how someone managed to get into that office. No one that is in there; saw, or heard anyone come in. I give a brief description of the man I saw leaving the office.

Actually it was based on the man I saw earlier, but it was the same man. It is just I got a better look at him then. What I didn't say, was that I thought the person driving the car was actually the same person. As it turns out no one else gives very much of a description of the driver and what is given, barely matches what I saw. The side windows were heavily tinted.

It is about this point when they find the speeding car. It hasn't gone far. It has been dumped very close to its point of being stolen from. It had been parked in New Street car park. It has just been found in Queen Street, on the corner of King Street. Two of the officers go off to have a look at it. No one has seen it stop there. No one saw the driver get out. Therefore no one saw where he went. No one saw if he walked away, or got into another car and drove off.

I don't hear this at the time. I only hear this from Andy, a while later, when he turns up on the scene. He says he doesn't know why he decided to come. It was just when he heard the shout about something happening in Wenlock, he had this feeling that I would be found at its midst. He wasn't wrong in that then.

By the time he turns up, the police have dealt with the cars that have been clipped. They have brought SOCO officers over, to have a look at the stolen car. They are also in the Corn Exchange, trying to see what happened in there. Ryan has long gone with his pals. His Mum, who was working in one of the shops, is surprised, but very proud, of the actions her son has taken.

Andy and I move away from the scene, to discuss the goings on. I tell him about my walk back into town and the feeling I got of being watched. I tell him that I think the driver looked exactly like the man I saw going into the Corn Exchange. Could it have been the same man he asks me? Only if there was someone else who threw the manikin through the window. And also could he have got out, gone and stolen the car; driven down the High Street and dumped it back by the bus station; then made it back to the Corn

Exchange and got in again unseen? And why would he need to do that anyway?

That doesn't take long as a conversation, to get dropped. Then the obvious question gets dropped into it. Do I think this has anything to do with the murders? I do as it happens, but I am not sure how or why. Obviously it is different, as I have seen a man and not Anne. Did I see Anne in any of this? No I didn't! Do I think Anne could have been the one who threw the manikin out of the window? Was she trying to stop the car with it?

The short answer is that I don't know. The long answer is that I think we are getting into realms that we just don't have enough information on, to speculate one way or the other. But if I were pushed to make a response, I would say that this has nothing to do directly with Anne. It just doesn't have her mark on it.

Have I been up to see where the manikin was thrown out of? No I haven't! Have I checked the building to see if Anne is in there? Again, no I haven't. It is actually something that didn't occur to me to do. Also I don't think they would have allowed me to do that, even if they understand who I am talking about, if I mentioned Anne. That is a good point!

We decide, well Andy decides, that it might be interesting to see if Anne is there. I don't for one second believe that she will be. Even if she was, I don't think she would have hung around afterwards.

SOCO have finished by the time we get there. There was little to look at. Not one thing had been touched. The manikin has been swept up and bagged, ready to be inspected later. We go through the building, from top to bottom. There is no sign of Anne. Do you think it is worth seeing if she is in the house? I am not that keen to go down there. I am not sure I want any more to do with anything today. I just want to go home and have a G & T. Andy wins though and we wander out onto the front again. We cross straight over the road and stop. We are on the pavement. I turn to look at the front of the building. There isn't one single crack to be seen. I point this out to Andy, as this was the reason why I was standing in the road in the first place. Ask the question again! Do I think the two things are connected? Hmmm, this thing about the cracks can only make the two connected. How they are connected is another matter, but they are definitely connected.

We walk down High Street and into Wilmore Street. Another minute and we are outside the house. Andy has put his hand in his pocket, to get the key out. We arrive outside the house, but there is going to be no need to use the key. The door is wide open!

'Don't tell me we have another one' he says, as he turns to look at me.

'I certainly hope not' I reply, with my thoughts springing to someone we know is missing; Tara!'

Chapter 56 Anne

The dawn approaches slowly, as it does at this time of year. It is still very dark and even when dawn arrives; things aren't going to get much brighter. It has been quite a rough night. The winds had come in from the west and as so often happens at this time of year, it brings the rain along with it. Wind and rain is what has been the experience of the night. It started shortly after dark and got progressively worse, as the night went on. Thankfully for now, the wind has dropped to little more than a breeze and the rain has stopped altogether for now.

What light there is going to be, still manages to brighten up the town, in a small way. Those who have to be up early; brave it out and make their way to their place of work. Those who do not, are safely tucked up in their beds still, or if they are up, are staying in the relative warmth under their own roof. A bit later in the day, some of them will be having to go out anyway, whatever the weather. When someone dies and the time is fixed for the funeral, then that is that. If you are going to attend, then that is what you will do. It doesn't matter what the weather is doing at the time.

There are two men who have to get up early. They are the grave diggers. Usually they would have dug the grave the day before, but on this occasion, the decision has been taken that it won't be done until the morning of the funeral. That decision was taken, as it was felt that the weather coming in would be too awful for them to work in. Along with that was the thought that too much rain; would have meant the grave filling up with water. As it turned out, although it looked bad the day before, the day held out for the hours of daylight. It only came in later, although the amount of rain that has fallen in the night might have been an issue with the grave.

The ground is soft when they put the first spade in and remove the turf from the top. They have their work cut out, to get it dug in time and be out of the way, before the funeral procession arrives. It won't exactly be a procession though. That makes it sound much grander than it is going to be. It is not an important person to the town who is being laid to rest today. There are people in the town who are very much involved with making the town a viable place. There are people in the town who make things happen. There are people in the town who employ others in the town, in their businesses. There are people in the town who work for themselves, to earn their daily crust. Then there are people in the town, who just manage to pick up pieces of work, wherever they can. They don't have regular employment. They don't really have their own place to stay. But they are in the town nevertheless and as such, they are equally a part of the town. It is one of these people who are being buried today.

As can be the case with the likes of these individuals, there is no one around to pay for their burial. It is something that the town does, as the person was living there and their death occurred there. Sometimes a town will go to some lengths, not to pick up the tab for this cost. This is not the case in this instance. Part of that, is due to the circumstance of the death itself. This isn't just the case of an individual dying and then the town having to perform the burial. This is because the individual, who is being buried on this day, has not died of natural causes. The person concerned has been murdered. There are some who are still working on finding the perpetrator, while others are trying to move the whole situation along and get the burial done and dusted, so that life can move on. That is not to say they don't want to find who is responsible, but more likely is that if they do discover who is responsible, then what are they going to do about it?

This isn't the first time this has happened either, in recent times. This is the second time this year. That is to say, it is the second time that a body has been found this year. The victim has died, by the looks of it, in the same manner, on both occasions. It is not as if the bodies were found in the streets of the town either. Both were found in the trees, on the edge of town. Both were found in shallow graves, funnily enough not that far apart, but at different times. Searching around had brought to light that it looks like there may have been another place that had been used as a shallow grave, but that one held no corpse. That is not to say that there hadn't been one put there, as a temporary resting place for that victim. That is the consensus of opinion; that the bodies were placed in a temporary shallow grave, awaiting the opportunity to move the body, to a place where it could lie out of sight more permanently. The fact is that persons have been found, but the perpetrator has not. The other fact is that the two persons found, were not locals of the town. They were both persons who had come to Wenlock and had managed to find casual work, wherever they could. The other fact is that both of these two persons were female. Both were young and in their own ways they had a beauty to them. They were certainly not unattractive. That may, or may not, have had an influence, as to their ultimate demise.

The grave has been hastily dug. They put a cover over it, although it does not look as if it is going to be needed on this day. It may not be the brightest day, as it is heavily overcast, but it does not look likely that the rains have any intention of resuming in the near future.

The cart trundles along Spittle Street, laden with the coffin on the back. The horse is being led by George. He is good with horses and this horse is temperamental, to say the least. It is sensitive to days like this. Usually the cart would have been ridden along, but as the weather is like it is today, it is unwise to do that. It would not be respectful to the person being transported, if the horse were to break into a trot, or worse still a run, because it got spooked.

There are a number of townsfolk who have braved the day, to walk behind the cart, as it makes the journey to the graveyard. None of them are relatives, but they are folks who believe there should be people there, when she is buried. Needless to say, there are certain individuals you would expect to be there. The reverend is one of them. Then on the other hand, there are people you might expect who would and even should attend, but they are missing from this entourage. I mean town dignitaries. It is unlikely they are going to join them at the graveside.

The cart comes to a stop, close to where the grave has been dug. The coffin is gently removed and taken the rest of the way to the graveside. It is at this moment the wind decides, not to strengthen, but instead it takes on a much cooler stance, as it blows across the exposed graveyard. The reverend stands at one end of the grave, as the coffin is gently lowered into the hole that has been dug. He says a few words and then a couple of prayers. There is not much he can say. He has been encouraged to perform this simple service, but to keep it to the minimum. It is not as if he ever knew the girl, in fact he doesn't think he ever saw her. She was not one of those who attended his church services.

One by one, the people attending step forward, and pick up a handful of soil. They drop it gently down onto the coffin. Each one saying a few words silently to themselves as they do so. There are not that many of them who have made the effort to come out today; certainly no more than a dozen of them. Once they are done, they all turn away and make their way back towards the town. The horse and cart has already gone. It went as soon as the coffin was unloaded.

And so it was on that day, that Lucy Bernow was laid to rest in Wenlock. The last person to leave had waited for the grave diggers to fill in the grave. Once they had gone, the young girl stepped forward and placed the flimsy handmade cross on the grave.

Chapter 57 Me

As I said, the door is wide open. We are both thinking that we know what we are going to find inside. That is purely based on recent history, but that is to be expected. Andy looks at me, but he already knows he is going to be the first one in. I can see that he is not looking forward to it, any more than I am.

'I guess we should get on with it' he ends up saying.

I just nod back at him.

He steps over the threshold and stops. I almost clatter into the back of him. I am not going to wait outside for him to make the discovery. I don't want to discover another dead body, but I think it only fair I am there with him.

'Is there anyone around?' he shouts ahead of him.

I stifle a laugh, as it crosses my mind about the condition that the people have been in that we have found in here previously. They haven't been in a position to answer this sort of question. Of course he is just trying to ascertain, if someone else (alive that is) is in here. Maybe the owner has returned, due to all the publicity, maybe not.

There isn't any shout coming back to us. There isn't a sound to be heard from in there, upstairs or downstairs. He tries again, but we get the same response as the first time; a stony silence.

He is just about to brave the next step forward, when we hear the sound of heavy feet running down the street towards us. It is enough to stop us taking the next step inwards. I step back, so that I can get a look at who is running so loudly. My eyes are met with the sight of a bobby, slowing down as he approaches us.

'Sir, you need to come back up there' he opens with, slightly out of breath.

I can almost see the relief on Andy's face, before he realizes that there is only going to be a different problem, waiting for him back in the town.

'I need you to stay here then' he replies 'and I will send someone else down to stand with you. The door was open when we got here. I have shouted in, but we haven't had a response. If someone comes out, I need you to keep them here and let me know. I don't think there is anyone in there, so don't get too concerned. Don't go in there, as we haven't looked around yet.'

'Sir' he replies.

I think he too is relieved, not to be going back up High Street. That makes me think that we have another surprise waiting for us there.

He takes his place outside the door of the house, while we start to walk away. We aren't running, like he had been on his way down. We are walking briskly, but not running. As we turn into High Street, we are kind of surprised that there is nothing visible, that we think the panic call can have been about. We stop in front of the Corn Exchange. We are met there by a couple of people from the SOCO team.

'Something odd has been going on here, Andy' is his first words.

'Like what?'

It would have been a surprise, if it wasn't for the fact that things haven't been exactly straight forward, since he came to Wenlock on this case.

'There are two things!'

We wait to be informed, but initially the information isn't coming. I look at him closely and I actually notice for the first time, that he appears to be unnerved. My mind immediately goes into overdrive. What on earth could have happened now?

'Why don't you show me' Andy realizes the same as I do, something is wrong and they are struggling to come to grips with it.

He turns and, along with his colleague, who hasn't uttered a word yet, they walk towards the door, to go into the offices of the Corn Exchange. We climb the stairs and go into the town offices and then into the archive room. That is the room that the manikin was thrown out of window from.

My eyes look to the window, as do Andy's. We take in what we see, but it is Andy who speaks first.

'They did that quickly.'

We are looking at a window that is intact. I also notice that it is a bit dirty too, but it doesn't connect with me, before the reply comes back.

'They didn't! The guy came to fix it, but when he got up here to see how he could board it up, this is what he found. The window is intact and there is no broken glass lying around anywhere. The vast majority of it was outside, but there were a few shards in here. Now there isn't one to be found. We opened the window. There isn't a trace of any broken glass on the sill outside either. The same goes for the street. We swept it up well when we cleared up, but now you can't see even the smallest bit of glass.'

'There will be bits on the manikin though' Andy says.

'That's the other thing. The manikin has disappeared.'

'But you bagged it up and put it in the van, ready to take back with you.'

'Yes, we did. We locked the van and came back here, to check everything had been done. That is when we bumped into the guy from the boarding up company. When we got back to the van, it was still locked. We opened up the back, to see if there was any glass in the bag. There would have been, because it was cleared up from the street. The van was empty.'

'Do you think someone took it?' Andy asks. The guy looks back at him, as if he is an idiot. In his eyes, that is he whole point of what he has been saying. Someone has obviously taken the manikin. He has no idea what has gone on with the window.

I know what Andy is asking. Until he asked the question, I wasn't thinking down this path, but now he has said that, it has made me think.

The guy just looks at us and shrugs his shoulders. His mate is giving us very similar uncertain looks. Andy decides what he has said, needs clarification.

'It isn't the first time that things have disappeared here in Wenlock, only for them to turn up somewhere else in the town. I was just wondering if you think kids might have taken the bagged manikin from the van.'

The message gets through.

'I don't think so. Anyway the van was still locked, when we went back to it. Kids wouldn't have shut the door, let alone lock it again. They would have wanted us to know that they had beaten the locks on the van.'

'I suppose you are right. Have you checked the rest of the building and round this area?'

'Yes and there is no sign of the manikin, or the bag it was in.'

I walk over to the window and have a look at it more closely. What I see makes it all the more puzzling. The other SOCO guy comes over and stands beside me.'

'That is what has spooked us out' are the first words he brings to the conversation.

I can see what he means. The window is as it looks; complete in the frame. But there is more than that. The window has been in there for some considerable time. That is easily visible, as you look at it. There is dirt that has accumulated over time, on the edges of the glass where it meets the frame. There is also paint on the frame and on the window too, in the matching place. That too is not new; in fact it is quite old. Andy comes over to join us.

'It looks like we have a similar kind of situation here. Instead of a body, read that for a manikin.'

'The only thing different is the window. The doors we had to mend, but the window has mended itself.' Andy says to me.

'But it was us who broke the door, to get back in after it slammed shut.'

'That is a good point.'

'I think we need to get back round to the house. There is a possibility that there might be a manikin for us to find in there.'

'I think that you may well be correct. Anyway, I forgot to send someone else round to him, so we had better go.'

Chapter 58 Me

The bobby is waiting for us when we get back round. Andy tells him to hang on for a minute, while he checks the house out. He is much more confident now, as he marches straight in, through the open doorway. I am just about on his heels. He goes into the room where the other bodies have been found. He stops suddenly. My thought is that he has found exactly what he is expecting to find. He moves forward, slowly enough for me to be able to get into the room with him. It is empty. That is definitely not what he was expecting to find.

We look around the room. It doesn't take long to establish that we aren't missing anything. The room is bare!

Andy moves out back into the hallway and checks the kitchen out the back. That too is as it should be. He still has a spring to his step. He goes up the stairs, two at a time. I remain where I am, standing at the bottom of the stairs. I don't think it needs two of us to look at empty rooms. That is what I am expecting him to find up there. I can hear him, when I can't see him. It doesn't take more than thirty seconds for him to reappear at the top of the stairs.

'There's nothing up here either. I wonder why the door is open then.'

'I have no idea.' That is all I can think of to say.

He starts to come down again and then stops, two steps from the top. I have already started to turn round, so I don't know he has stopped, until the sound of his feet on the bare stairs let me know he has.

'Why would the door be open?'

I turn back round to face his direction.

'I have no idea.'

'Exactly and neither have I really. But then I start to think that there has to be a reason.'

I don't respond to that one. I reckon he is going to enlighten me about something, any second now. I am not wrong about that.

'I'm thinking it has something to do with what has been going on round the corner. It is all bizarre, but then everything up to now has been bizarre and they are all connected. I'm convinced of that. Nobody has come along and opened this house because it is theirs and they have come back here. This isn't that sort of house and why would they come back and leave the door open, when there is no one in the house?'

'I agree, especially with the history we have, with the door being left open.'

'So, why is the door open, but there is nothing to be found?'

'I have no idea?'

'Well, I expected to find the manikin in here just now, I really did. But that isn't here. I have no idea where that has gone either, before you ask.'

He smiles at me as he says this. I just smile back. He continues:

'So, it just occurs to me. That if the manikin isn't here as I thought it would be and there isn't another body, something that is a bit of a relief too, then there must be another reason why the door is open.'

'That is fair enough.'

I am thinking that I was half expecting to find Tara here, when the door was open. I still don't know where he is leading us with this conjecture.

'Then my mind goes back to when we were upstairs that time, in the front room.'

I make the jump and I think I am now up to where he is thinking. As I take a step towards the stairs, he tells me what I have just thought about. He has been way ahead of me on this.

'You saw something that I couldn't. Is it possible she is in the house?'

'I'll come up and have a look.'

I take the stairs one at a time. I join him at the top on the landing, where he has waited for me. I check out the bathroom first and then the spare room. I leave the front room to last. I step slowly into the room. I stop almost immediately, but then move one step to the side, so that Andy can join me.

'She's in here isn't she? He says quietly to me.

'Yes, she is. Can you see her?'

'No, I'm only saying that, because of your action of taking a step to the side.'

'Yes, she is in here. She is lying where she was before. I think she is asleep. She is wrapped in a blanket, but I can see her face, so I know it is her.'

'Try to wake her if you can. I need to know what has been going on and why the door is open.'

'Anne' I say in a quiet voice. She does not respond. I try again, but a bit louder this time. 'Anne, wake up please.'

Again I don't get a response and nor so the next two attempts, using a louder voice. I am going to have to change tactics here. I know I felt her brush past me before, but I don't know if I can touch her. I am not that keen on trying either, to be honest. I take a look at Andy, but he is looking to where I have said Anne is lying on the floor. I take a tentative step forward. I stop maybe three feet away and then I kneel down beside her. I bet this is a bit weird looking for Andy, watching me bend down to something he cannot see.

I reach out with my right arm and stop short of touching her. My hand has become quite cold, because the air around Anne is quite cold. I relay this little bit of information to Andy. He asks what that means. I tell him I have no idea, my stock answer of the moment. I get over the shock of the change of temperature and my fingers get closer to touching the blanket.

The blanket is even colder than the air around Anne. I am a little surprised that the blanket is firm under my touch. I had the thought there would be nothing firm to touch, but there is. I give the blanket and Anne within it, a firm shake. Initially there is no response like before, but as I do it a second time a lot harder, I do get her to respond.

I move back, but stay down at her level. It takes her a minute or two, before she opens her eyes. It takes her another minute or two, before I believe she is actually taking note of the fact I am here. Then I realize that she is seeing Andy behind me.

'Maybe you should go back and stand on the landing' I suggest to him. He doesn't ask why, but he moves out of the room.

I concentrate on Anne. She appears more relaxed, now Andy isn't there in her direct view. I suspect that she can still see him, but she isn't concerned about his presence now. She starts to sit up and the blanket falls off her as she does so. She is wearing the same clothes as before. She stays sitting on the floor and keeps on looking at me. I thought maybe she would say something to me, but it looks like I will have to talk first.

'The door was open. Was it left open for us to find?'

She nods back at me, but doesn't say anything.

'Did you have anything to do with the manikin in High Street?'

I don't get a definite nod this time, but she isn't saying no.

'What about the car that was aiming at me?'

Again I don't get a definite response. I am struggling to know what to ask next.

'But you left the door open here, so we would find it.'

I get the nod again.

'Can you tell me about it?'

This time I get a shake of the head.

'Can you tell me anything?'

I get a confused look to this one.

'Are you going to talk to me?'

I see that to this question I get a sorrowful look, followed by a slight shake of the head. I don't know what to make of her. She wants us here, but now she won't talk. Am I supposed to guess what she wants us here for? Then I get something come into my head. I am fairly certain it isn't my thought. I think it has come from Anne.

'I am not allowed to tell you. But I need you here, because it will start to happen soon.'

That is all I get.

Chapter 59 Me

I wait for a few seconds, to see if there is going to be any more forthcoming. But she just sits there, looking at me. I decide I should tell Andy what has transpired, so I turn round and go out onto the landing. Andy is waiting for me at the top of the stairs. He is looking down the stairs at something. As I reach him, the bobby from the door comes to the bottom of the stairs.

'I need to talk to you, Andy.'

Andy looks at me, to see what I am going to say.

'I don't like the sound of that' is the first comment out of my mouth, followed by a quick resume of the conversation I have just had with Anne. Then I tell him her last words to me.

'"I am not allowed to tell you. But I need you here, because it will start to happen soon" were what she just finished with, whatever that means.'

'OK, you stay here with her, while I go to see what has happened now.'

Andy goes off down the stairs, while I return to the front bedroom. When I get there, I find that Anne has wrapped herself back up in the blanket and is lying back down on the floor, with her eyes closed. I call out to her, but she does not respond, or answer me. I debate whether I should go through the process of kneeling down and giving her another shake, but I come down on the side of not doing it now. I don't want her to do anything, while Andy is away dealing with his new issue. I lean up against the door frame and watch her, while listening out for sounds of Andy returning.

Anne is very restful as she lies there. I can't say that I can see her breathing, but she looks alright, as she lies there. I start to wonder what she means, when she says that something is going to happen soon. I suppose I shouldn't be surprised, because it makes sense that this has all been leading up to something.

Andy is away for the best part of half an hour. When he does come back, I hear him climb the stairs as quietly as he can. I move out onto the landing, to meet him. He makes eyes towards the front room.

'She's lying back down, all wrapped up' I answer his unspoken question.

'Has she said anything more?'

'No, she'd gone back to sleep by the time I went back in. I haven't tried to wake her. Was there anything interesting they wanted you for?'

'You could say that. So the guy has got the stolen car onto the back of the tow truck. He is just about to drive off, when he thinks he might have forgotten to fasten one of the holding straps. So he gets out, to check on that. Then he notices something straight away. The damage on the front wing of the car has gone. The car has straightened out. He checks the rest of the vehicle and where there was damage before he put it on the truck, now there is no damage. Then someone comes back from one of the cars he hit. Their car has now rectified the damage on it. I have sent someone to check on the rest of the vehicles that were hit, but I can guess what I am going to get back from that. They are all going to be as they were; when they left home today. I'm betting there will be no damage. What on earth is going on here? I don't expect you to answer that.'

That is just as well, because I haven't got a clue either.

'What are you going to do about her?' He asks me when I don't carry on the conversation.

'I don't know. She wants me to stay here. I'm not totally happy about that, but then it does appear to be me who has got involved in all this. It could be minutes or hours, before whatever it is starts to happen. How long do I stay for?'

'I guess that is up to you. You don't have to stay. I wonder what she would do if you didn't stay?'

'I don't think I have much choice. She lured us here with the other events, if they were down to her. I am not sure if they are or not. Then she tells me to stay and she goes back off to sleep. I guess I should stay for a while and see what happens.'

'I'll check in and say I am going to stay with you. I can't leave you here alone. You can't be locked in. I could leave the bobby with you, but I need to see what is going on and what is going to happen.'

He leaves me, to go to make his phone calls. I go back in and make sure that Anne is still lying on the floor; she is. I go back to my leaning place, by the door. It is another fifteen minutes later that I hear the footsteps on the stairs again. I go out to see who is there. It is not Andy. It is someone else.

'Do you want a coffee?' he asks me.
'That would be good, thanks.'
'I'm George. I work with Andy.'
'Thanks George.'
'Is there any movement?'

'No, she is still lying on the floor.'

'Andy is having a conversation with the boss. The boss isn't taking all this very well. He hasn't got a clue with what has been happening here in Wenlock.'

'Neither have the rest of us' I smile as I say it.

'I'll go and get the coffees. I daresay that Andy won't be too long.'

The coffees come back and are drunk, well before I see Andy again. Anne is still out on the floor. I have no idea how long she will stay that way. Eventually Andy arrives and joins me on the landing.

'The boss says I'd better stay until something happens. He suggests we don't stay later than midnight though, if nothing has happened before then. It was hard trying to explain the situation to him. He wanted to know what was going to happen. He couldn't take it in that we haven't got a clue.'

'I think that is alright. I will have to go to make a call. I am not getting any signal here.'

'I'd say I'll keep an eye on things, but I can't. I doubt she will move if you are not here when she wakes up, anyway.'

'I'll be as quick as I can.'

I move past him and go down the stairs and out onto the street. I walk for about a minute along Sheinton Street, until I have sufficient signal on my phone to make the call home. Neither of us is exactly happy with me staying with Anne, but it has to be done. I finish the call and make my way back to the house.

As soon as I enter the house, I can feel that something has changed. I can't put my finger on what it is exactly, but I know things are not the same. I make my way up the stairs. Andy is on the landing. I nod to him as I walk past him and into the front room. Anne is now sitting up, like she was before. The blanket she had round her has disappeared. I glance round the room, but it isn't there.

'Is it time?' I ask her.

She nods back to me and then I get some words come into my head once more.

'You have to tell that man to go downstairs and step outside. He will have to shut the door, when we have gone.'

I relay that message to Andy. Andy goes downstairs to be ready. My heart starts to beat a little faster as Anne stands up. She walks past me and starts to walk down the stairs. When she gets to the bottom, she doesn't go forward towards the front door. She turns to go towards the back of the house. I follow her. As I turn towards the back of the house, the front door slams shut. I don't think that was Andy. Anne looks at me and smiles. I am not sure if I should be worried now, or not. I don't think Andy is going to be able to get back in with his key. I hear him trying, as I follow Anne into the kitchen.

Anne opens the back door and we go out into the courtyard. It has got a lot darker since we came downstairs. It is getting darker out here by the second. I don't like this! She walks towards the wall and through the opening. By the time we are on the other side, it is dark in Wenlock

Chapter 60 Me & Anne

I stop when we are outside the courtyard. I am almost sure that Andy and the bobby would be shouting out, if they can't get in through the front door. I can't hear anything from them, or anyone else for that matter. Anne must have sensed that I have stopped, as she stops too. I can make her out, about four feet in front of me. It is dark, but not the total blackness I experienced the last time I came back, when the fireman rescued me.

I am not happy about what is happening, but I don't believe I have any choice, but to follow. I am ready to move on, so I take the first step. Anne resumes ahead of me. I recognize where we are, as we come out onto Back Lane. It is never particularly light down this stretch of road anyway, as the street lighting is insufficiently spaced, but tonight there is no light from ahead of us. What lights there normally are, do not appear to be on. There are no lights to be seen around us either.

We start to walk up, what I know as the car park behind the Corn Exchange. The ground feels rough beneath my feet, well just a bit uneven. When we reach the top, I am expecting the passageway to be lit, but I am to be disappointed in that. It is dark, even darker now, as we walk through the passage. We get through to the other side. Anne stops, so I stop about a step behind her. She turns towards me and holds out a scarf. I hadn't seen her holding one, but she must have had it on. She steps towards me and rolls the scarf up, before covering my eyes with it and then tying it behind the back of my head. She then touches my hands with hers. The touch is cold, but I let her do it. I know she has put the blindfold on for a reason, so I go along with it. I will, until I really don't feel safe about it. I can't say I am comfortable with it now.

She turns me round this way and that for a quite a while. I have no idea which way I am facing now. She takes hold of my hand and pulls me forward slowly. We turn one way and then again about a minute later and then she stops again. I hear a noise fairly close, but I have no idea what it is. She then takes hold of both of my hands and leads me forward. I feel her go down a fraction and she puts one hand on my leg. She stops me and lets go of my hands. I wonder what is happening, but I let her do what she wants to and that is to guide my feet onto something. It is a step. I know that by the distance my one leg has gone down. She speaks to me, for the first time since we have left the house.

'There are eight steps. I will guide you down them.'

She does so and when we reach the bottom, she puts her hand on my hand and I understand she wants me to stop. I feel her brush past me, as she goes to climb the stairs. I hear the sound again. I am assuming that the door to where we are is now closed. I try to think where she might have taken me, from the time she blindfolded me to now, but I can't think of anywhere where I might be. She obviously does not want me to know at this stage. She rejoins me and removes my blindfold. It doesn't make any difference, as it as black as can be where we are standing.

She lights a candle. She must have had it in her clothes. I can see around where we are. We are standing in a small chamber, at the bottom of the stairs. Leading away from the chamber is a tunnel. It is not as high as we are tall. We are going to have to bend over, to get along it. We are going to go along it. Anne leads the way. She stoops over as she makes her way into the tunnel. She isn't going fast. I find out why, quite quickly. We come to another sets of steps in the ground after only a few yards. We go down quite a lot deeper. Certainly more than the eight steps had taken us down from ground level.

Once we are down, we continue along the tunnel. It is not so high in this section. I am struggling to make progress, even by stooping. I am thinking I am going to have to get down onto my hands and knees. Ahead of me, that is what Anne does. Progress is of course much slower. I am only glad that the earth we are crawling over is dry and dusty. I could do without the dust really. Anne is kicking it up in front of me. I keep a bit further back from her and this helps.

I have no idea what sort of distance we have travelled. I know we have crawled along on our hands and knees for quite a few minutes. I still don't know where we started from and I have no idea where we will end up, or why we are approaching this way.

We stop when we come to some more steps. Anne comes back to me, but she doesn't say anything. She just takes hold of my hand and leads me forward. We start to climb the stairs, with her ahead of me. We climb more stairs than we had on the way down. I find that a bit confusing. It is not that many more stairs, maybe four or five I reckon. At the top of the stairs there is a door. She tries to open it, but it will not open. She tries pushing with her shoulder, but it remains stubbornly closed. She turns to look at me. I edge up beside her and try the door handle. It turns to a degree, but the door doesn't open for me either. My shoulder does nothing for the problem either. I get Anne to bring her light a little closer to me, while I look at the handle. I turn it and can see that it is not turning far enough. I bang it with my hand a couple of times and then try to manhandle it, in an effort to get it to turn just that extra fraction. Something I've done has worked, as the door moves. I am about to push it open a bit more, when Anne stops me. She hands me the scarf blindfold and indicates I should put it on. Reluctantly, I do as she asks. She checks it is on, with her cold fingers. I feel them against my face, as she checks the scarf. She takes hold of my hand and she opens the door. I know she does, as the hinges protest quite loudly. We walk out on the level, very slowly. She stops me and closes the door. Again the hinges protest at this effort.

She leads me slowly for only a few seconds. She then tells me we are going down a few steps; we do so. The ground under my feet is firm; it is not rough at all. She doesn't turn me, or try to disorientate me this time. She stops and then removes the scarf from over my eyes. It is still dark. I am not surprised by that. I take a look around me, to see what I can see and also to try to work out where I am. My thoughts are going to several places in the town that we may have crawled to, in the time we were in the tunnel. I had noticed that the tunnel wasn't straight, but just like when she turned me round; it was hard to try to keep a true angle on our direction, particularly as I didn't know the direction of our starting place.

The candle was blown out before my eyes were uncovered. There is no light coming from around me. I feel the slight echo and I know this place, but I am a bit confused.

'Are we where we started from?' I ask.

'It had to be this way' Anne replies to me softly.

My eyes are becoming used to the light, or rather the lack of it. I start to be able to make out the walls, at the edge of where I am standing. I am also able to just about see across the road, but I don't recognize what I am seeing there. Things are not what I recognize. I am of course standing in the Corn Exchange. Why we came up more steps than we went down, I don't totally understand. We have come out of the tunnel, but not where we went in. That is all I know.

Chapter 61 Anne & Me

As I am looking around me, I am struggling to understand what is different from the place I know. I am standing a few feet away from the doors to the offices. Anne has edged away slightly and is standing about eight feet away from me now. She is just standing there, as if she is waiting for something. Suddenly I hear a noise behind me. I hear the sound of footsteps coming towards us, from within the building. A second or two later, I see two men coming down the steps. I am in the way, if they carry on in the same direction. It is as if I am not there. They brush past me. I might almost say, I think they could easily have gone through part of me. I turn as they pass me.

Anne is standing at the edge of the Corn Exchange now. She is looking out onto the street. The men walk straight towards her. One goes to her right and the other to her left. Each takes hold of her arm on that side.

'We've told you before, that the likes of you are not permitted to stand here.'

'I'm not doing anything wrong' Anne replies.

'The likes of you cannot do anything right and you should not answer us back. We are important people in the town.'

'I'm just standing here, minding my own business.'

'That is just cheek. You are standing here begging, isn't she Christopher?'

'She looks like she is begging to me.'

They both laugh. I stay where I am. I know I should step forward, but I don't believe it will do any good. I believe I am watching something being played out here.

'Let's have a proper look at you' the first one says and pulls back the hood from over her head.

'She's a pretty little thing' Christopher says 'well pretty, considering she is just a beggar.'

'I am not a beggar. I do work to pay for my food and shelter.'

'You wouldn't know what work is, well not that sort of work.'

'I know the sort of work she probably does.' Christopher says.

'You're right there' the first one replies. 'Maybe we should see about that.'

'I am not like that' Anne retorts and tries to break their grip on her arms.

I step forward and close the gap between us. But when I reach them I find, pretty much as I had suspected, that I can't feel them. My hand just goes through, as if they aren't there.

'You need to be taught a lesson girl' the first one says. 'Come on Christopher. We'll take her somewhere quiet, where we can deal with her.'

He takes the scarf from round her neck and gags her, so she can't shout out. I try once again to intervene. They don't hear my voice, or if they do, they ignore it, and once again my hands go straight through them. All I can do is follow, which is what I think I am here for; at least it is what I think Anne has brought me here for.

They go through the passageway, almost holding Anne off the ground. They walk along Back Lane and out onto High Street and on towards the corner, past the Fox and over the junction at the Gaskell. Again this area is not as I know it. I do know roughly where I am though. We turn off at the Stretton Road and walk along there. There are no houses, where I know there are houses now. I try to keep track of where I am, but that is harder, because it is dark and I am in unfamiliar territory.

We walk for a little way, before turning up a rough path. We are soon up on the Edge. I am fairly sure that these two know where they are going. They appear to be sure footed and confident, in a way that makes me think they have done this before.

We come to an open section and they stop for a couple of seconds.

'This way' Christopher says.

We don't go very far. The land drops away and we go down a little distance and then they stop. Christopher keeps hold of Anne, while the first one moves some rocks. A deep dreading fear strikes my being. I try once again to intervene, but I am powerless to. They don't hear me and I cannot touch them.

The first one comes back and they step forward to the face of the slope. They push Anne through and then they go through the gap he has made. I try to follow them, but when

I get to the place where they went through; there is no gap for me to go through. It is almost as if I am in a different dimension. I try to move the rocks, but they are firmly in place. I keep trying for several minutes. I can't hear anything from where they went in. Who knows what may be happening in there.

I need to do something, so that I can find this place again. This is an important moment in the entire goings on we have been experiencing in Wenlock.

My eyes have become accustomed to the night; or is it just darkness? There is a faint glow in the sky, probably from the moon behind the thin clouds. I hunt around for something I can use, to make a mark. I find a rock that is easy to hold, but hard enough to do the job I need it to. I go back to the entrance they have gone through. About a foot to the left, I start to scratch a large letter A into the rock. I can't exactly see what I am doing, but I know I am making an impression on it. With that done, I step back to wait, but only after having another try to get through. Then a thought occurs to me. What if they see the mark and try to erase it? What if they see the mark and succeed in erasing it? I need another one, a little bit away from the entrance.

I take four paces to my right. That is the direction away from where we arrived from. I still have my rock in my hand. I find a suitable rock face to scratch on and then score it as deeply as I can with my rock. I score much more than I had the first one. Something inside me says I have to, or it won't last? Just for good measure, I keep at it for a bit longer. In fact I only stop, because I hear their voices to my left. It is only two voices I hear; two male voices.

I step back over towards them, in time to see the two of them come out of the opening.

'She was a fiery little thing.'

'She was and very enjoyable too.'

'She won't be missed. Maybe someone might wonder where she has gone, but her type just up and leave an area all the time.'

'You say that every time, Christopher.'

'It's time we were getting back, before Meg starts to wonder why we have been out so long.'

They fill up the entrance and pack it as well as they can. As they walk away, I walk up to the entrance and feel for the letter I have scratched in the rock face. I think I can see it, but it is hard, as the little light I had has now gone. I feel around for a minute or so and think about trying to make it deeper, but I have put my rock down now. I give it one last try, to get inside the cave. Even if I did manage it, I believe it is too late now for Anne. Anne is already dead.

I give up and make my way back up the slope. I walk along the Edge for a way and then find the footpath back down to the Stretton Road. I get a shock when I get there, as I see the houses on the other side of the road. There is no sign of the two men as I walk along it. These houses hadn't been there earlier. The streetlights are on too. Wherever I was earlier, it would appear I am back in the present now. I think I feel happier about that. I haven't come across anyone else, but then I am not sure what time it is. I look at my watch for the first time, but I don't get any help there. It has stopped. I find that out while I am standing beneath a street light.

Chapter 62 Me

By the time I have reached the Gaskell corner, I have still not passed anyone. I have not seen anyone either and I haven't been passed on the road, by any traffic whatsoever. I get the feeling that although I may well be back in the present; at least I am hoping I am back in the present, things are still not under my control. I think I am still watching something being played out. I think it probably has to be something else too, that is being played out. I have no idea what it can be. I am not exactly happy about that.

I cross over the road and see Waggies up to my right. I start back along High Street. I walk past Salon Ten and then the Fox is as it should be too. It looks like it did the last time I went in there. I pass Twickel next. That is Twickel, so I know I am current. I go straight ahead at the corner of Back Lane and into that section of High Street. I mentally tick off all the places as I pass them. The Undertaker is first. The Candle shop is on my left, with the Bilash and the Pharmacy on my right. Then there is the Talbot, Wenlock Books and the Deli on that side and Mrs P's, Stentons, Ippikin, Ryans Butchers on the other. Then there is The Bank, Cuan House, Bella Rosa, Wah Lei and Much More Books on my right, with The Copper Kettle and the Corn Exchange on my left. Then towards the bottom, I have Colours Florist on my right, along with Twenty-Twenty, The George pub and Wenlock Wardrobe. And on my left are No.63 clothes, Fodens, the Spar and the Museum.

Just for good measure I check the other shops at the bottom, to make sure I am in the here and now. In Wilmore Street I have Mary's Antique shop Memories. Beside that is the Optician. Going the other way, on my left I have Croft Design, Tea on The Square, Catherine's Bakery, A J Superstore, Nick Tart and then Tea Junction. In the square there is Penny Farthing, The Smoothie, Wenlock Fine Art and The Salon.

Past them, I have Twickel dentist and then The Raven. I tick them all off in my head. Every one of them is as it should be, for me to be in the here and now. I still have not passed a single soul, nor have I seen anyone or any vehicles.

I reach the corner and stop to make sure it is clear for me to cross the road. I am just about to step off the pavement, when I hear something. I stop with my foot in the air, ready to take my first step into the road. I am not sure what it is I have heard. I listen intently, to see if the sound comes again. I do hear something, even if I don't think it is the same sound. It is coming from somewhere up St Mary's Lane. I start to walk up there, with a little tingle in my heart. The last time I tried to walk up here, I was up against the dark wall. No such thing happens this time. I can't see anything out of place. I do hear a noise again, as I slowly make my way up the road. I reach the point where the lane turns right, but the road carries on straight ahead. I stop, to try to listen out for the noise again. I have to wait a few seconds, but it does eventually come to my ears. For the first time, I think I can make out what sort of sound it is. It is the sound of a human voice. It is the sound of a human voice in distress. I can't be quite sure which direction it is coming from. I think it might be from my right, but then it might be ahead of me too. The common denominator of that is the car park.

I keep to the main road and run up to the road into the car park. I stop again, to try to work out the direction. The voice is louder now and still in distress. But I can now hear another voice. This one is much quieter. From what I can hear, this one is trying to settle the distressed person down.

I am right about the location of the voices. They are definitely coming from the car park. I start to walk towards the sounds I am hearing. I can't hear the words that are being spoken, but I can hear one talking, while the distressed one keeps sobbing. I pass the end of the wall, on my right and I am now in the car park. I stop again, to see if I can see them. At first I don't, but then my eyes pick out two people, standing by a car. One person has their back to the side of the car, while the other person is standing in front of them, with their hands stretched out in front of them, onto the car. I don't need telling which one is the person in distress.

These days the question is always, whether you should get involved. After all you can never tell what the reaction is going to be. But then I am still thinking that even though I do appear to be back in the here and now, there is also something being played out here. I think I am meant to be here. I am meant to be seeing this scene in front of me. Am I meant to intervene? I don't know the answer to that one, but like before, I will probably try to.

As I approach within twenty feet of them, I think two things. First of all, is that I am expecting them to turn their attention towards me. Where they are standing, is in the dark. Well they are in the shadow. I am still not; as I am being lit from behind, by a streetlight, I would presume. Along with that, I am not walking quietly. I am allowing my approach to be heard. To my mind, one or both of them should be turning, to see who is approaching.

The second things I think is this: I think the man is familiar to me. I can't see much of him; I can only see his outline really. He is side on to me and I can only see his shape, but there is something about him. It is not a big town, so if he is local, then I would probably have seen him around and about. But that is not the sort of familiarity I am thinking about. This man reminds me of someone I have seen recently. Then I get it. He looks like the man I saw at the Corn Exchange and possible even the man in the car, though that bit is less clear.

I stop and give out a cough. They still don't turn. I decide not to approach any closer, just yet. I will see how this plays out. As if they have been waiting for their audience to arrive; me that is, I suddenly start to be able to hear what is going on. I can also make out that the person with their back to the car, is a woman, well a girl really. Then she turns just a fraction and I know who it is; Tara.

'I need you to tell me that you're not going to tell anyone.' The man says.

'You attacked me! You …..'

I can't quite pick up the words she says, as she drops her voice when saying them.

'You didn't seem to mind at the beginning.'

'You were just chatting to me' she says through her sobs 'and then you just pulled me in there' she says, pointing over to the other side of the car park.

'You're a very attractive young woman. I thought that you fancied me.'

'Fancy you?' she raises her voice to the loudest yet. 'You're an old man. Why would I fancy an old man? I was talking to you, because I know you, not because I want you to ……' her voice drops away again, so I can't hear the end of what she is saying.

'You won't tell anyone, will you?' His voice is getting more agitated.

'Of course I will! You can't do things like that and expect to get away with it.'

Suddenly he takes one hand off the car and side swipes her face with it. She reels under the force of it. I can't stand here and watch any longer. I need to try to do something, if I can.

I step forward briskly and shout out to him. I suppose that in my head I wasn't expecting him to be able to hear me, like the others couldn't. I am almost on him, when he turns towards me. He has something in his hand that I hadn't noticed before. As he turns, he hits me with it. It catches me on the side of my head. My world goes immediately very dark. It is Dark in Wenlock for me now!

Chapter 63 Me

I don't awake, as you might imagine, either in the same place I have last remembered being, or in a hospital bed. It is not that I remember what my last thought was, straight away. That is because where I return to the land of the living. I am not experiencing either of those scenarios. I appear to have dropped back into something else. The somewhere else I am at, is dark. At first I don't realize where I am. Then I do and that is when I wonder what is going on. It is almost as if the clock has turned back, in the time I have been out of it. The only difference being, that I am aware I have been here before with it being like this, but not after being knocked out by the man holding Tara. It is just like before and the same thought processes go through my mind. This is how I come back to it.

I turn out of the lane onto Sheinton Street or is it Shineton Street? It all depends on which sign you read. At one end of the street is says one spelling and at the other end the other spelling. I realize now just how dark it is without any streetlights on and with no lights on in any of the houses. I feel it is quite creepy, so I am already a little bit on edge (just like the first time I came along here in the dark). I cross over by the Bull Ring and start walking up the pavement, going past the church. I hear a noise to my left. I can't explain what sort of noise exactly, but it is like a swooshing noise. I stop and turn. I remember that this is exactly like it was before and that in itself is scary. I feel my heartrate go up a few notches. I can just make out the outline of the nearest gravestones. I can also make out the shape of the big tree beyond that. That is about the extent of my view.

Then she appears from the doorway of the church and walks along the path and away from me. She must have been hiding in the doorway as I approached. The whoosh, I take to be her movement. She has a long cloak on, as far as I can make out. Beyond the gravestones, she just blends into the rest of the darkness. I do call out to her. I call out to her by name. But she doesn't slow down and she doesn't respond. I am saying she, but to honest I am only saying that, because of her size and the cloak. I do believe it is Anne though.

I stand there for a few more seconds and my heartrate continues at its accelerated pace. This is just like before and I don't know if this is a return to last time; or if for some reason I have had to come down here, late at night again. The darkness reminds me that I need to get moving again. I start walking, but keeping one eye to my left and the church green and the other ahead of me, towards the square. I reach the Guildhall and the darkened area where they hold the markets. Somehow I am spooked and I keep to the edge of the pavement as I walk past it. As I pass the end of the Guildhall, where the passage comes out, I either hear the whooshing noise again, or I imagine it. I cross over the road towards the square and the momentary relief of a light. The Smoothie leaves one on in their café overnight. I am grateful for that relief. It may sound silly, but I need the safety of that light just at this moment, just like I did last time. If she chooses to come towards me, I will be able to see her. I am thinking that she will come and talk to me.

I wait for a few minutes, but nothing happens. I am not going to sit here waiting, all night. I am just about to get up and turn for home, when a thought strikes me. I wonder if the door is open or shut? The first time I experienced this, the door was found open later, by Bob, on his way to pick up his paper. Was it open for me to see, the first time? I don't know, nor probably ever will, but I can go to see if it is open now. This is probably not the wisest idea I have ever had, but I need to know the answer.

I walk out of the square into Wilmore Street and walk towards the Bull Ring. When I get there, I step out into the middle of the road, so I am not going to be right next to the buildings, at the start of Sheinton Street. It is not the first door, but the second door along there, that is what I am looking out for.

I know it even before I see it. That is because something happens. It is nothing to do with what happened last time, because I am in new territory for that episode. I hear the whoosh approaching me, from the direction of the church. I stop in the middle of the road. I see her approach, skirt round me, and then disappear through the door. I am not going to go in there if I find the door is open; it is!

This is different from last time. Last time Bob found the door open! Last time there was a body inside. I am not going in on my own, to discover this. I haven't got a torch on me. I have just checked my pockets. I do have my phone though and I am going to use that; to phone for the police.

I decide to call Andy. The last time I was with Andy, Anne led me out through the back door and slammed the front door on Andy, leaving him totally out of it and unable to follow us. I don't think he would have been able to anyway. I wonder how Andy will react to me calling him now. It is the middle of the night, but hopefully he won't mind too much and will be glad to hear my voice and know that I am back in the land of the living once more. That is not how it turns out, when I ring his number.

'Hello' the voice says, as the phone is answered.

'Andy. It's Bill. I am outside the house and the door is open again.'

'Who is this?'

'It's Bill in Wenlock.'

'Where did you get my number?'

'You gave it to me, so I could call you direct.'

'When did I do this?'

'It was when you met me, to talk about the murders in Wenlock!'

'What murders in Wenlock?'

It is about this point, when I am getting a strange feeling about what is going on, not for the first time.

'I've been working with you. You were with me, when I saw Anne on the floor of the house. Last time I saw you. She shut you out and we went out of the back door.'

The line is silent from the other end. I think he is doing something, because I can't hear anything.

'Where are you?'

'I am outside the house.'

'Which house exactly, are you outside?'

'I'm outside the one in Sheinton Street.'

'You said Wenlock. Is that Much Wenlock?'

'Yes of course it is Much Wenlock. I have been working with you on this.'

'Stay where you are. I will get someone to come over.'

He puts the phone down on me. I am puzzled by his reaction, but then it is starting to dawn on me, that I may very well be back at the first time this happened. If that is the case, then Andy has not come into this yet.

While I am waiting for someone to come, I step forward towards the open door. I call out softly for Anne. She doesn't come out and she doesn't answer me. I try one more time, but then give up and step over to the pavement, on the other side of the road. I see the blue flashing lights, before I hear the engine. A few seconds later, the police patrol car pulls up beside me. The officer doesn't look to be in a good mood, the way he is looking at me.

Chapter 64 Me

He talks to me for a couple of minutes. I show him the open door. He tells me to stay where I am, but only having taken a note of my name and address. I think the fact I was still here when he turned up, has actually done something for my credibility. No doubt what happens next will determine where things go from here.

The policeman leaves me and crosses over the road. He knocks on the open door, before venturing in. I see him walk inside and then turn into the front room. He is only in there for a matter of a few seconds, before he is rushing out again.

'Stay there!'

He issues me with that order. He opens the car door and gets in. I can see him talking furiously on his radio. He is in there for maybe ten minutes, before he ventures out again. By that time, there are sirens on the way to us. They aren't far away, as he gets out of the car. He comes over to stand beside me.

'I take it you haven't been in there.'

'No, I saw the door open and called it in.'

'You called a detective directly, I understand.'

'Yes I did, but I think he was asleep and didn't recognize who I was.' I am trying to make the situation as simple as I can. I think I might have some more questions to answer soon enough. I have been here before of course.

Several vehicles come to a stop, near to where we are standing talking. The policeman leaves my side and goes to stand by the front door. He is joined by several others. More sirens are on their way. I'm sure they aren't really needed at this time of night, as there really isn't any traffic around.

The policeman talks to the newly arrived officers, before they go in. From my position over the road, it looks like the police officer is reluctant to go first, but he has to show the way. He hasn't told me what he has found in there, but I have the general idea, from what has been found there before.

Surprisingly they aren't in there very long; maybe only a couple of minutes and they are all out on the street again. There appears to be a degree of confusion. A couple of officers go back into the house, including the one who arrived first. Five minute elapse this time, before they are all out again. I am left standing over the road, observing the goings on, but not being part of it. Another car pulls up. I look across, as the driver gets out. It is Andy. He glances across in my direction, but doesn't give any sign that he recognizes me. I watch as he approaches the group of officers. There is a short discussion and he goes into the house with my police officer. Five minutes later, they are out again. There is another discussion, which results in all but Andy and the police officer leaving. Only now does he come across and introduce himself to me. I know as soon as he does, that he doesn't know that we have already met. That is a weird moment, because it actually tells me that what I have been thinking is true; I am back at the time when I first came across Anne.

He asks me what I was doing out at this time of night. I tell him and he goes off to check on what I have said. He is back soon enough. He still hasn't told me about what they found in the house. He asks me if I have been in the house. I don't answer him straight away. I am not sure what I should give as an answer. I have of course been in the house before, but that is not what he is asking me, I think. I think he wants to ask if I have been in the house, before I rang the police. It is a complicated one for me to answer, because I have of course been in the house and with him, but he doesn't know that. I decide to clarify his question.

'Did I go into the house to check, before I rang the police?'

He nods that this is indeed what he is asking, although I also see that he has picked up on why I might be asking the question.

'No, I saw the door was open, so I rang the police.'

I have not told him about seeing Anne run in there. I will wait to see what he tells me first.

'Did the officer say anything to you, when he came out the first time?'

'No he just told me to stay here and then he got into his car. I saw him call in on his radio and then the others turned up.'

'You said I gave you my number?'

'That's right.'

'You said it was to do with the Wenlock murders.'

'That's right.'

'I think we need to have a chat. Something odd is going on here and you seem to be, how can I put it nicely, in the know about it?'

'What did you see in there?'

He eyes me up for a few seconds. He obviously lands on the side to tell me something.

'Well, when I went in there, I saw nothing.'

He stops to see my reaction. He doesn't see anything, as I am waiting to hear the rest of it. I know there is more to come.

'The officer, who went in first, did see something though.'

I try not to give a reaction, but I am not a poker player. I am sure that he notices it. He doesn't tell me what the officer saw. Instead he asks me what I think the officer saw.

'I think he saw a dead body. Then when he went back in with the others, the body had disappeared.'

He smiles at me.

'This has happened before then?'

'Kind of' I reply, without expanding on it yet. 'Was it the body of a man or woman?'

'It was a woman, probably more a girl than a woman.'

I am thinking it must be Tara. The last time I saw her, she had been hit by the man in the car park; just before he knocked me out too. But then something strikes me, as not being right about that. I saw Tara in the car park. In reality I don't know when that was, but something inside me, is telling me that the body the police officer saw was not Tara's. I need to ask a question.

I come to from my thoughts, to see Andy looking at me.

'What was she wearing?'

'Does it matter? Do you have an idea whose body it might have been?'

I don't reply in words, but I do nod.

'You need to know what she was wearing first.'

I nod again. Thankfully he humours me. He goes over to speak to the police officer. They are only together a matter of a few seconds. Andy comes back over to me.

'She was dressed in a black dress or cloak, he thinks it was.'

'It's Anne I think.'

I almost let the words slip out of my mouth, that it is not Tara, but I manage to finish without it sounding as if there is more to be said.

'Who is Anne?'

'It's a long story, but I am thinking you are going to want to hear it.'

'I think I am probably going to have to, even though this Anne is not here anymore.'

'But as you will understand, when I tell you the history of this, that she is very likely somewhere. I don't know why the bodies appear here and then are found elsewhere, but that is what has happened before. But that is telling things out of order. Shall we go back to my house and I'll tell you what I know, over a mug of coffee or two.'

'That seems a good idea. I'll just get the officer to shut the door for now.'

We turn towards the house. We have been side on to it as we stood there talking. The officer is standing at the edge of the pavement, looking across in our direction. Andy is just stepping onto the road, to talk to the officer, when the door crashes shut, with a loud bang. It gives us all a shock. I should probably have been expecting it, but I wasn't.

We all go to the door and try it, but it is firmly shut, as if it has never been open.

'Has it done that before?' Andy asks me.

'It has done that before.'

'We need to get to the bottom of this.'

Chapter 65 Me

I tell my story to Andy, over several cups of coffee. We are joined by my wife, when she hears voices downstairs. I realize straight away, that this is all new to her too. I am the only one who has been party to it all. I try to remember everything in order, but I may have made a few jumps backwards and forwards, in my relating of what I have experienced. When I have finished, Andy has a few questions for me. I answer those as best I can. It is more that he is trying to get everything straight in his head. Three things are in my favour, for him believing me, to some extent. First, is the fact that the police officer who came out saw a body, when he went in the first time. Second, is the fact that three of us witnessed the door being slammed shut! Third, is that he now understands where I got his mobile number from.

He thinks things over in silence for a couple of minutes.

'So you know where we should look for Anne?'

'I think I know roughly where they took her; these important people.'

'So I guess when it gets light, then we should maybe go and have a look for her.'

'I'm up for that.'

'Good, then we will do that. Is there a reason why she has appeared and done all this, do you think?'

'I'm not sure, except for some reason I can see her and I think she wants to be found. As to why the other murdered people are part of this, I have no idea.'

'So we will go up onto the Edge at first light. It shouldn't be long.'

'I'm actually more concerned about Tara.'

'Why is that?'

'Well Anne has been dead for a long time. Tara is from this time. I think we should check to see if she is at home first.'

'Do you mean now this minute?'

'I am fearful for her safety. I know it is bizarre, but she was the last person I saw, along with the man, before I came back here to the present day.'

'Did you recognize the man?'

'I am sure I know him, but his face was never clear to me. Something about him is familiar, but that is the best I can get.'

'It is a bit early to wake people on, well this sort of information.'

'But if she isn't at home and they don't know where she is, then it can never be too soon. At least check now that she hasn't been reported missing, or for not returning home.'

'I suppose that won't hurt.'

He goes out to his car, to radio in. I am not sure why he doesn't want us hearing his call, but I suspect it is because he is going to make more than one call. I can understand that, as I am not sure what I would make of me, if I were the one listening to this story.

He is away from us for nearly half an hour. We have another mug of coffee while we wait. I can see the edges of the sky beginning to herald the dawning of a new day. Andy comes back in, when it has just begun to get light.

He has a funny look on his face. I don't know if I should be concerned about that.

'Your Tara has been called in as missing. It is early yet, as she just hasn't gone home last night. Saying that, it is totally out of character for her not to tell her mother she isn't going to come home after a night out.'

'Do you know where she was going?'

'Apparently she was coming into Much Wenlock, to meet someone. She didn't say who. I've arranged for someone to go to her house, to make sure she hasn't turned up yet. I don't suppose you know where she parks her car, when she comes to town?'

'I only know her, as she works in the Deli. I would assume she parks her car somewhere in the streets behind there. I guess Paul who owns the Deli would know maybe. Have you got the make of car and the registration?'

'I have got them both. I thought that maybe we could take a trip down there and see if we can find if it is parked there somewhere.'

'The car was in the car park. The one I last saw her by. I don't know if it was her car, or just a car they were standing up against. We could maybe check there first.'

'That sounds like a good place to start. I have arranged for a small team to come here, as soon as we can get them together, to go to search for Anne.'

'It will be just her remains at best' I reply 'and from what was said, I think there may be others too.'

'Hopefully we will find out. I have also got them to try to trace the owners of the house in Sheinton Street. That might take a bit longer. It is unoccupied and has been for some time, a quick search has revealed.'

We leave my house and go in Andy's car to the centre of town, well St Mary's car park first. I can see straight away, that there are no cars where I saw Tara and the man standing. We drive slowly round the car park, to check on the few cars that are there. Her car is not one of them. We check the next car park too, but it is not there, nor in any of the private spaces around that. St Mary's Road is next, along with St Mary's Lane, but we have no luck there. We turn into Racecourse Lane and about fifty metres up that road, we find her car. It is locked and more to the point, it is empty. I am really not getting a good feeling about this.

'Do you have any idea where she might be?'

'I have no idea where she might be. I don't know what she was here in town to do and who she was going to see.'

I lapse into silence, as I try to rack my brains, to come up with a useful bit of information. Nothing comes to me straight away. So much has gone on and I am sure I haven't remembered every little bit.

'You said in part of the story, that you thought Anne was trying to lead you somewhere?'

I know the part of the story he means. That one has confused me since, because we didn't manage to get anywhere. On reflection I thought that she was trying to show me where she was buried. I say that, because we started off in that direction. But we didn't get through, because of the dark wall. We met that in another place too. I try to think more about this episode, because I think I might have missed some of it. I work my way through the journey. Andy is watching me patiently. I can't think of anything. I concentrate harder, because I am sure that Anne has shown me something, because of Tara. Why else would she be part of what I saw in the car park. Is she possibly up on the Edge somewhere too? I am just about to give up on it, when I remember how that journey ended. I sort of woke up in the back yard of the house. But the bit before that, I haven't told Andy. I remember it now. I tell it as it happened, to Andy.

"We walk more confidently back along to the Raven and then continue towards the square. We veer off onto Church Walk. The green is on our right and the church is ahead of us. We turn right and skirt round the church and out beside the old tower. The school is on my right. We are only a few paces along the road to the Priory, when Anne suddenly turns round. It is as if she knows this isn't the way.

She stops and puts her hand to her head. I put my hands on her shoulders. She feels cold against the warmth of my hands. I sense that my doing that is calming her. I almost think I am calming her directly with my thoughts.

'Where else could it be?' is all I say, when I break our long silence.

'I am not sure. I don't know what I am looking for.'

'I can see that. Do you feel something that might guide you? I mean, you seem to know what it is not and the darkness stops us from going places it does not want us to.'

She thinks deeply for a second.

'The only place I have had a different feeling, is the other side of the church, on the road we were on.'

'Let's go back there then.'

We retrace our steps and come out of Church Walk, onto the street. She stops and gathers herself, before taking one step at a time along the street. She steps and then she stops. Nothing! She does it again and again. I think she got the feeling of being close.

'What about the well?' I said quietly to her.

'The old well.' She looks around her. 'It is so different here, that I struggle to get my bearings.'

'The old well is down this lane' I said, but stood still.

She starts walking down the lane. With every step I take it that the feeling gets better. About twenty yards down the lane, I can see that she tenses up. I guess the feeling is at its strongest. She almost misses it, but I touch her arm and point down to the right. There is a small depression in the ground, guarded by a fence. I open the gate and I walk slowly down the steps. I look into the hole in the stone wall that is the old well, St Milburga's Well. You can't see much, as it is dark in there."

'Where is this well?'

It is not far from here. It's in Barrow Street.'

'I think we should have a look there.'

'There must be a reason why she took me there.'

Chapter 66 Me

We are about to set off there, when something else comes back to me. Anne took me into the tunnel, somewhere not that far away from the Corn Exchange. We came out of the tunnel after moving along it, in a different place, but still I believe in the Corn Exchange. Anne had put it down to the fact that we had to use this channel, to get to where she disappeared, but I am thinking that it too, might have some relevance in the search for her and or, maybe Tara.

I decide not to cloud the current situation with even more murky details. I can see that Andy knows I have just thought about something else, but he isn't pressing me on it.

Andy starts the car up and we turn round, ready to go back down to Barrow Street. We turn left at the Raven and then a right into the lane that leads to the nursery. The well is by the lane, about twenty metres from the road.

We pull to a stop and get out. There is a black railing, guarding the steps down to the section outside the well. The well is accessed by a hole in the wall, to the right. The hole is maybe half a metre square, or something like that. Andy looks at me, as if to say this is not that impressive.

'Some say it was the original water source for the town, back in the day.' I know little about it really, but I have read that somewhere.

'Let's have a look. Is it deep?'

'It's not like that. It is just a space under there.'

I open the gate and step through first. As I go down the steps, Andy comes through and joins me. He has brought his flashlight from the car. We bend down in front of the hole in the wall and peer in. Andy's flashlight illuminates a lot of the interior. It isn't very big in there, maybe two or three metres deep and a couple of metres wide. We can see the back wall without difficulty. There is nothing in there. Andy shines the light to the left. We can't see the entire inside from where we are. What we can see to the left, is empty too. We can see most of it from where we are standing, but not it all. I get down onto my knees and crawl in. Andy gets down and moves into the entrance, to shine his light round the corner.

I see something straight away.

'There's something here.' I can feel the tremor in my voice.

Andy crawls in too. I move over to the mound I have seen. Andy shines the light for me. I can now see that whatever it is has been covered with a blanket. With my heart in my mouth, I pull back one corner. The first thing I see is hair; the second is a head. Andy quickly pulls back the rest of the blanket. The person is huddled up, lying on their side. Andy reaches past me and tries to find a pulse.

'She's warm and there is a pulse, although not strong. Go call an ambulance and more help.'

I scramble out of the well and run up the steps. My phone is out and I am checking for signal. Thankfully I have some, but only one bar. I dial 999 as I run down the lane to the street. I am ready to aim for the Raven, if my signal doesn't hold out. It does and help is on the way. I return to the well. Andy is still in there. I tell him help is on the way and then ask if he knows who it is. He doesn't. It is a girl. My thinking is that it can't be Anne, so it must be Tara. At this moment in time, it doesn't matter who it is. All that matters is that they are alive and help is coming. On that note, I leave them, to go and direct the ambulance and police reinforcements. They don't take long in coming. In fact the help more or less arrives together. The First Responder gets to me first. I direct him to the well where Andy is. The others arrive less than five minutes later. I stand patiently near to the top of the well, in the lane. Andy comes out soon after the first responder arrives. There is only limited space in there.

Ten minutes later, they bring the girl out and put her on a stretcher. She has already been identified by the first responder. She has been beaten to within an inch of her life and hidden in the well. No doubt the attacker was intending to move her some time later. She is still alive though. She is now being moved to hospital, where she can be assessed fully. I look at the face as the stretcher passes me. At least we have found Tara now. She is in no state to tell us who did this to her though.

'Let's get on with this then' Andy now has something tangible that has come out of all this. We leave people working round the well, not helped that we have contaminated the scene somewhat. Some extra help moves with us.
'Should we take a look at the Corn Exchange first?'
Andy stops to take a look at me. We have managed to extricate his car from the line of vehicles that had parked behind us. I tell him about the tunnels. I don't tell him about all of the tunnels, yet. We can talk about the rest of them later, if we have to. I just need to see this one first. I'm not convinced that Anne will be in there anyway, but I think it needs investigating.
'We'll come back to that later' Andy decides 'I think we should follow the other lead first.'
We park up in the Stretton Road. I try to visualize where they went, when they took Anne up here.

"We walked for a little way before turning up a path. We were soon up on the edge. We came to an open section and they stopped for a couple of seconds. We didn't go very far. The land dropped away and we went down a little distance and then they stopped. Christopher kept hold of Anne, while the first one moved some rocks."

I relay this to Andy. We walk along and up a path, opposite some houses. We are soon up on the Edge. There are five or six of them, all following me. I am walking side by side with Andy. We do actually come to an open section. It is hard for me to say that this is the one I saw, but I feel confident that it might be. We go to the side, where the land drops away. We do go down and not far down, we come to a small level section. I feel my hopes rising inside me. I turn to look at the side of the hill in front of me. There isn't what I want to see in front of me. There is no apparent opening, even if it has been covered over. I think back to when I followed them here. When we came down the slope and stopped, we didn't go far. Was it at the end of the level section, like the one we are on now? It wasn't quite at the end. I move over three feet and look again. It is just the same. I can almost feel them all shaking their heads at me. I ignore them. I take four paces to my right. I am faced with rock, when I turn to face the side of the hill again. I step closer and hunt.

'What are you looking for?' one of them asks me, as he comes to my side.

'I used a stone to scratch a letter, as deep into the rock as I could.'

'Was it a letter A?' he replies.

'Yes, it was.'

'Like this one?' He is looking just to the right of where I am looking.

I move to it and I immediately recognize my letter A. I turn to my left and walk 4 paces back towards the others. I stop and face the hillside.

'It should be here.'

The tools come out of the kitbag. The dirt is scraped back. It isn't deep. There is rock, just an inch or two under the surface. They clear a section, until we have an area of rock clear in front of us. But it isn't one piece of rock. It is a mosaic of rocks, filling the gap. I move closer and tell them there should be another letter A, somewhere by the opening. It takes them a couple of minutes, but they find it. It is much less clear than the other one, but it is there.

Andy is looking at me. I wonder what he is thinking. Is he wondering if I have done all this and am just leading him to one place and then another. If we find something in here, then I am certain I won't be able to stop him from looking for the tunnel at the Corn Exchange.

The rocks are removed, until there is enough room for someone to squeeze through. Two people squeeze through and disappear into the hillside. They are away from us for twenty minutes, maybe longer than that. Eventually they re-surface.

'They are old. I mean very old. They have been in there for a lot of years. There are three in there. There's nothing left except, and this is really odd. There is a scarf lying on the floor beside one of them. It is in perfect condition, well it looks like it. We haven't touched anything. You need to get the team up here.'

I feel a pit in my stomach. I know that they have found Anne. I knew that at the mention of the scarf. I bet I can describe that scarf to them, but I don't think that will be helpful to me, in the circumstances.

A couple of them stay there to guard the entrance. The rest of us move back into the town.

Chapter 67 Me

We get back down to the car and drive into the town. As I suspected he would, Andy now wants to have a look for this tunnel, in or around the Corn Exchange. We park up in High Street, just outside the book shop. I get out and move to the back of the car, to wait for Andy to get out and come to the back too. He is just about with me, so I step out into the road. I have looked to my left to see it is clear; it is. All I see is a man walking towards us, on the far pavement. His walk tries to give the impression, that he thinks he is an important person. Something about him is familiar. I mean that, in relation to recent events. As I lock in on him, he notices me. I see a look of panic sweep across his face as he, I think, recognises me too. He breaks into a faster walk, I think it would have been a run if he could, and he cuts into the Corn Exchange. He quickly makes for the door and goes up into the offices. He does this, while I tell Andy that I think he might be Tara's attacker.

Andy tells me to stay there, while he and the three others with us, race into the building. They search it top to bottom, but he isn't there to be found. They come out again ten minutes later and leave one of them on the door. Andy goes back to his car. He takes me along with him. I think I still have some questions to answer.

We are just crossing the road, when two things happen, almost simultaneously. First we hear the sound of a car racing towards us, from the right. The second thing is that we hear a crash of glass from above us. We race across the last few feet of the road, before turning round. Two sights greet our eyes. The first is of a man falling to the ground. He is in mid-air, as we turn. The second is the sight of the speeding car, now in view.

The man hits the ground, about a tenth of a second before the car smashes into him. It swerves and hits Andy's car on the passenger side and comes to a jarring stop. The driver can't get out his side, but he does scramble across and escape out of the passenger door. He looks remarkably like the man we saw earlier. He is well dressed and has the air of importance to him too.

He doesn't hang around, but darts into the Corn Exchange and pushes past the man at the door. He slams the door shut behind him.

One look at the man, who has come through the window, is enough to know he won't be alive. The shard of glass through his throat is part of the problem. The damage the landing did is another part and the collision with the car, just made sure he didn't live.

While one stays by the man on the road, Andy and I run across to the door. The officer, who had been guarding that, is trying to get the door to open, but it is firmly shut. I remember other doors doing this too.

'I'll try it' I don't know why I think I can do better, but I think this is all still part of the reveal. They stand aside to let me. I turn the handle and the door opens. Andy goes in first and then suddenly stops. He ushers us in too.

As you go through the door there are a couple of wooden panels to your right. One of these is open. Immediately it makes sense to me. I could have come out of the tunnel here. I came out higher than I went in. But something isn't right here. The passageway goes past, on the other side of this wall. There isn't room for a tunnel, but when I look through the open panel, I see that there is. Well it might be the start of one, but it is actually just a cavity. The cavity is occupied. The occupant is very much dead. I can see enough to know that it was a man. I can see enough to know he was the man in the car. I can see that his clothes are those of someone who thinks he is important. We all see this, as we look into the cavity. Then in the space of a single second, most of that is gone. His face disappears, as do his clothes. We are left looking at the skeleton of a man who has been hidden away in here for a very long time.

It is a bit of a shock. We go back outside and into the fresh air. I am feely a bit heady, after what we have just witnessed. We step down onto the pavement. A crowd has gathered, but is being held back behind some tape. I look up the street at some of the faces. I recognise some, but not all. I look at the crowd gathered the other way. I do a double take. I don't believe who I am seeing, standing there chatting together behind that line of tape. Quite clearly I see

Joan, Peter and Bob, talking to each other. I am just about to say something to Andy, when my legs give way and I start to fall to the floor, blacking out as I go.

Chapter 68 Me

I am sitting on a bench. That is where I am, when I regain consciousness. They have moved me over here to recover. They think I fainted. I assure them that I am alright. They leave me to get on with the work that has plumped itself on their laps. I can't see much from where I am sitting. I look around me. I am sitting on the bench by the wall, under the Corn Exchange. If I'm right, I am not far away from the place where Anne showed me her initial, etched onto the wall.

There must be a dark cloud or two coming over, because the light has gone, even as I have sat here the past couple of minutes. It keeps getting darker and darker and gloomier too. It almost reminds me of when we had the eclipse. The light went bit by bit, until the eclipse occurred.

I feel someone sit down beside me on the bench. I turn towards them. I am shocked, but then I shouldn't be, to see Anne is sitting beside me. She is looking at me. She sees that I know she is there.

'Thank you for finding me.'

'I'm glad we have.'

'What will happen to me now?'

'I don't know. What would you like to happen?'

'I would like to be buried properly.'

'I'll see what I can do.'

'Thank you.'

'Will I see you again?'

'I don't know. I don't know what will happen now you have found me.'

'I'll come and sit here sometimes, if you want to come and sit with me.'

I don't get a reply because she has gone. I look down onto the bench where she has been sitting. There is something there. I reach out and pick it up. It is her scarf. I wrap it round my neck and as I do so, it gently disappears into my skin.

The end.

It's Dark in Wenlock: Copyright © 2018 William (Bill) Stenlake

It's Dark in Wenlock by Bill Stenlake

All rights reserved. No part of this book may be reproduced, distributed or transmitted in any form, by any means without the prior consent of the author.

All characters in this publication are fictitious and any resemblance to persons, living or dead is purely coincidental. Some places named in the book exist and are real and some do not exist and are not real. The placement of all things geographical is relevant to this story only and as such should be deemed fictional.

Book Cover Photo:
© Bobrooky/Dreamstime.com

Other books by Bill Stenlake:

HOLLOW MILL
THE KEEPER
KENAN'S LEGACY
CORNERSTONE
THE GRAND MASTER
DETECTIVE BRAMLEY BOOK 1
RANDOLPH
VOICES IN MY HEAD
LOWARTH TOLL
THE CORIDAE KEY
BRAMLEY BOOK 2
THE MANNACHS
DIMENSIONS
THE ROOTS
A PAIR OF SHORTS
THE WATCHER
THE KEEPER TRILOGY
COMING SOON: JOHNSTONE

Made in the USA
Middletown, DE
21 January 2018